NOTHING BETWEEN US

Manda Mazanec

Published 2023

ISBN: 979-8-9867630-1-9

Cover design: Amanda Walker

Editing: Beth at VB Edits

Proofreader: Sarah Burr at Reed Editorial Services

For my mom.

For your unwavering love and support.

Disclaimer: Addiction, domestic violence, and the loss of a parent, grandparent, and pregnancy, are discussed in this book.

CHAPTER ONE

Three Years Earlier

Meera

There's a dull ache in the pit of my stomach. I want to move my hand out from under the thin cotton sheet, but the second I try, the room flips upside down and a wave of heat powers through my diaphragm. I clench my jaw, keeping my hand in place. *Don't move. Stay stiff as a board and it'll go away.*

"Breathe, Meera. It'll subside. Keep your eyes closed. Just breathe."

When I'm finally brave enough to lift my heavy eyelids, it feels as if a herd of dinosaurs has been unleashed, stampeding, trampling my brain into a pile of mush.

Letting out a shallow groan, I blink at the bright flicker of sunshine streaking through the half-open curtains. My gaze shifts from the white pillowcase to the floor-length window at the far end of the room. Small flecks of light float across the white walls, dancing along a beautiful antique mahogany dresser and dark-brown hardwood floors as the trees sway in the wind.

I smile. For a brief moment, I'm at peace.

But then I feel it.

The slow movement of sheets being pulled from the other side of the bed. Without thinking, without hesitating, I roll over.

As I turn, the sheets that cover my bare legs fall loose. And then my attention shifts and my mouth drops. I suck in a sharp breath when I catch sight of the man lying next to me.

"What . . . the . . . fuck?" I whisper.

Gabriel Henry opens his eyes and squints at me. A small curve forms at his lips.

"No. No, no, no," I say and bolt upright, pulling the sheet high over my chest, which I now realize is bare. Along with the rest of my body. I'm dreaming. I have to be dreaming. I went to bed by myself last night. I may have wanted Gabe to come back to my room with me, but he was dancing with a blonde. And a brunette. Actually, now that I think about it, I'm pretty sure he danced with every single girl at the wedding.

Panic-stricken, I ask, "What are you doing here?"

Gabe rolls his neck from side to side before inching up onto his elbow. "We call it sleeping where I come from." His lean legs poke out from what's left of the sheets.

I shake my head. "No. I mean, why are you here, in my room? You need to leave. Oh my God, did we—no, don't answer that." I clasp a hand over my mouth. This isn't me. I don't sleep around. I don't have one-night stands. Especially not with people like him. Gabriel Henry may be attractive with his chiseled abs and concrete jaw. And his liquid blue eyes may have, on more than one occasion, made my heart skip a beat. But sleeping with him? That's a hard no.

"Get out. You need to get out." My words come out sharp. I pull the sheet again, tugging it away from Gabe's rock-hard body, and close my eyes, embarrassed, afraid to see just how naked he is underneath.

When the bed dips, I instinctively grip the sheets tighter. I'm not sure why. It's not like I expect Gabe to take them. Though I'm still in the dark about what happened last night and how he managed to get into my room.

How many drinks did I have? Images of last night swirl in my head. It was Sadie and Jack's wedding. I stayed away from Gabe the entire night, didn't I? I drank a lot. But there is absolutely no way he came back to my room with me.

Gabe's gravelly voice startles me. "Actually, this is my room."

I blink open my eyes. He's standing on the other side of the bed now, showing off a pair of baby-blue boxer briefs that barely fit over his tight thighs. He runs a hand through his dark-brown hair before he crouches beside the mattress.

That's when I take in my surroundings. Holy shit. He's right. At first glance, this looks like my room. The same four-poster oak-framed bed and its floral print comforter, which currently lies in a heap on the floor. The full-length window that runs the width of the room. Even the freshly painted white walls are identical. The only difference is the couch. The one in my room is a three-seat beige sofa, while this one is a small midnight blue loveseat.

How did I end up here?

Gabe stands back up with something in his hand. It's my dress. *And* it's inside out.

Suddenly, the pain in my stomach returns. My heartbeat quickens, and a warm sensation rushes to my cheeks, but it's not because I'm hungover. No, I'm mortified. I don't know what to say or how to even ask for my dress back. And he's just silently watching me, unmoving.

Then, after what feels like an eternity, I say the only thing I can think of. “I’m married.”

He puts his hand out, offering up the dress, his expression blank. “I know.”

CHAPTER TWO

Present

Meera

"Are you sure?" Sadie asks as she folds a box in half and lays it on top of a mounting stack of cardboard next to the garbage can. "I can stay. Jack can put Grace to bed tonight."

"I'm fine. I'll have everything put away by the next time I see you," I lie, taking in the mess in front of us. "Plus, I need to shower and get ready for work. Can't be late on my first day." I take a drink from my water bottle but push the cold pizza aside.

"You mean your first night." Sadie pouts for a second and then turns her lips up in a grin before I can respond. "I seriously can't believe you're here." She squeals and pops up on her tiptoes to hug me. "Promise you'll call tomorrow and tell me all about your first shift. Dr. Coleman is going to love you."

I've known Sadie for the last decade. We met during our senior year of high school while touring San Francisco State University. Sadie and I were the only girls in the group we'd been assigned to, so when they told us to pair up, it was only natural that we linked arms and became instant friends. Since she's from a small town outside Savannah, her mom wasn't sold on the idea of her only daughter moving across the country. But it helped that she fell in love with my grandma *and* the fact that she lived a short bike ride from campus.

When the tour ended, Sadie and I had claimed each other as roommates and friends for life. I was there when she met Jack during our freshman move-in. He was a year older and a resident advisor, so he was assigned with helping us move into our dorm room. It wasn't love at first sight, but I witnessed a few sparks that first day. I was also there, three years later, after Jack popped the question with the most gorgeous diamond I'd ever seen, slathering butter on her finger, trying to slide it off because Sadie thought marriage meant having to give up her identity. And then three years ago, I flew across the country to be her maid of honor and fell in love with the small town Jack grew up in, which was surprisingly close to Sadie's own hometown.

She's the reason I'm here. Choosing Morganville once I received my doctorate was a no-brainer. I have no ties anywhere else. Even if my grandma was still alive, I could never go back to San Francisco. Not since Tom still lives there.

Sadie's my only family now. She and Jack. They were there when things got bad. And now they're all I need.

I hug Sadie one more time.

When she's gone, I finally get a good look at my new place. It's a one-bedroom apartment above a cute little boutique that grabbed my attention when I flew in for her wedding. Sure, it has mustard-yellow and citrus-orange walls. And yes, the matching carpet is stained with what looks to be car oil. At least that's what I hope it is. But it has charm. Large windows that overlook the center of downtown Morganville. An oversized terrace above a small garden. Not to mention it came fully furnished and is less than three blocks from Morganville Animal Hospital, my new place of employment for the next year.

I toss my suitcase onto the bed. When it lands, the mattress sinks and then falls straight through the metal frame. A bit startled, I crouch to inspect it. There are no wooden slats underneath to give it support. It lies slanted now, half on the floor and half on the frame, but it's still better than sleeping in my car, something I've done for far too long.

I pull clean clothes from the suitcase and head to the bathroom. I half expect cold water to fall from the showerhead when I slip beneath the heavy stream several minutes later, but I smile when the heat hits my back. No more sneaking into the gym to wash my hair.

This. I can get used to this.

An hour later, I lock my door and head downstairs. Gray clouds sweep across the sky, and darkness envelops me when I step outside. An earthly smell permeates the air. I make a mental note to invest in outside lighting as I turn onto the main road, where it's only slightly lighter.

A warm breeze blows my long brown hair across my face. I brush it away from my eyes, but it's already too late. I walk straight into a pole. Like full-on head to metal.

"Shit." I wince at the pain that radiates through my skull as I rub at the knot already forming on my forehead. A tall, black utility pole stands in front of me. *Where did that come from*? Embarrassed, I scan the area around me and breathe a sigh of relief when I realize there were no witnesses to my awkward stunt. The town is quiet. The only businesses that are still open are the two bars down the road and the animal hospital.

I let out a slow and steady breath. "Get it together, Meera." If Tom were here, he'd scoff and say something like *Can't you walk normally for once in your life?* and shake his head as he avoided eye contact with me. But Tom isn't here. Tom doesn't get to ruin my first night in Morganville.

I rub my head, straighten my shoulders, and take off again. *I got this.*

The sky opens up, and large raindrops fall to the cement just as I reach the animal hospital. I tug open the door, dodging the downpour at the last second. I don't get lucky very often, so I say a quick thank-you as I cross over the threshold.

Inside, I'm greeted by a young blonde with her hair piled high on her head. "Hi there. How can I help you?" she asks in an upbeat voice that matches her grin.

"Hi," I say, returning the smile. "I'm Meera Taylor. I'm here to see Dr. Coleman."

She glances at the clock against the scuffed beige wall. "Oh, Dr. Taylor. You're early. We weren't expecting you for another half an hour. I'm Lydia, Dr. Coleman's granddaughter." She stands. "I work the front desk at night. Let me go tell him you're here."

Just as she steps away from her spot at the counter, a gust of wind sweeps through the reception area, blowing my hair in my face and ruffling the papers on the desk. When I turn around, a small girl stands on the mat just inside the door. She's clutching a red leash with a large golden retriever attached to the other end. They're soaking wet, and a puddle quickly forms below their feet.

"Hi, sweetie," I begin. The girl looks like she's seven, maybe eight years old. "Is your mom or dad here with you?" I glance at the door, hoping an adult is about to pop inside.

"No," she says.

That's it. Nothing else. Water drips down her stringy auburn hair, and she makes no effort to move it away from the intense blue eyes she has firmly locked on me.

Her dog shakes, and water flies in every direction.

Throwing a hand up and turning my head, I shield myself just as Lydia comes back.

"My grandfather will be out in a few minutes. He said to make yourself comfortable," she says. Then she catches sight of the little girl. "Sophie, what are you doing here?"

"Charlie ate another Lego."

Lydia rounds the desk, and she and the girl talk. They know each other, which is good, but why didn't Lydia ask why she's alone or where her parents are? Who lets a little girl wander the streets in the dark? I sure hope this is an isolated incident and not something people do so casually in small towns.

"How many does that make this week? Three?" Lydia laughs, scratching the wet dog behind one ear.

"Does Charlie make it a habit of eating Legos?" I ask, ignoring the urge to bring up the girl's parents again. I slip my bag down my shoulder and hang it on a hook near the door. Then I set my water jug on the counter. I don't like that this girl is by herself, but I also don't like the idea that this dog is eating plastic toys like they're cookies.

Sophie doesn't answer. She does, however, narrow her eyes like she's analyzing me. The expression coming from such a small human kind of creeps me out.

"Should we take Charlie in for an exam?" I ask, hoping to settle my own uneasiness.

"Come on, Charlie." Lydia takes the leash from the little girl and guides the dog toward a door on the opposite side of the room, and I follow. When she hands me the leash, Sophie yanks it out of my grasp.

I open my mouth, ready to insist she let me examine her dog, but then another gust of wind hits me, and a tall figure enters the room. His clothes are soaked, and his deep-brown hair is dripping down his face in much the same way Sophie's was a moment ago.

"How many times do I have to tell you not to leave without telling anybody?" he admonishes the little girl, his voice deep and rough. He crouches so he's at eye level with her. "And what did I tell you about your manners? You can't just snatch things out of people's hands like that. Please tell her you're sorry." When he stops for a breath, he looks up, and that's when it happens.

There are two of him, maybe three. My head is slightly fuzzy. Okay, it's a lot fuzzy. I grab the wall to brace myself as a familiar dizziness takes hold. I'm suddenly sweating. The guy is barking. And then the room goes black.

When I regain consciousness, I'm met with the brightest blue eyes I've ever seen. They're so bright they might not even be blue. They're ice and glass, and I can't peel my gaze away from them.

"Dr. Taylor. Dr. Taylor, are you all right?" he says. But his lips aren't moving. He's focused on me, scanning my face, when I hear my name again. This time it's louder. High pitched.

Lydia.

I close my eyes and groan.

"I'm okay. Just a bit light-headed." I open my eyes again, but this time I don't look up.

"I'll grab you some water," Lydia says.

"Wait," I call out a little louder than necessary, catching her before she can leave the room. "Can you grab my black bag? It's hanging on the hook out front. There should be an apple juice in it."

When she disappears, the guy helps me sit up.

"It looks like you hit your head pretty good on the way down," he says, placing a small ice pack on my forehead. "Though I don't know how because you never made it to the floor."

"Oh," I say as I touch my forehead, heat rising up my neck. "This is from earlier." I leave out the part where I lost the fight with the utility pole. I try to wash away my embarrassment by standing, but he presses down on my arm, forcing me to stay put.

"Why don't we wait on that juice?" he murmurs.

I let out a deep sigh. I'm still a bit disoriented, so I doubt I'd be able to get up without stumbling anyway. And I have a hard limit when it comes to making a fool out of myself. Once a day is enough.

"Here you go," Lydia announces. She doesn't hand the juice to me, though. Instead, she places it in this guy's large, tanned hand.

He tears off the plastic wrapper and pokes the straw through the top of the carton, then he brings the straw to my lips. I despise apple juice, but after a few sips, I feel life return to my cheeks. This is so humiliating. My first day, and I already look like an incompetent klutz. My night cannot get any worse.

"Thank you," I finally say as I push to my feet. My eyes gloss over the man in front of me and go directly to Lydia. "I'm so sorry about that. Can you tell me where the bathroom is? I need a minute before I start the exam."

"Charlie will be fine. It's just a Lego." The man beside me places a gentle hand on my forearm. "You should get checked out. There's an urgent care across town."

I turn toward the familiar voice, and for the first time, I catch all of him. Not just his ice-blue eyes. Not just the dark-brown hair that's still damp. But all of him. His tall frame. His broad chest. His hard jaw.

"Gabe," I mutter under my breath.

He doesn't hear me. He doesn't smile. Though I don't expect him to. It's been three years since I last saw him. Three years since I asked him to turn around so I could get dressed. So I could escape his hotel room with the last bit of dignity I could muster. Three years since I ghosted him. Though ghosting would mean he tried to call me. I don't know what to call it, because in all honesty, I don't have the slightest clue as to what happened.

The memory of that night is interrupted by a pleading voice.

"Daddy, what happens if Charlie can't poop out the Lego?"

In sync, we all turn toward the little girl holding the leash.

"Charlie will be fine. This isn't his first rodeo." Gabe places a hand on her shoulder. "Tell Lydia you'll see her tomorrow and let's go."

"Actually, I would still like to do an exam on Charlie," I interject. "I'll be quick. Give me two minutes, and I'll be right back."

Gabe narrows his eyes, but I ignore it. Instead, I shoot Lydia a desperate look, hoping she'll keep them here until I get back. Once inside the bathroom, I set my black bag and apple juice on the sink. After pulling out my lancet, I stab my fingertip and let the blood ooze out, then watch as a thick droplet slides onto a new test strip.

I know the numbers will be low, but I still shudder when they flash across the screen. This is what I get for not checking it earlier and for skipping dinner. I turn my attention to the apple juice sitting on the edge of the sink and sigh. This is my life now. My doctor warned me that not eating regularly with this new medication could cause my blood sugar to tank.

Quickly, I finish the juice, clean up my mess, and wash my hands.

Then, as I open the bathroom door, trying not to think about Gabe, I collide full-on with the man himself. Like earlier with the utility pole, my skull makes impact, smashing against the corner of his concrete jaw. There's no doubt that by the time my shift ends tomorrow morning, my forehead will match the blue scrub shirt I'm wearing.

I cringe, but not out of pain or for what my face will look like. I'm used to that. If anything, two bruises is a downgrade from what I'm accustomed to. I'm a bit accident prone. Okay, more like I was born with two left feet.

"I'm sorry," I say as I stumble backward.

Gabe catches my elbow and steadies me as he roughs a hand over his jaw at the same time. "Nope, that was my fault. I wanted to check on you. Didn't anticipate you coming out at the same time."

My attention shifts from the hand holding my elbow to Gabe's face. For a moment, neither of us speaks. I'm thrown off by how soft his hand feels and the evergreen scent floating between us.

"Dr. Taylor, right?" he says.

And there it is. He doesn't remember me. Women must fall into his bed so often that he can't distinguish one naked body from the next. Or maybe he doesn't recognize women once we have our clothes on. Either way, my blood boils in anger.

"Yes. I'm fine." I shrug his hands off and push past him. "You're Charlie's owner, I take it?" My voice is sharp, but I don't give a crap. Gabe was the one person I wanted to avoid this year, but then again, I do have the worst luck in the world.

"I am," he says, following me down the hall.

Sophie and Lydia are sitting on the floor of the exam room, petting Charlie. A tall gray-haired man stands next to them. As we step through the doorway, they all look up in unison.

"Ah, you must be Dr. Taylor. Lydia was just telling me you got a bit dizzy. Is there anything I can do to help?" He laces his fingers in front of his torso and looks at me with genuine concern. "We don't have any patients right now. You can rest for a bit, and we can do a tour when you're feeling better." His face is weathered and worn. Deep lines burrow along his forehead and crease at his eyes. His gray hair is thinning but gelled firmly in place. And his smile is so soft I almost forget Gabe is standing behind me. Almost.

"I'm okay. Blood sugar was a bit low, but I'm good now." I smile.

I hold out a hand and properly introduce myself. "My name is Meera Taylor. It's nice to finally meet you, Dr. Coleman."

"Call me Edgar." He takes my hand in his, but he doesn't shake it. Instead, he places his other hand on top so he's more or less holding mine between his. "You've met the rest of the gang already. This is Lydia, my granddaughter." He nods to where she's still sitting cross-legged on the floor. "She works the front at night. That's Gabe, my grandson." A nod of his head toward the man still hovering behind me. "And this here is our little Sophie, my great-granddaughter."

My eyes go wide. Grandson. Gabriel Henry is Dr. Coleman's grandson. Holy hell. Worst of the worst luck ever.

CHAPTER THREE

Meera

My eyelids are heavy when I push through the door of my apartment. It's not even seven, and the sun is already screaming at the people of Morganville as they begin their day. I, however, am ready to sleep off my exhaustion.

While last night was uneventful once Gabe took Sophie and Charlie home, it dragged on as a result. Not one person stepped inside.

Dr. Coleman showed me where the medications were located, where he performs surgery, and how he likes to do things. Lydia gave me the lowdown on medical records and what *not* to do to piss off Helen, the morning technician.

"Sometimes, I think blinking even makes her mad. I'm sure I only get a free pass because of my grandpa." She laughed. "She has tomorrow off, so you probably won't meet her until your next shift. Good thing you'll only see her in passing, though. At least till you get moved to days."

In less than ten minutes, my face is washed, my teeth are brushed, and I'm ready to count sheep. But as I stumble toward the bed, I realize I have one tiny problem. I never fixed my mattress. I stare down at it as fatigue begins to win its battle. With a heavy sigh, I press the mattress through the frame with my foot until it's pushed all the way through and lying flat on the floor. I'm about to flop down when the iron railings beat me to it.

I jump back in the nick of time.

One rail misses my toes by mere centimeters. But I'm too tired to even care. I sink into the mattress, anyway, not bothering with pillows or sheets. Regardless of how old this thing is, it's way more comfortable than the back seat of my car. Though the smell is an entirely different story.

I'm not sure what time it is when I'm jolted awake by a muffled clanking and banging. I hold my breath, both because I'm pretty sure I'm lying next to a puke stain and because I don't know if I dreamed the noise or if it was real.

There it is again.

I heave myself from my death trap of a bed and tiptoe my way out of the room, tilting my head to listen more closely. When the clanking grows louder, I head toward the bathroom. I'm no expert, but once I open the cabinet below the sink, I know there's a problem.

"I can handle this," I say to myself. With phone in hand, I do a quick search online for *plumbing problems*. And after I click on a few sites, I find a common theme right away. Call a plumber.

I don't know any plumbers. Hell, I barely know anyone, so I call my landlord instead.

When he doesn't answer, I leave a very detailed message. "Hi Tanner, this is Meera, the new tenant on Kline Avenue. Above Limitless Boutique. The corner apartment. My bathroom pipes are making a weird noise."

I huff out of frustration. I suck at talking on the phone. It's like anxiety rips through my lungs and I can't find enough oxygen to string a coherent sentence together. I try to shrug it off, though I'm annoyed that I made it sound like the plumbing issue was no big deal. There's no way Tanner will be calling back anytime soon.

My grandparents raised me to be relatively self-sufficient. Once, my grandfather showed me how to take apart a washing machine and dryer so I could get a feel for how things worked. It came in handy during my college years when the only dryer in our building broke down. With a screwdriver in hand, I tore off the access panel and replaced the belt all on my own. But plumbing is something I have zero experience with.

I guess it's time to learn.

Crouching low, I feel each pipe and immediately find where the water is coming from. A wave of relief washes over me as I realize it's just a small leak. I can fix this.

Wrench in hand, I tighten one ring and then another, but the pipes are corroded, making everything I do pointless. I try again, this time yanking once I know my wrench has a good grip. But instead of tightening, I swear it loosens. "Righty tighty, lefty loosey," I say as I visualize the direction my hand turned.

But it doesn't matter whether I turned right or left, because I have a bigger problem now. A steady stream of water slides down my arm. Instinctively, I wrap my hand around the gaping hole in the pipe, and just as quickly as it started, it stops.

In its path, a thin bead of blood tracks along my skin, followed instantly by a searing pain. I close my eyes and suck in a sharp breath before releasing it. When I pull my hand away, there's a small gash from where the rust dug into my palm.

"It's not me. It's just life," I mutter to myself as I sit on the cold linoleum floor, repeating my therapist's mantra. *There is no such thing as an unlucky person, Meera. It's just how life works. Things break. Then they get fixed. You fall. Then you get back up. It happens to everyone.* She reminded me of the same thing at every visit, which has been every week for the last three years.

I'll be okay. I can do this.

Pushing off the floor, I head to the kitchen and clean my hand before wrapping it with a bandage. Then I call my friend.

"Hello?" Sadie's voice is soft and sweet when she answers.

"Sadie," I sigh. "I need help. Do you know any plumbers? Is Jack home? My bathroom sink is leaking. I thought I could fix it, but I'm pretty sure I just made it worse."

"Jack is still at work, but let me call him. I'm sure we can get someone over there." Then she's gone. Presumably sending her husband to help.

Half an hour goes by before there's a knock at the door.

"In here," I call out.

When I crawl out from under the sink, standing in front of me, dressed in a black business suit, is none other than the devil himself. Gabe. Gabe is the devil. But at least he's holding towels.

"Oh, thank God."

Wearing an unreadable expression, he watches me as I reach for one of the dry towels.

"Is Jack with you?" I ask. "I'm not sure what I did, but I made it worse."

"He's in court today. What happened to your hand?" Gabe asks, nodding at the bandage. He snags my hand and pulls it toward him, but I yank it away.

"I cut myself."

Without a word in response, he takes off his suit jacket and rolls up his sleeves, as if this is something he does every day.

My bathroom is small, and while I can easily move out of the way, I don't. I stand my ground and watch as Gabe squeezes past me and squats, positioning himself in front of the cabinet.

When the fabric of his suit pants presses against the skin of my leg, I'm suddenly aware of how little clothing I have on. In my defense, I just woke up. But Gabe doesn't know that, and now I feel almost naked.

"You forgot to cut off the waterline."

He must catch my blank stare because he points at a lever and says, "You should always turn off the water before doing anything with pipes. It'll save you a lot of cleanup."

I say nothing but do my best to give him a tight-lipped smirk.

"Hand me a towel," he bellows. He sticks his hand out, not bothering to turn in my direction. "These pipes are all corroded. Looks like you're going to need to replace them."

I throw my head back and groan.

"You're renting, right?" Gabe's still halfway under my sink, wiping away the rest of the water.

"No, I chose to buy this apartment for its meth-lab appeal," I chortle.

Gabe pauses and looks at me. His eyebrows are bunched so low I wonder if they're frozen that way.

"Yes, I'm renting," I sigh.

"Your landlord should fix this. Don't let him give you any excuses. But don't let him in here by himself either."

I gape at him. *What?*

"Have you met Tanner yet?" He grimaces.

I fold my arms over my chest. "No. I signed the lease online, and then he left the key under the mat."

"Doesn't surprise me. He isn't so much a landlord as he is a slumlord," he deadpans.

I laugh but stop short and glare when he doesn't smile back. "What does that even mean?"

Gabe grabs the last dry towel and wipes his hands. His face is still devoid of an expression, making it impossible to read him.

"Tanner isn't known for taking care of his properties. This one here." He points around the room. "Was where he lived until the girl downstairs reported him for"—he hesitates and finally makes eye contact with me—"meth. That and she filed a restraining order against him for sexual assault."

I turn around and stomp out of the bathroom.

Fuck my life.

CHAPTER FOUR

Gabe

I can't *not* watch as Meera walks away. She may hate me for what happened three years ago, but that won't stop me from looking. In a pair of gray cotton shorts that show off the curves of her ass and a tight white tank top with pink roses, she makes it virtually impossible to train my attention anywhere but on her. She's hot as hell. And even if she were wearing sweats, I'd still have to tell my lower region to calm the fuck down. But everything about this girl screams commitment, and that's not my thing.

Three years ago, before I set eyes on Meera, commitment didn't scare me. It was so far off my radar that I don't think I could even spell the damn word. But that night, when Meera walked into the Tipsy Brew Garage wearing a goddamn yellow floral sundress, my fucking heart about leaped from my chest, and I would have laid everything out on the table for a chance with her. And not just to get my dick wet. Crazy, right?

I was minding my own business, flirting with a tiny blonde, trying to close the deal, when the entire bar fell silent.

When I looked up to see why everyone had gone quiet, my heart came to a screeching halt. I soaked in every detail of the gorgeous woman with hair so dark it could have been black. She strode straight through the entrance with Sadie at her side. She smiled, and her green irises gleamed against the dim lights of the bar.

"Look who's here!" Sadie announced. She waved a hand in the air as she thrust the girl forward.

Jack was the first one up. "Damn, Meera. You look great. When Sadie told me you were coming, I almost didn't believe her." He lifted her off her feet and twirled her in the air. "It's been too damn long. Everyone," he shouted, "come say hi to Meera."

The sound of her responding laugh sent goose bumps down my spine. And it wasn't until the music started again and everyone talked at once that I exhaled. And for the first time in my life, I lost myself in the presence of a woman.

From the bar, I watched as Sadie and Jack introduced their college friend to the bridal party.

"These are my bridesmaids. Marissa, Leila, and Heidi," Sadie said, waving her hand at the three girls I've known just about my entire life. "And Liam, Jacob, and Declan are Jack's groomsmen. Y'all are going to love each other."

And I swear, for a second, Sadie thought about introducing me. She glanced in my direction, but when she caught sight of me staring at her friend, she furrowed her brows and shook her head. But the night was still young. I'd find my own way of making myself known.

Oh, and that blonde? I had no idea when she left, nor did I care, because from that moment on, I was completely transfixed by Meera.

But of course, rather than tucking my balls away and being a good boy like I'm sure my friends were praying I would, I did the exact opposite. I cornered Meera in the bathroom the first chance I got and propositioned her, promising her a night of blissful sex.

Not my finest moment.

But a lot has changed in the last three years. Now? Fuck. I've settled into this fatherhood thing, and the whole town thinks I should be ready to throw a ring on a finger. But that's the thing. I thought, once upon a time, after tucking Meera into my bed the night of Sadie and Jack's wedding, that maybe I could be ready.

Come to find out, the only thing it did was help me grow a conscience.

"You okay in there?" Meera's voice jerks me back to the present.

"Yup, just cleaning up the rest of this water," I call as I push to my feet.

When I step out of the bathroom, Meera is sitting on the wooden armrest of a burnt-orange and gold couch that is no doubt older than the both of us put together. Her arms are folded against her chest, her bare feet are firmly planted on the ground, and her dark-brown hair is in a messy knot on the top of her head.

"I didn't make a mistake renting this place."

"I didn't say you did." My voice comes out lower than I intend.

"No, but you're thinking it." She huffs. "If Tanner won't hire someone to fix it, I'll do it myself."

I keep my gaze fixed on her, but I don't respond. Sadie's warmed to me over the years, but in her eyes, my past still precedes me, and I've never cared enough to change her opinion. So when it comes to Meera, she's always tight-lipped around me. Though I've overheard enough over the years to know that this woman has dealt with more than her fair share of hurdles in life, so I don't doubt that she *would* fix it herself.

The room is quiet now. The only sounds are those that come from the busy street below.

Meera presses her lips together like she's thinking about what to say next. As if the silence is too much to bear. But for me, it's a chance at redemption. Maybe if I clear the air, tell her what happened that night at the bed-and-breakfast, she won't hate me so much.

I open my mouth, ready to apologize, when my focus snags on the bruise on her forehead.

"Is that from last night? When I ran into you?" I step closer, realizing there are actually two bumps decked out in purple and blue hues.

This time, when I angle in, Meera doesn't pull away. It's not an invitation, but I brush away a few loose strands of hair anyway. When my fingertips sweep across her skin, my insides tighten and my heartbeat quickens. And for a second, I think Meera's breathing deepens too.

At her subtle response, I let my eyes wander. I can't help myself. She's gorgeous.

But it's not like a scene from a movie. Meera doesn't let out a heavy sigh. She doesn't look up at me longingly. There is no melting of hearts. No. Instead, she's an icebox. She squares her shoulders and holds her breath. Then, through clenched teeth, she says, "My eyes are up here."

"Maybe wear something that covers that up next time," I growl.

"You can show yourself out."

Yup, she still hates me.

What in the actual fuck is wrong with me? Taking a step back, I roll down my sleeves. I need to get back to work. I need to get my head out of my ass. She's hot, sure. But her personality is bitter and cold. I don't have time for this bullshit.

"You should put ice on that," I say and then turn and stride out the door without a backward glance.

It doesn't take me long to walk back to my office, but I'm sweating by the time I push through the door.

"Ashley, I told you to have Dee's file on my desk by the time I got back. She pays us too much damn money for us not to be prepared." I tug on my tie, pulling it from side to side, desperate for some kind of relief, but every nerve ending in my body is on fire.

I yank, and the knot tightens. I can't get Meera out of my head.

"Fuck," I groan, releasing it from my grasp and letting it hang in shit fashion.

"Hey, don't take it out on Ashley. I have it right here. I wasn't sure if you'd be back for your meeting, so I grabbed it." Jack stands in the doorway, holding Dee's red folder. "How'd it go at Meera's? Were you able to help?" he asks, dropping the folder on my desk.

Jack and I are family-law attorneys. We specialize in divorce and have been partners for the past five years. Jack's what I like to call a cat. He's more of a domesticated shorthair than a tiger. He's approachable. Nice. With his clean-shaven face and blond hair cut like I wore mine during my Marine Corps days, he looks like everybody's best friend.

When potential clients call our office crying, they talk to him first because he can calm anyone down. He's got a great heart. If he hadn't landed Sadie in college, women from all over the world would be beating down his door for a date. But he's already housebroken.

Me, on the other hand? I'm not clean shaven. I'm not cute and cuddly. I'm a fucking shark. When an estranged spouse acts like a dick and can't manage an amicable divorce, I step in and take down the asshole who doesn't deserve my client's time.

"She needs new pipes," I say, my attention focused on the folder in front of me.

Jack was just trying to help me by pulling the file. That's what we do. When one of us is running behind or stuck in court, the other makes it their business to cover. Hence the reason I was at Meera's in the first place. But my shirt is soaked with sweat, and I don't have time for small talk.

I'm scanning the new documents in Dee's file when Ashley pokes her head into my office. "Dee is here when you're ready." She shakes her head and huffs when her eyes land on the folder in my hand. "Oh, I see you found the file I placed on your desk." She rolls her eyes and then walks out.

"Tell me why we keep her employed here," I grumble.

"Because she's great at what she does." Jack laughs. "Come see me after Dee leaves."

I nod, snap the folder shut, and head for our conference room, where Dee Thomas sits, tapping her fingers on the oversized mahogany table. Her attention is cast toward the window, where she's probably watching the people going about their day on the street below. When I clear my throat, the tapping stops.

She studies my shirt and lets out a loud huff. "I hope she was worth it."

"Hello, Dee," I say. My voice is soft and husky. I turn on the charm I know she enjoys.

"Don't you *hello* me looking like that." Her lips are set in a fine line.

"Like what?" I hold back a grimace as I glance down at my shirt. "This?" I point. "I was helping a friend with a plumbing problem. But I'm all yours now."

"Is that what you kids are calling it nowadays? You should be ashamed of yourself."

I have to suppress my laughter. Dee is a firecracker. She doesn't beat around the bush. She's a decade or so younger than my grandpa and lives by a set of rules she believes everyone should follow. One being that people should keep their sex lives to themselves. This I know because she's not only a client but a family friend.

I've known Dee for years. When I was in junior high, my mom bought the house next to hers because it was directly behind the animal hospital. That first day, when Justin was helping us unpack, Dee showed up with a casserole. When my mom introduced Justin as her boyfriend, Dee blushed and said, "What you do on your own time is none of my business."

Dee hired me as her lawyer and shocked the shit out of me when she told me without a hint of embarrassment that her husband, Dick—yeah, Dick is his name—impregnated his mistress. I about fell out of my seat. And then I got pissed for her. It must have been difficult for a woman who kept her life so private to reveal something that would become so public.

"Don't be mad at me today, Dee. I have good news. I think you'll like what I found." I sink into the seat next to her and scoot closer. She smells like a combination of fabric softener and soap, reminding me of my grandmother. Of days when my mom took night classes and she would chase me into the bathtub and wash my hair, scrubbing at my scalp with her long fingernails.

"How can I like something when it involves my husband leaving me for a twenty-year-old floozy? When he's choosing to create a new family when he already has one?" she asks, her words heavy with pain and regret. "I gave him thirty-nine years of my life. Thirty-nine fucking years. That asshole."

"I'm sorry. But you asked for the shark, so you're getting the shark. Let me help you and Jeremy. He deserves it just as much as you do." Jeremy is Dee and Dick's only child. He's in his midthirties, just a handful of years older than me, and has Rett syndrome, a rare neurological disorder that keeps him wheelchair bound.

Opening the folder, I pull out the list of Dick's assets and debt his lawyer supplied us. Then I pull out the title to a home located in Washington state with Dick's name on it. "This here was not on the discovery. He purchased this last month. With cash. It's valued at one and a half million dollars." I place my hand on Dee's. "He's been hiding money. Your money."

Her eyes grow dark as she says those four beautiful words I live for. "Get that fucking bastard."

When Dee heads out, she isn't smiling. My clients rarely do. They're jaded. They have no reason to believe their reality—the hell they've been living in—will change. But they're wrong. Because I do anything it takes to help them. To fix the problems their douchebag husbands carelessly created.

When I step into Jack's office, I'm hit by an overpowering fruit-scented waft of air. Like peaches and oranges or some shit like that. "Sadie's candles?" I ask.

Jack peers up from his computer screen, a loose grin on his face. "Those candles are what's about to take us to Hawaii."

"We're going to Hawaii?" I stop in my tracks. *Since when?*

"Not us." He rolls his eyes. "Sadie's killing it with her sales. Her company is sending her to Hawaii for a conference next week, kind of last minute. That's what I wanted to talk to you about." He slides his keyboard to the side and clasps his hands on the desktop in front of him.

I drop into the chair across from his desk and cross my legs. While I wait for him to continue, I suppress the urge to grin, because my best friend is so predictable. Ever since we were kids, Jack has started every serious conversation by affecting a matter-of-fact tone. Then comes the hand clasping and the eye twitch. It never fails. Like the time he sat on his brother's hamster. He called Johnny down from his bedroom, folded his hands, and said in a voice far too mature for a little boy, "Johnny, there comes a time when all animals have to follow the rainbow to find their forever home."

While I doubt what Jack has to say is bad, it's clear by his posture that it's serious.

He clears his throat. "I don't have much on my schedule for next week, so maybe I could move a few clients around. And if you can finish up Jill's case for me, then I might go with Sadie."

I shake my head. "Might go with her?"

"Okay, I am going with her. I already bought a ticket. Jill is the only one on the docket for next week."

"Yeah, that's not a problem."

Jill is a super attractive, super young, super low-key girl who married the wrong prick. But they don't have kids and they've already agreed to sell their only joint assets and split the proceeds equally.

"Jill will be in solid hands with me."

Jack's half smile fades. "She's a decade younger than you. There's a difference between young and robbing the cradle. Think of Sophie. Jill was probably, what, twelve years old when she was born?"

The visual my mind creates makes me cringe. I wasn't serious about Jill. She's a client, and I don't mix business with pleasure. But now I can't get the image out of my head. How would it look from Sophie's perspective? She's too young to understand the idea of casual dating or hooking up, and I'm definitely not looking to find her a stepmom. Sophie's my world, and I'll do anything to protect her.

"Is Grace going with you?" I ask, in desperate need of a subject change so I can wipe the disturbing thoughts from my head.

"Nope. Sadie's mom is staying with her so she can watch the dog too." Jack pushes back and props his feet on his desk. "We're having people over this weekend. Figured we'd grill and swim. You should bring Sophie. I think we'll have a full house, so she'll have plenty of friends to play with."

Friends. It's such a Jack thing to say. He means well. I'll give him that. But Sophie isn't a friend type of girl. She's quiet and standoffish while somehow also being brash and abrasive, though she probably gets that last part from me. She doesn't care to make friends, and I don't push her.

After being dropped off on my doorstep, it took Sophie almost six months to speak and another six months before she was willing to accept her first hug from me. Now, almost three years later, she's finally communicating with my mom, my sister, and my grandpa. They've all accepted how hard the first few years of her life must have been and are patient with her. But strangers? People who don't know her? Sophie can go from shy to screaming in two seconds flat, and that's if she's having a good day.

And I can't help but wonder whether she'd have the same tendencies if I'd known about her earlier or if she'd come to me as a newborn. Would she still have that hard outer shell? Or was it built up over years of neglect? Was her brashness inherited from me, or was that how she had to respond to be seen and heard? My heart breaks every time I picture what life must have been like for her. But I can't change the past. I can only provide her with love and support now.

I duck my head and rub the back of my neck. "We'll be there." Because while I know Sophie won't make any dramatic changes overnight, the exposure will help.

CHAPTER FIVE

Meera

"How was it?" Sadie asks. "No wait, tell me about the plumbing issue first. Did Gabe fix the problem, or did you ever get a hold of Tanner?"

My spoon is halfway back to the bowl when I choke on the cereal already in my mouth. I pull the phone away from my face, hoping she doesn't read into my reaction. "You knew Gabe came by?" I ask once my fit of coughing subsides.

"How do you think he knew where you lived?" she laughs.

"I figured it was Jack."

"Jack was in court, so Gabe volunteered. He's pretty good with stuff like that."

Gabe volunteered? And Sadie was okay with that?

The last time we talked about Gabe was at her rehearsal dinner three years ago. She refused to introduce us because she said, and I quote,

"Gabriel Henry is a man slut, and I refuse to let him take advantage of your situation. Avoid him at all costs."

Has that changed? Or is he still the man I met that night? The night he followed me into the women's bathroom and invited me to join him in the back of his truck. He'd stepped into my personal space, his bright-blue eyes blazing while he waited for me to respond, the combination of evergreen and alcohol floating between us. He promised that he'd help take my mind off everything. And part of me wanted him to make good on that promise. I wanted to forget about my ex and to let loose.

But Sadie's spidey senses must have activated, because as soon as Gabe brought his lips to my ear and whispered promises of what he'd do to me with his fingers, she sauntered into the bathroom. Her eyes went wide when she mistakenly thought I'd been backed into a corner. Gabe, on the other hand, was too shit-faced to hear her. Small little Sadie grabbed Gabe by the collar and dragged him out the door.

Later, she vowed that she'd make sure he stayed clear of me at the wedding and reception. Though I would never have admitted it to Sadie, I was a bit disappointed, because Gabe seemed like the perfect distraction.

After that, she never mentioned him again. And I never told her about waking up next to him the morning after. How could I when I don't even know what happened myself?

But with that memory comes a more recent one. My run-in with Gabe at the animal hospital. The guy doesn't even remember who I am. And then when he touched me with those soft hands of his—

"Meera, you still there?"

"I'm here. Sorry about that," I say, scrambling for an excuse. But I don't need one because Sadie is talking again.

"Did Gabe fix the problem?"

I drop my bowl into the sink with a clatter and sigh. "No. He said I need new pipes. I'll figure it out."

"Not by yourself. Absolutely not. Jack and Gabe can do it for you. I'll send them over Friday after work. They owe me." Gotta love this pint-sized woman. She always gets her way. "By the way, you're coming over Saturday. We're having a barbeque. Jack needs to put his grill to good use before the summer is over. And it'll give you a chance to catch up with some of the girls from the wedding. They've been asking about you."

She goes on to mention Hawaii and a work conference, but I stopped actively listening when she insisted on sending Gabe over on Friday. I want to be upset about this. I'm fully capable of doing this on my own. But despite my efforts, I can't muster the will to argue with her. Maybe my mind hasn't caught up with logic yet. Logical Meera doesn't want Gabe in the same room as me. Sensible Meera knows men like him don't change. He could have been a good time. Hell, maybe he was. But I'm not that Meera anymore, and I'll be damned if I let another man treat me the way Tom treated me for all those years.

Once Sadie and I say goodbye, I wash my dishes and set them on the counter to dry. Then I scan the apartment and try not to cringe. This place just needs a makeover—massive as it may be—and then it should be as good as new.

I have a few hours before work, so I do the one thing I know I probably shouldn't. I grab a hammer. The carpet has got to go.

The next few days go by in a blur, and I find a rhythm at work quicker than expected. Nights can sometimes get hectic, but Lydia is a godsend. She knows every facet of the place. Not to mention she's sweet and charismatic and knows how to talk to both pets and their owners. Probably because she's studying to become a teacher.

Teachers have to be nice, right? Most veterinarians, and even office staff, tend to be great with animals but lack people skills.

She's also the exact opposite of Helen. Sure, Lydia warned me about her, but no amount of caution could have prepared me for Mount St. Helen. If I didn't know better, I would have thought *she* was related to Gabe and not Lydia.

"Did you just touch my files?" Helen asked in passing during my second shift. "When we have appointments during the day, no one touches my files. Got that?"

"Sorry, I was just trying to—"

"Don't help. It doesn't look good on you," she snapped back. She tossed her long copper ponytail over her shoulder and stomped in the opposite direction, carrying a bottle of pet-friendly cleaning solution.

On my third shift, as I was getting ready to leave, she came in wearing black sunglasses that were almost the size of her head. Before we could say good morning, she demanded that neither Lydia nor I open our mouths. "I don't have time to listen to either of you, and I am not in the mood for a headache."

Today, I plan to keep it cool. I made myself a list as a reminder. One, don't look at Helen. Two, don't say hi to Helen. Three, don't touch anything that looks like it might belong to Helen. I'm on four when the bell above the door jingles.

It's Helen, and she's walking straight toward me with a smile that reaches both ears.

I almost fall out of my chair.

"Don't look so surprised," she says. "I don't always bite."

Next to me, Lydia just shrugs. "This is a first for me too."

I want to get up, to follow her. To get to know this Helen. With that smile, she almost looks approachable. Almost. But I stay in my seat because all good things are worth waiting for, and I don't want to rock the boat just yet.

When I do finally push myself out of my seat and stretch, Dr. Thompson glides in and heads straight to an exam room, not saying a word to any of us.

I shake my head. The two of them will take some getting used to.

Then, as I'm gathering my things, Dr. Coleman makes an appearance.

"Good morning, ladies," he sings. "It was another great night, wouldn't you say?"

My first thought is about how similar his sparkling blue eyes are to Gabe's. But I push that notion out of my head. It's too early to be thinking about that man. And Dr. Coleman smiles. It stretches across his face in a way that makes me want to mimic the expression. Unlike Helen's, his smile brings warmth to my heart. He's content; his heart is full. I like Dr. Coleman. Like Lydia, he's sweet. He cares about his patients and their owners. He's soft-spoken and gentle, and while he might be set in his ways, he's been open to suggestions I have about improving productivity.

"Meera, you look exhausted," he adds. His voice drops a decibel, and then that smile is quickly replaced with a frown.

If Gabe is my age, then Dr. Coleman must be in his midseventies. Don't get me wrong, I firmly believe that a person should work for as long as they want. Nobody should be put out to pasture before they're ready. But right now, as I focus on him, I see a tired man hiding behind a smile. In a way, he resembles my grandfather before he passed away—weary and drained.

"I am," I admit, hiking my bag onto my shoulder. "I don't know how you work nights all the time. Maybe I'm still getting accustomed to the time zone, but it's harder than I imagined. I feel like I could sleep the day away."

Dr. Coleman laughs. "Why don't you take tonight off? Get some sleep. And then come back bright and early Monday morning."

I stare at him, dumbfounded. "I can't take the night off. I've only been here four days."

"Four days, and you're already doing better than Dr. Thompson, and he's been with us for the past two years. But don't tell him I said that." He winks. "I'm going to need you to teach him a thing or two on those day shifts."

That's when I catch it. Day shifts. I work nights. I'm set to work nights for the first six months of my contract.

"Days?" I raise my eyebrows.

Dr. Coleman gives me the cutest old man smirk I've ever seen. "As long as you can handle Helen. Business is picking up during the day now that the clinic in Harbour Village cut back to emergency hours."

"Oh, but I like working with Meera," Lydia complains.

"Good, because I'm changing your hours too. The semester starts in a few weeks, right?"

Lydia angles her head as if she's expecting to hear something she won't believe.

"Yes . . ." She elongates the *y*-sound.

Dr. Coleman rubs his hands together. "I plan to talk to the doctor at Harbour Village about working together. Patients can come to us during the day, and they can take over the nighttime emergency visits. It's a win-win for both of us. I'm getting too old—"

I stop him midsentence. "Do not say you're getting old. Dr. Coleman, you're—"

"Edgar. Call me Edgar." He rubs his temple and continues. "And yes, I'm well beyond retirement."

He turns back to Lydia, who's wearing a look of shock. "Your mom's been nagging me to cut back my hours. And she's right. It's time to shake things up a bit. It might even be good for the business. For us *and* Harbour Village. And then maybe I'll finally get to take up golf." He chuckles.

Dr. Coleman has dedicated his life to this hospital. But right now, it's obvious he's ready to live outside of his job. But instead of throwing in the towel, he's spreading the wealth. He wants Harbour Village to succeed right along with his own hospital.

"Once you have your schedule, let me know, and we'll work around your classes. Then I'll announce the change of hours. But Meera," he says, patting me on the shoulder, "you'll make a great addition to the day shift."

Lydia jumps from her seat and hugs her grandpa, almost knocking him over in the process. "This is great."

For an instant, I let a hint of a smile spread across my face. But just as quickly, my heart grows heavy and I have to fight back tears. Their interaction. That hug. It's as if I'm looking through a mirror that reflects my own past. Lydia is me, and Edgar is my grandfather. What I would do to have one last hug. To smell his Old Spice cologne. To tell him I love him. But most importantly, to thank him. To thank him for taking me in and raising me like a daughter. For never pitying me and for teaching me so much. And to tell him to give Grandma a hug from me.

A tear escapes and tracks down my cheek at the exact moment the door flies open. Quickly, I run my hand across my face, wiping the dampness away.

"It's Charlie. He ate another Lego."

CHAPTER SIX

Gabe

"Charlie did not swallow a Lego," I say once Sophie is out of earshot. Meera has examined him the last two times we've been here. I don't *have* to explain anything to her, but the look she gave me when Sophie told her this makes five times in less than two weeks made me feel like one of my clients when their case goes to trial. Judged. Like Meera was cross-examining me, picking apart my parenting skills. And while typically, I couldn't care less about what people think, with her, I suddenly care too much.

Meera stops in her tracks and spins to face me. Her forest-green irises swirl with hints of gold near her pupils. And for a moment, I'm so enraptured by them that my mind goes blank.

She clears her throat, bringing me back to the present. Then she shifts her weight and places one hand on her hip while holding Charlie's chart in her other hand, the stance indicating she doesn't have all day.

"We don't have Legos."

With her brows furrowed and a slight frown marring her lips, she looks more confused now.

"I mean, Sophie doesn't play with Legos. We have some, but she doesn't play with them. So it's not like we leave them lying around the house."

"Then why would she say he's swallowing them?"

Meera's question throws me. The answer is far more complicated than I can understand, let alone explain. Sophie's a worrier. When we first brought Charlie home from the shelter two years ago, he was bone thin and malnourished, kind of like she was. Sophie took him in and brought him back to life. Everywhere she goes, Charlie is at her side. So the Lego thing could be an irrational concern.

And yet, part of me thinks she's finally trying to connect. She spends so much time at my mom's house, she's probably bored. She doesn't like playing with the kids in the neighborhood, so maybe this gives her a reason to come by and hang out with my sister.

I release a deep exhale, wishing I could shut down the conversation, but Meera is still standing before me, hip cocked, waiting for a response.

"It's complicated." I tighten my tie, hoping she takes it as a sign that I need to leave. I'm already late for work, and I'll have to leave early this afternoon since Jack and I are helping Meera with her plumbing.

"Then uncomplicate it."

I suck in a breath at the demand. Normal people would have taken my comment as a sign to stop asking questions. But Meera is anything but normal.

She doesn't back down. Instead, she stands a little straighter and tilts her head like she's still waiting for my response, her eyes never leaving me.

I force out the oxygen trapped inside my chest and do what lawyers do best. I deflect. "Jack and I will be by around six. Will you be home to let us in, or do you want to give me a key so we can let ourselves in?"

"I'll be there," she huffs and turns around.

It works. Yeah, I'm an asshole. But I don't have time for this shit.

At five fifty-five, I'm midknock when the door swings open and Meera appears with an armload of yellow carpet.

She jumps back and drops the smelly pile to the floor. "Oh my God, you scared me. You're early," she says.

I set my supplies on the floor in the hallway and help her pick up the carpet. "I'm only five minutes early."

Her eyes go wide. "It's already six?"

"In five minutes it will be," I deadpan.

Her lips tighten. She's clearly not amused by my response. "Where's Jack?" She leads me across the deck and down the stairs into her poorly lit parking lot.

"He had to finish something at the office. He'll be here in about half an hour."

Once she's chucked the carpet into the dumpster, she studies me, as if she's trying to figure out whether she should let me into her apartment or throw me out with the carpet.

I ignore her expression and drop my armload in as well. Then I brush my hands on my basketball shorts and head back up the stairs without giving her a chance to respond.

"Holy shit." When I step inside her apartment, it looks nothing like it did the other day. The walls are no longer piss yellow. Instead, they're an eggshell white, a fresh canvas that's both inviting and refreshing.

The hardwood floors are in pretty bad shape, but without the carpet, the room looks larger. Suitable to live in. There's a metallic gold rod hanging above the window with rose-gold curtains that reach the floor and plants that sit on a three-tier stand against the wall. And flowers. An assortment of red, pink, and yellow roses spills over a metal vase in the center of her table.

"Holy shit good, or holy shit bad?" Meera asks, her voice hitched with uncertainty.

I turn to her, baffled that she can't see how incredible this place looks. But then she makes eye contact, and I'm caught in her orbit, and I can't possibly compare the beauty of the room to her.

Meera's dark hair is pulled into a low ponytail. She's wearing an oversized white T-shirt that says *coffee* in black lettering and black workout shorts that show off her long, slender legs.

I clear my throat. "Goodbye, meth lab. Did you do this all yourself?"

The corners of her mouth lift like she's going to smile, but she doesn't allow herself the satisfaction.

Is the reluctance my fault? Or is this just her personality?

"You should be proud." I spin, catching sight of the kitchen cabinets lying on the floor with a canister of stain next to them. "I can't imagine how much time it's taken you to put so much work into this place."

Meera squares her shoulders and scowls as if I just insulted her. "I am."

I want to ask her what's got her so wound up. I want to tell her she should relax a little. Maybe have some fun. That I don't bite. But the truth is I do bite. And I'm not a liar. Instead, I take the supplies I brought with me and head to the bathroom.

"Do you want something to drink?" Meera calls after me.

"Sure," I say, but I don't turn back to face her. The sooner I get this shit finished, the sooner I can go. I promised Sophie a movie night.

I'm under the sink when Meera enters the bathroom, her bare feet padding softly across the tile. She walks like Sophie, quiet and with purpose. If I didn't know better, I'd say she was watching me too, just as Sophie does when she doesn't think I'm paying attention.

I clear my throat. "Can you hand me that wrench?"

Her bare calf brushes against my knee, sending goose bumps trailing down my spine, as a glass bottle clinks against the porcelain sink above my head.

A second later, the soft touch disappears, and I'm left with an overwhelming sense of desire. For her to touch me again. For her skin to make contact with mine just once more.

A cold metal object pokes me in the arm, forcing my attention up to where Meera is bent at the waist, holding the wrench.

"Thanks," I say, and then I hold out my hand.

When she places the wrench in my palm, her fingers glide across my flesh, and I suck in a sharp breath. My heart rate ratchets up, but my inner voice screams at it to slow the fuck down. This girl still hates me, and rightfully so.

Our eyes meet, and for a moment, I forget what happened three years ago. I forget that Meera thinks I'm an asshole. Strike that. I forget that she knows I'm an asshole. That I didn't proposition her for sex the night of our best friends' rehearsal dinner. But the moment ends all too quickly when she pulls her hand back and looks away. The same way she did the other night when I asked about the bandage.

It's not there anymore. And while I want to ask her about it, I don't pry.

When she pulls back, I want to punch myself in the face. Because of her, my skin is on fire, and I don't want to put out the flames.

I close my eyes and repeat my mom's words silently. *You can't change the past, but you can damn well learn from it.* She's philosophical and optimistic and all that shit. She had to be, raising a hellion like me. If she were here, right now, she'd tell me to seize the day or some bullshit. But Meera and I are not cut from the same cloth. She's roses and sunshine, and I'm piss and vinegar. Something my grandma used to say.

"I wasn't sure what you'd want, so I brought you a beer." Meera's voice is flat.

Fuck. I'm over here all hot and bothered and she can barely look in my direction. I shake my head, trying to focus on what's in front of me and force all these thoughts of her out of my mind.

"I don't drink," I say, but when she arches an eyebrow, I correct myself. "I don't drink during the week. Only on the weekends."

"It is the weekend."

I close my eyes because I don't want to get into this, but when I open them again, she's still watching me. Just like she did when she wanted an explanation about the Legos.

"I limit my drinking to one night a week. I'll be drinking tomorrow, so alcohol is off-limits tonight."

Surprisingly, Meera only shrugs and turns to leave.

"But I'll take a water," I add before she disappears down the hall, because let's be honest, I want her to come back.

CHAPTER SEVEN

Meera

I can't get out of there fast enough. Breathing in the same air as that man does something to me and I don't like it. Okay, that's a lie, because I do like it. I more than like it.

If only he wasn't so smug. So righteous. So full of himself.

Three years ago, I wanted nothing more than to slam my lips against his arrogant mouth. I wanted to forget about Tom. I deserved a night where I could put the piece of shit behind me.

Back then, I craved a night of fun. I wanted everything Gabe promised when he followed me into the women's restroom, as his jaw rested against my cheek and his words spilled into a blissful whisper. He was buzzed. I smelled it when his lips hovered over my mouth. And I wanted to be drunk with him.

Sadie had told me he was a womanizer. That he cared about no one but himself.

But none of that mattered. For the first time in years, I was having a good time. Being spontaneous and reckless and not the Meera who was still married to a lying, cheating, abusive asshole.

So as Gabe slid his hands up my legs and dug his fingers into my flesh as he hoisted me onto the bathroom sink, my only thought was that I wanted him. That if men could do this sort of thing, so could I.

But that all went to hell the moment Sadie flew in on her rageful unicorn. She peeled Gabe away. And I didn't stop her. I didn't know how. Once Sadie got that look, nothing got in her way.

"Oh my God," she said, her eyes wide. Her words were directed at Gabe. "Do you not have any moral compass?"

When he didn't respond, she snatched at the front of his collared shirt and yanked him down to her level. "Leave. Before I get Jack in here."

Like me, Gabe didn't put up a fight. Instead, he turned to me, and for a split second, an unnamed emotion flashed across his face. Regret. Maybe remorse. But then he threw up his hands when Sadie yanked at his shirt for a second time.

"All right, all right, I'm going," he said as she marched him out of the bathroom.

"Nothing happened," I said when he was gone.

She eyed me suspiciously as I pulled down the hem of my dress.

It was true. His hands may have inched their way up my legs, but he hadn't made it very far. He hadn't even kissed me.

"Good, because he was with another woman before you got here, and I'm sure he'll find someone else to go home with."

She was right. Right? What did I expect? How would I have even handled a one-night stand anyway? Would I have been okay with allowing his lips to touch mine and then pretending like nothing happened the next morning? I don't consider myself a prude, but like

Sadie said—men like Gabe weren't for me. And I was still technically married.

And when I walked out of the bathroom with Sadie at my side, her words rang true. A tall woman, much older than me, with beautiful chestnut hair, slinked her arm through Gabe's and led him out the restaurant door. And for some ungodly reason, jealousy shot through my veins.

When Gabe's voice brings me back to the present, water is cascading down my wrist and I fumble to shut it off.

"I'm sorry. What was that?" I ask, startled, but also trying to play it cool. Dammit, why can't I get this man out of my mind? I don't want to think about him. I don't even want him here in my apartment. But I can't kick him out. He's doing me a favor, for crying out loud.

I turn around, expecting Gabe to be in the hallway, but instead, those clear-blue eyes are piercing me from only a foot or two away.

He's so close I can smell his cologne. The same hint of evergreen he wore that night I first set eyes on him. The scent I woke up to the morning after the wedding. The fragrance that hung in the air when he stood in my apartment just days ago.

"You okay?" He takes the glass of water out of my hand. Then he places it on the counter and grasps my elbow. "Here, sit down."

I open my mouth, but nothing comes out.

Brows furrowed, he pulls me to a chair. "Sit." It's a demand, full of authority.

I listen and sink onto the cold metal barstool, too stunned and embarrassed to argue.

"Do you have any juice?"

"Juice," I repeat obtusely.

"Yes, juice. Do you have some in the fridge, or do you keep it in your bag?" he asks. He's hunched over, his hands on his thighs so he's at eye level with me, but he's scanning the room.

"Juice," I say a second time, my voice hitching. Why is he asking if I have juice?

"The last time you got light-headed, you said you had juice in your bag." He says this as if he's just read my mind.

I'm suddenly mortified. Gabe thinks my blood sugar is low. He thinks I'm going to pass out again.

I throw my hand over my face and close my eyes. I can't look at him. I want to tell him I'm fine. That I don't need juice. That I was lost in thought—about him. Remembering his nose pressed against my neck as he whispered about getting me alone.

But what would I even say? *Hey, Gabe. I was just thinking about the night we met and how your hands were on my thighs. Can you put them there again?*

Oh my God. No. Never.

I open my eyes and clear my throat. "I'm okay. I was just spacing out." I plant my feet and push up out of the stool.

But he tugs at my arm, pulling me back down. He squints, the look full of skepticism.

"I get lost in thought sometimes. You know, I kind of daydream, I guess." It's not a total lie.

"I'd feel better if you'd at least drink some water," he growls. He loosens his grip on my arm, but he doesn't let go. With his other hand, he reaches for the glass and sets it in front of me.

When I don't take the glass right away, he lets go of me. His fingertips graze my flesh as he nudges the water closer, sending goose bumps ricocheting down my spine. Then he places his warm hand back where it was.

"Honestly, I'm fine," I say, finally finding my voice, though his touch makes me want to melt into a puddle at his feet.

"Then drink."

The tone of Gabe's voice matches the hint of emotion that shines from his eyes sometimes. Concern. Sadness, even. The man standing in front of me doesn't look like the man who had his hands on my thighs three years ago. That man was hungry. This one looks beaten down and tired.

With a huff, I pick up the glass and take two large gulps. "See? I'm okay."

Gabe eyes me, his expression flat again. "Good. I could use your help. Jack can't make it. Sadie has a flat tire."

Mr. Grump is back.

An hour later, sweat beads down my temple as I crawl out from under my bathroom sink for the hundredth time. I stand and wipe away the extra putty from the drain like Gabe showed me. Then I turn to him for approval.

He laughs, the sound of it surprising me. He hasn't so much as smiled since he's been here, and now he's laughing.

I'm taken aback, because I don't know what he finds funny. I narrow my eyes and bite my lip, mentally running through each step. Did I do something wrong? Did I forget to tighten all the rings?

At my obvious confusion, he stops, though the curve to his mouth remains.

"What? Do I have something on my face?"

He laughs again, a little lower this time. "Actually, you do," he says, stepping closer.

My natural reaction is to pull away, but the way his eyes dance in the light roots me to the spot and makes my stomach tighten.

Tilting close, he drags his thumb across my cheek. It's rough and soft and slow.

It catches me off guard, and I stumble, but Gabe presses his other hand to my hip, anchoring me in place.

I close my eyes and let him peel away the putty, fixated on the way it crumbles between our skin.

He moves to my chin, and this time, with his index finger, he wipes away the goop that hasn't yet dried.

"Breathe, Meera," he whispers.

My eyes flash open at the familiarity of his words. The deep undertone of his whisper draws a current down my spine. I hadn't realized I was holding my breath.

When our eyes meet, he laughs again.

"Hold still, there's more."

On a normal day, I wouldn't let this happen. I wouldn't allow a man to get this close. But I don't budge.

He presses a finger to my neck and slides it across my clavicle. It's warm and tender, and time seems to stand still as we breathe in the same oxygen.

"I think I got it all," he says, but he doesn't move.

I don't move either. I'm frozen in place. When his throat bobs, my heart takes off and my breathing quickens. It's ridiculous. He's just standing in front of me, but every second that his skin connects with mine, my body reacts in a way I can't control. His proximity makes my body buzz.

Maybe it's because I haven't been touched in forever. The last time I felt like this was when Gabe's hands were gripping my thighs in that restaurant bathroom. I wanted him then. And I want him now.

He dips his head, inching closer, and I feel the tug at the center of my core. I want this. I need this. When his mouth hovers over mine, I tremble, ready to give in to the urge to lean in. Ready to let him take me. Devour me.

But I hold myself back. As turned on as I am, this is Gabe. The man slut. He can have any woman he wants. He *does* have every woman he wants. And he doesn't even remember me.

I can't. I won't.

Released from the spell, I suck in a sharp breath and go rigid.

At the change in my mood, he pulls back, his brows dropping low.

I swallow harshly and gather my bearings, clenching my fists at my sides. "You can leave now."

He takes a step back and scowls.

"It's not you. It's me. I mean, no, it is you," I babble, shaking my head, embarrassed at the moment I've created between us.

"I don't follow."

"You don't remember, do you?"

"Remember?" He tilts his head, his blue eyes full of confusion.

I fold my arms and walk out of the bathroom. In the hallway, he tugs on my arm and cages me against the wall.

"What should I remember?" he growls.

His warm breath skates across my neck, his lips so close to mine. We're closer than we were moments ago. So close I can see every blade of stubble on his jaw. But I don't let his good looks charm me this time.

"The wedding," I seethe.

"The wedding?"

"Stop repeating what I say. Yes. The wedding. Sadie and Jack's wedding. Three years ago." I'm loud and flustered, and I'm talking fast to keep up with the heart that's about to lurch from my chest.

"I remember the wedding." His voice is gravelly and slow, his warm breath encircling me.

"Yeah, but do you remember the girl who woke up in your bed the next morning?" I fight to slow my words to match his, but it's useless. Something in his voice, or maybe the way he's looking at me, is making me lose control.

"I'm still not following," he whispers, almost like he's too wrapped up in me. Too wrapped up in wanting something I can't give him.

"Oh my God. Of course you're not following. That was me. I woke up in your bed." I finally push past him.

He turns, following my movement with his eyes, his expression unwavering.

I didn't move to Morganville to get mixed up in lust-filled nights with this man. I moved here to be independent. To prove to myself that I can do anything I want. That I can take care of myself. That broken promises don't have to mean broken dreams.

After a moment of silence, I shift my weight and look away. "Please leave."

Gabe hesitates, scanning my face, as if he's contemplating something. But whatever it is doesn't come to fruition. Instead, he presses his lips together and walks away. At the door, he looks back at me one last time. "I know it was you." His voice is peppered with anger.

And then he's gone.

CHAPTER EIGHT

Gabe

"Can I have popcorn?" Sophie asks when I pick her up from my mom's house.

"Of course. Get your things, and then we'll head home. You can pick out the movie tonight," I say, ruffling her hair.

She skips up the stairs to my old bedroom, Charlie chasing behind her. My mom redecorated it the day after we found out about Sophie. Instead of baseball posters plastered over half-naked women, the walls are decorated in hues of pinks and creams and adorned with pictures of ballet dancers and unicorns. Though Sophie would probably prefer the baseball.

"Hi, dear. You're back early," my mom says as she places a kiss on my cheek. She's wearing a pink T-shirt that reads *Kindergarten Rocks* and a pair of black slacks covered in beige dog hair.

"It didn't take long to replace the pipes," I say. "How was your first day back at work?" I divert the conversation, not interested in elaborating on anything that involves Meera.

My mom's been teaching since I was in fourth grade. The day she graduated from college, it was still just the two of us and my grandparents. But she worked her ass off going to night school and taking care of me because my dad was—and still is—a low-life piece of scum. Though I've long made peace with the fact that some men should never procreate.

"I'm not at work yet. Just setting up the classroom. And you replaced her pipes?" She eyes me with suspicion. "Lydia *did* say Dr. Taylor is gorgeous."

"Mom, seriously. You're starting to sound like Dee." I let out a huff and watch as my mom's shoulders sink.

"How is Dee?" Her voice softens.

"Dick is still a dick, but we all knew that. But Dee is finally ready to play hardball." I don't say the obvious, because my mom knows all too well that it takes time to heal after a betrayal like that.

"Good, she deserves the best. But don't change the subject. I want to know more about this lady doctor. Lydia loves her. She said she's friends with Jack and Sadie. Does that mean she's a friend of yours too?" There's a hint of hope in her voice.

I release a heavy sigh. My mom is anything but subtle. "I only helped with a leak. I showed her how to replace the pipes, and then I left." I leave off the part where she kicked me out.

My mom pouts. "You could have stayed out later. Sophie is always welcome to stay the night. You should get back out there. Have some fun."

Here we go again. "I'd prefer to keep my love life between me and—"

"What love life?" she interjects. "Work and Sophie are the only things that keep you going these days."

"I like my job. And I enjoy spending time with my daughter," I say with a straight face. "Where's Justin?"

She waves her hand dismissively. "He got called in for a surgery. But stop changing the subject. Is it too much to want my baby boy to be happy? You can be happy with your job and Sophie, but what about in—"

I throw my hand out in front of me and wince. "Stop right there."

I don't know how she planned to end that sentence, but I'm pretty sure it wouldn't have been PG. My mom is a bit of a free spirit. She had me young, and while she worked hard to be where she is now, she raised me more as a friend than a son. It wasn't until she met Justin and had Lydia that she settled down. But by then, I was a teenager, and the damage had already been done.

"I am perfectly content, thank you very much."

She sighs. "Okay, okay." She holds her hands up in defeat. "I know you're busy, but do you think you can pencil us in for dinner tomorrow night? I'm making Grandma's chicken chili."

The mention of chili makes my mouth water. I can almost taste the savory chicken melting in my mouth. When my grandma was alive, it was my favorite meal. She only made it on special occasions or if I was sick. She said that if she made it more often, we wouldn't love it the way we did. That the secret wasn't in the recipe, but in how rarely she made it.

"Thanks for the invite, but we can't make it," I say, almost regretting it once the words leave my mouth. "Jack and Sadie are having people over. I think it'll be good for Sophie to socialize with other kids."

And then, as if on cue, Sophie comes down the stairs. She's dragging her feet, and Charlie is nipping at her heels. "What does socialize mean?" she asks, her eyes locked on me.

It's at that moment, when I see her emotionless face, that I realize I am my mother's son.

Night falls, and the morning sun rises, slow and steady as it has for the past three years. When I stumble to the kitchen, Sophie is already sitting at the table with a bowl of cereal. Her feet are tucked beneath her on an old oak chair as she digs her spoon into a heap of Lucky Charms, and her long hair is already combed back into a neat ponytail.

"Good morning," I say, wiping the sleep from my eyes. "Looks like you started breakfast without me."

I reach for Charlie's bowl, ready to fill it with kibble, when Sophie stops me. "I already fed him and took him out."

Of course she did. My eight-year-old, the responsible one.

"What do you want to do this morning?" I ask, eyeing her as I fumble with the coffeepot. "Want to go to the zoo before Jack and Sadie's barbeque? I hear there's a new butterfly exhibit."

Sophie shoves another spoonful of cereal into her mouth and shakes her head. "Can we go to the library?" she mumbles, a dribble of milk running down her chin. "I want to return my books and see if they have anything new."

I press the button on the coffee machine and smile. Not only is she responsible, but she's inquisitive and curious and always on the hunt for knowledge. "Absolutely." And then I add, "I think Ms. Penelope said they were getting a new shipment of books this week."

The sweet scent of fresh coffee fills the air, and like every Saturday morning, I sit across from my daughter and watch her as she silently finishes her breakfast.

After the library, we drop Charlie off with my mom and head over to Jack and Sadie's house, which isn't too far from my own.

"Hey, the other kids are out back," Jack says, giving Sophie the best side hug she's willing to give while also taking the store-bought cookies I hold out in offering. "Some of them are about to go jump in the pool."

Sophie gives a fake smile but says nothing.

"And Sadie bought a really cool arts and crafts set. She set it up in Grace's bedroom. Grace is at her grandma's, so you have the room to yourself today." He lifts his brows like he knows that he hit the jackpot with that last part.

Sophie's lips curl almost imperceptibly, but as tiny as it is, the smile is real. She tilts her head and looks at me.

I nod. "Go ahead. Have fun. You know where to find me."

"Thank you," Sophie says politely before padding toward the other end of the house.

I'm thankful too. I'm not sure how I got so lucky. Jack has been a great friend. He's a few years younger than me, but I've known him for most of my life. Growing up, most of us boys stuck together. We had to. The girls outnumbered us four to one.

"There are drinks out back. But beware—Darlene is coming by at some point."

I grit my teeth. Darlene is the one and only girl I've attempted a relationship with since I was a teenager. She's one of Sadie's friends, so I knew I had to tread lightly, but since she didn't live in Morganville, for once my reputation didn't color our every interaction. It was nice to connect with someone who didn't know me or my old ways. Sophie had been with me for two years by then, and I felt like I was finally ready to get out there. Maybe settle down.

But goddamn, was I wrong. Darlene is a nice woman, and she's attractive, but there was zero chemistry between us. At least, on my end. A few dates in, I knew it wasn't going to go anywhere, but tell that to the girl who thought she was already madly in love.

"Thanks for the warning."

I head through the house and out onto the back patio, where white clouds absorb the evening sunlight. Birds flutter from tree to tree, gleefully chasing one another just as two boys who don't look much older than Sophie zoom past me and climb the ladder to the pool at lightning speed. The first boy barely makes it to the top before he launches himself into the water, belly first. The second laughs, and without a morsel of hesitation, mirrors him, slapping the water with a loud splash.

"Ouch, that didn't sound good," a feminine voice, high-pitched and nasally, snorts from the other side of the patio.

It's Marissa. She's sitting next to Heidi and Leila. The three of them have their hands wound so tightly around their wineglasses, they're almost strangling them.

I lift the lid to the cooler and pull out a cold beer.

"What I'd do to be a kid again," Leila says.

Her soft voice instantly transports me back in time to our freshman year homecoming dance. Leila was my date, and when that last song played, I leaned in for a kiss like every other boy in the auditorium. But the moment I pursed my lips, she put a hand between us, stopping me midpucker. "Gabe, I don't like you like that. We're friends. That's it." Then she took my hand and promised not to tell anyone about my duck face. To this day, as far as I know, she hasn't. And for that, she's probably my favorite of the girls.

"Fuck that shit," Marissa snaps. "Can you imagine growing up in today's society? Hell no. Our childhood was nothing like what these kids have to endure. Social media is one evil bitch. And texting? Don't get me started. Kids have no idea how to interpret them. Maisy insists every message is mean and that all of her classmates are picking on her. And you know what? They might be. I can't understand half the acronyms they use." Marissa is the opposite of Leila. She cusses like it's nobody's business. So much so that I've asked her to come work with Jack and me, but she refuses to give up her cushy corporate position in the next town over. That, and she doesn't like me very much.

"Can we not talk about kids tonight?" Heidi jumps in as Marissa takes a breath, no doubt ready to continue her rant. "I deal with a crying colicky baby day in and day out, and I'd really like to enjoy this moment while my mother-in-law watches the little monster."

They all laugh. Then they clink glasses in midair before bringing them back to their lips.

I twist the cap to my bottle, ready to make my way over, when Heidi continues.

"Have either of you seen Meera yet?"

I freeze midstride. Meera's coming? I guess I should have realized she would. She's Sadie's friend, so she belongs here.

"Not yet, but Sadie mentioned she was coming by. She doesn't have kids. That lucky bitch," Marissa adds dryly.

"Did she ever divorce that guy? What was his name? Tim?"

"Fuck if I know. It's been what, three years? I sure hope she finally moved on from that bastard."

"Didn't she live out of her car? I think Sadie said that, but I was so shit-faced I wasn't really listening."

At the mention of her name, Sadie materializes beside me. "Hey, Gabe." She follows my gaze to the three women. "They're talking shit, aren't they?"

Not wanting to get involved, I only shrug.

"Lies." She snorts. "Sophie's in Grace's room if you're looking for her."

I smile. "Jack said you bought craft stuff. You didn't have to go out of your way and do that."

Sadie shakes her head. "I didn't. I was at the store anyway, and I know she likes to color and create stuff, so when I saw the kit, I knew I had to get it for her."

I take a pull from my beer and say, "Either way, I appreciate it."

Sadie lifts the lid to the cooler beside me and pulls out a fruity spritzer and flips back the tab. "She's come a long way. I wasn't bribing her or anything, but she *did* give me a hug, so it was a win-win." She laughs. "Were you able to help Meera with the plumbing in the bathroom yesterday? I haven't had a chance to talk to her yet."

I nod. "Yup. I replaced the pipes and—"

"*I* replaced the pipes," a soft but firm voice interrupts me from behind. "But he showed me how."

Meera sidles up to Sadie, her green eyes sparkling when she turns to face me. If I didn't know better, I'd swear she was smiling. Her glow is so contagious, I find myself returning the expression. And for the briefest moment, I swear she notices. But then she pulls her bottom lip in so quickly I wonder if I imagined it.

"Ah! You made it. The girls are going to die." Sadie drags her in for a hug, drawing her attention away from me. Meera is tall and slim, and because Sadie is so short, Meera towers over her. Then, with a quick turn, they're off, moving in the direction of the table on the other end of the patio.

"Gabe, bring Meera a drink, would you?" Sadie yells over her shoulder.

As she slips away, the only thing I can think about is how badly I want to taste those lips. God dammit. Tonight is going to be a long night.

CHAPTER NINE

Meera

"You look great."

"How long are you here for?"

"I love your dress. Where did you get it?"

The questions are rapid-fire as each woman stands and leans in for a hug.

"Thanks, I'll be here for at least a year," I say.

"She's working with Dr. Coleman. I'm hoping she'll love it here so much that she'll stay," Sadie says as she pulls out a seat and drops into it.

"You're from San Francisco, right?" Heidi asks.

I nod, but my focus is on where Gabe is digging through the cooler. He looks different today. Not quite as put together as the last few times I've seen him. In a suit, he's attractive. In a suit without his blazer, with his sleeves rolled up, he's hot. Even yesterday, in a pair of basketball shorts and a T-shirt, he was sexy. But he still had that look. His hair was styled perfectly, like he'd just come from work. Today, he's wearing a pair of faded jeans and a white T-shirt that highlights the lean muscles that stretch across his chest. And a backward baseball hat—something I've never found attractive until this minute—covers his head.

When he straightens, I turn my attention back to the girls in front of me.

"No one moves to a small town willingly, unless they're running from something. Or someone," Heidi says, bringing her glass to her lips. "So which one is it?"

Heidi, from my understanding, lives in Morganville to help with her mom, who has multiple sclerosis, but she isn't a native. She moved here when she was in middle school, when her parents divorced. Sadie said that she always planned to move back to Savannah once she turned eighteen, but that was almost twelve years ago.

When she lifts a brow, waiting for a response, my inner voice screams Tom's name. But out loud, all I can utter is, "I like the small-town feel. It's nice. Different from what I'm used to."

"This has got to be quite the culture shock for you," she continues.

"You'll love it. I promise," Sadie pleads, giving Heidi the shut-up face.

Sadie wanted me to come the moment I left Tom. But I wanted to finish college first. I didn't have the chance while she and Jack were there because I got pregnant, and as a result, married. And once I finished, I was admitted to the veterinarian medicine program at Western University of Health Sciences in Anaheim. Sadie knew becoming a veterinarian was my dream, and though she wanted me close, she respected my decision to stay and finish the program.

The closer I came to graduation, the deeper Sadie dug her claws into my plans and the more detailed her plotting became. While the thought of living in a small town worried me, I was excited to finally be near her and Jack again.

"*One year,*" I told her. "*I'll give it one year. And if I love it, I'll stay. But you can't get mad if I leave.*"

"She'll love what?" Gabe slips between us and holds a gin and tonic out to me.

"Morganville, of course," Sadie says, as if it's obvious.

"Ah, yes. Morganville. It has a lot to offer." He's watching me closely, and for a moment, it feels like he's talking about himself.

"Ugh, like what?" Marissa groans. "Unless you have kids, this place is eerily quiet. And believe you me, there are virtually no men available to sweep you off your feet. The good ones are already taken."

"*Most* of them are taken," he says, his fingertips grazing mine as I take the offered drink. My insides twist at his words, and I bite my lip. He *is* talking about himself.

"I swear, if Liam hadn't knocked me up, I would be in LA right now."

That comment drags me back into the conversation, and I pull away from Gabe, taking the drink with me. "I just moved from LA. It's congested and dirty," I admit, "but there's so much culture."

"You were in LA?" A thunderous voice joins the conversation. "I thought you were in San Francisco." Jacob steps up next to Leila. He's tall and handsome and disheveled in much the same way Gabe is, though he doesn't fill out a shirt quite the same way.

Declan stands a foot behind him and smiles, and I return the gesture, still not used to the friendly atmosphere of a small southern town. It's then I realize that they're both looking at me expectantly. Right. Everyone here is a hugger.

I stand, almost bumping into Gabe, who hasn't backed up since he brought me a drink, and quickly embrace both Jacob and Declan.

"Leila never told me you were in LA. I have family out that way," Jacob says, stepping up beside his wife's chair.

"I did too, you big oaf." Leila swats his arm.

He tips forward and runs a finger down the slope of Leila's nose before setting his mouth on hers. She lets out a soft laugh and kisses him back. The two of them are cute together. Both innocent and sweet and very affectionate. They've been married for a while now, I realize. Since before Sadie and Jack's wedding.

A hint of jealousy creeps its way through me at the love they share, but I push it aside. I have no desire for a love life of my own. Not anymore.

Declan, on the other hand, is single. And he's a far cry from innocent and sweet. He's tall, like the other boys, with a solid, square frame.

"I give you three months before you're itching to go back," Marissa continues.

"I give her two," Declan groans.

Their voices fade away in seconds. My attention is once again drawn to the man still hovering close, but as I turn to Gabe, he inches back, creating space between us. Then he lifts a corner of his mouth and nods.

My heart sinks. Despite my resolve to keep my distance from him, I couldn't help but hope Gabe would join in on the conversation. That he would stick around.

Eventually, Jacob and Declan disappear, and other girls join us. The sun sinks behind the tree line, and off in the corner of the yard, Jack gets a bonfire going. A few kids are still in the pool, splashing and shrieking, while others are swinging on the playset or catching fireflies.

As I'm scanning the guests, taking in each scene, I realize I haven't seen Gabe in a while. I'm only three drinks in, but if someone asked who I was looking for right now, I'd say Gabe's name without a second thought.

That's not good.

I stand, needing a reset. I'll find the bathroom and not think about what's-his-name. But when I push out from my chair, my head spins, and I quickly realize I've been sitting here, without moving, for far to long. And now that I think about it, I'm more likely on drink number four, which means if I'm not careful, my glucose levels will spike.

"Hey, where are you going?" Marissa laughs. "You can't leave now."

Putting her at ease, I smile. "Bathroom. You need another drink?" The words come out clear, though I have to concentrate to make them sound that way. Damn. This isn't good. *Just smile and nod and maybe they won't notice.*

"Yes. And grab Sadie another too. The men are on little-monster duty tonight." She laughs, and the group gathered around us joins in.

Inside the house, my heart swells at the faint sound of classical music floating through the air. This is very much a Sadie thing. Like me, she loves Bach, Tchaikovsky, and Mozart. When we roomed together as freshmen, agreeing classical music was great for studying, we played Beethoven on repeat. The image of us sitting on opposite ends of our room, listening to our favorite music, makes me long for those carefree days.

I turn down the hall, feeling light and happy and free, but when I pass the second doorway, my emotions take a sharp detour. Inside, Gabe sits on a tiny white chair. Sophie sits across from him. They're both engrossed in projects that include glue and pom-poms and glitter.

The sight stills me, and for a moment, my thoughts shift to all the what-ifs in my life. What if I had stayed with Tom? What if we tried for another baby? Would Tom do this kind of thing with our daughter? Would I still have left him?

A burning sensation forms behind my eyes, so I quickly shut them tight. When I open them, Gabe's focused on me.

Crap. I turn and head back toward the kitchen, hoping he didn't really see me. But I quickly realize this isn't the way to the bathroom, so I turn around again.

But now Gabe is standing in front of me.

His hat is missing, and his dark hair is thick and wavy and—

"You okay?" he growls. And it's the sexiest sound I've ever heard.

Shit. I'm buzzed. And it's suddenly hotter than Hades in here.

"Your face is red," he muses.

"Just looking for the bathroom." I step forward, giving him a wide berth so I can walk past him, not trusting myself to be in his presence. But, of course, I stumble over my own feet.

Gabe grabs hold of my wrist. His touch is soft and tender and delicate in a way I wouldn't expect from a brute of a man like him.

And I like it. I don't want to pull away.

"You sure you're okay?" he asks in such a deep voice that it almost knocks the breath out of me.

I lift my head. Fuck. His eyes are piercing right through me.

"Breathe, Meera," he says slowly.

I let out a long, exaggerated breath, and then my heart rate accelerates because no one on earth breathes the way I just did.

"Must have had more to drink than I realized," I murmur, covering up my embarrassment.

He releases my arm, and of course, with my dumb luck, I stumble again. Like when he let go, I forgot I had two feet.

He grabs my elbow this time, steadying me.

I don't dare look at him, because if I do, I might laugh. And I don't want to laugh. Anything but laugh. So I look at a spot down the hall just over his shoulder and hold back the sound threatening to spill from me.

He scans me from head to toe, the examination sending heat rushing to my face. If my face was red before, I can only imagine what it looks like now.

Then he tugs my arm, and before I know it, we're in the bathroom. Holy shit. We're in the fucking bathroom together. I shut my eyes. He's going to kiss me. Gabe is going to kiss me. My chest rises sharply at the thought. I let my lips fall apart. I'm going to let him press his mouth to mine.

Is he the slow type, the kind of man who will lean in and brush his lips against mine before running his hand up behind my head? No. He's too forceful. He'll probably press me against the wall and pull my bottom lip between his teeth as he devours me.

I wait. I'm still waiting. I want to taste him, but when nothing happens, I peel back my eyelids. Gabe isn't millimeters away from me any longer. He isn't ready to kiss me at all.

He's hovering over the sink, unzipping my black Accu-Chek bag.

I gape at him, too stunned to speak. When he pulls out my lancing device, he sets it on a towel and washes his hands. Then, as if he just remembered I was standing behind him, he pulls my hands into the warm water and massages soap between my palms and fingers. Holy fuck. Gabriel Henry is massaging my hands. I'm not sure whether I'm in shock or whether I'm totally shit-faced, because I can't find a single word for what's happening.

"Sit," he says. It's the same demanding tone he used on me the other day.

I obey. Thank God the toilet seat is closed.

Gabe presses the button on my lancing device once before taking my hand in his.

"Which one?" He finally focuses on my face. And for once, his eyes aren't dark and swirly or twin blue flames.

"This one." I let out a slow breath, still slower than necessary, but it's real this time. No one except the nurse who showed me how to do this and me have lanced my finger.

Gabe crouches before me, his knees on either side of my calves, and gently massages my finger, and then—

"Ouch."

He squeezes the area around the pinprick and tips my finger to the side, letting the small drop of blood fall to the testing strip. Then he stands and checks the numbers.

"It's a bit high, I think. But, surprisingly, not too bad."

I squint at him. "I don't understand. How did you know? How do you know? I mean . . ."

"My grandma," he mutters as he cleans up. "And I saw this bag that day at the clinic."

"Yeah, but . . ."

"My grandma died of ketoacidosis." Gabe runs my hand under the water again. "Want to walk some of this off? I'll grab you a water."

"What about Sophie?"

"Sophie will be okay. She's finishing up a project, and she wants to get it just right. She's a perfectionist." He glances at me through the mirror, his lips tugging just a little.

The end of summer typically ushers in evenings filled with cool air. At least in LA. In Morganville, however, it's still hot and humid, and the only thing keeping me cool is the occasional breeze that floats by. Gabe and I silently walk down the sidewalk, each with a bottle of water in hand. When we reach the end of the road, he nods toward an open field full of wildflowers and a sea of endless green grass.

"There's a path on that side. It doesn't go into the woods or anything like that, and it's well lit." He waves a hand at a light post straight ahead.

I tighten my lips. Is it ever a good idea to walk down a deserted path with a stranger?

"I have mace," I lie, but I keep walking.

"You know my grandpa. And my sister."

The gravel crunches beneath our feet. The path is thinner than the sidewalk, and while it extends straight through the field, it meanders around a small pond. Beyond, I can just make out the shape of a house.

"Go ahead and ask me," Gabe says after a few moments go by.

My feet stop. I don't mean for them to stop, but they do. A step or two later, Gabe notices and shifts his attention toward me, but he keeps moving.

"Come on. We can talk and walk at the same time."

"How do you do that?" I ask, propelling my feet forward again.

"Do what?"

"That."

"Well, if you must know, I place one foot in front of the other, making sure to shift my weight evenly as I go."

The moment the words leave his mouth, I'm brought back to the morning after Sadie's wedding. When I asked him what he was doing, and his response was *We call it sleeping where I come from*.

"That's not what I meant, and you know it. How can you pretend like nothing happened?" I demand, letting my annoyance seep into the words.

"I don't pretend. I wasn't. Have I given you any indication that I was pretending?" There's a seriousness to him I hadn't expected.

"Well. Yeah. Sort of. I mean . . ." I stutter, at a loss for how to finish that sentence.

"Then ask me."

As our pace slows, I cycle the words in my head, trying to formulate my question in just the right way.

"You're making this more difficult than it needs to be. Just ask me what it is you want to know."

I huff and finally say it. "Did we sleep together?"

"Yes," Gabe says matter-of-factly.

My face heats up, and I'm pretty sure my jaw drops, though I should have known this. I was naked when I woke up next to him, except for the panties that barely covered my ass.

"You slept in my bed. And I slept in my bed. So yes. Technically, we slept together," he continues.

I stop. And this time, I don't budge when Gabe keeps moving. "What does that even mean? Stop speaking in code."

Gabe is several feet ahead when he finally turns to check on me. He stills. And then he lets out a calculated breath. "Just ask me the real question."

"I just did. Did we or did we not sleep together?"

He looks into my eyes, and for a split second, I see Gabe of the past. A hungry Gabe. A Gabe who might be remembering all the things I can't remember. Who had his way with me. And I can't even recall how good it was. Shit. Maybe it wasn't good. Maybe that's the problem. Maybe it was terrible. Maybe *I* was terrible.

But then he shakes his head and looks away, his attention set on the tree line. "Sex. You want to know if we had sex."

My heart seizes. "What's the difference?"

"The difference is you can't say the word."

That has my defenses rising. "I can too." And I instantly regret the childish response.

"Then say it."

I let out a frustrated huff. This is stupid. "Sex. Did we have sex?" My stomach tightens and my throat goes dry. "I'm not a prude, if that's what you're insinuating."

"I never took you for a prude," he deadpans. When he finally drags his gaze back to me, his eyes are liquid fire.

I don't know what he means, but my heart races, nonetheless.

"No," he says, then pauses for a long moment. "We did not have sex."

I let his words sink in, and then I breathe out a sigh of relief.

"Don't sound too excited over there. Come on, there's a bench up ahead."

I follow him to a small wooden bench, and as he rounds it, he nods as if to tell me I can sit. And I do, but not because he wants me to. I sit because my feet are tired and I need a second to digest this new information.

"If we didn't have sex, then why was I in your bed? What happened?"

"Do you really want to know? Because having sex with me would be a better story."

His bluntness takes me by surprise, and heat sears through my body. I bite my lip and nod. I can take it. Anything is better than drunk sex I can't remember.

"Okay," he begins, "but don't say I didn't warn you." He sits next to me and rests against the back of the bench, stretching his legs out in front of him. "What do you remember? I'll start there."

I think back to that day. To the hustle and bustle of the morning. The girls getting dressed and the application of fake lashes. Drinking mimosas and snacking to keep from getting drunk before the ceremony. Then the church. Gabe's evergreen scent encircling the two of us as we walked down the aisle as maid of honor and best man. The bus ride to the reception. Being sandwiched between Heidi and Leila as Gabe sat across from me. The dinner. The dancing and then. . .

"I remember dancing. But not with you."

He laughs, but he doesn't respond. Just watches me thoughtfully instead.

"You danced with just about every woman there. I ordered a drink, and then you sat next to me at the bar. And then—" I stop, surprised about this last part. I'd forgotten about the bar, and now I wish I hadn't remembered, because I think it was me who came on to him, not the other way around.

"Ready for the real version?" He lifts his brows and cocks his head, his eyes never leaving mine.

I cringe. Am I?

"You danced, *once.* With Sadie. And I didn't sit next to you at a bar, because it wasn't a restaurant. I did, however, ask the bartender to give you a water instead of another gin and tonic."

I scrunch my nose, confused.

"Sadie told me to stay away from you the night before, when she hauled me out of the bathroom." He looks down at his hands and presses his lips together. "So I made every effort to steer clear." He fidgets with his fingers before continuing. "And I knew just about everyone at the wedding, so yes, I danced with most of the women."

I'm not interested in details about how I embarrassed myself, but I've just boarded a train that's about to go off its rails, and there's no way to get off. So I ask my next question. "Then how did I end up in your bed?"

"Ah, the million-dollar question."

"Are you always like this?"

He ignores me and continues. "Remember. I told you that sex with me would have been better than what I'm about to tell you. Just keep that in mind."

"Keep flattering yourself," I say flatly.

"By the time the bartender handed you a water, you couldn't string a coherent sentence together. It was late. Most of the people had gone home, and Sadie was too shit-faced to walk. Jack asked me to help you back to your room since we were both staying at the bed-and-breakfast. Something about if you didn't make it back safely, he'd kill me. I didn't think you'd last long—and I'm not talking sex here—so I literally scooped you up and placed you in a Lyft to get you back to your room. Safe and sound like Jack asked."

"Then why didn't you take me to my own room?"

"You left your purse and room key at the reception."

"Nice try. My purse was on the nightstand, next to the bed."

"It pains me to have to tell you how much of a gentleman I really am," he says solemnly.

I scowl again.

"By the time we got back to the bed-and-breakfast, you were out cold. I realized you didn't have your purse, and since I knew you had an early flight out, I tucked you in and ran back out to get it for you."

"But . . ." I say in disbelief. "Then how did I . . ."

"There is absolutely no climactic ending here, no pun intended. I pulled the covers over you before I left. When I came back, well, that was all you. I told you. A sex story would have been more fun."

I swat at his arm as heat rises in my cheeks. "So nothing happened?"

"Nothing happened."

We sit for a few more moments, letting the night air seep into our lungs. I should be happy. Thankful. He didn't lure me into his bed.

He didn't take advantage of my bad choices that night. And I didn't come on to him like I thought. These are all good things. And yet, the relief I expect doesn't come.

"It's beautiful," I say, looking at the calm water in front of us. "It's so different from California."

In my periphery, Gabe nods. But he's not looking at the pond like I am. His focus is solely on me.

"We should get back to the party before anyone wonders where we ran off to," he says.

I exhale, wishing we didn't have to. But he's right.

He stands and offers his hand.

CHAPTER TEN

Gabe

No one notices our return, which means no one noticed our absence either. Fine by me. Less to explain.

Around the back, laughter fills the air and the soft glow of the overhead lights illuminates the yard. Meera paces herself next to me, almost shoulder to shoulder, our steps in sync. She smells like a tropical destination, her pleasant scent seemingly impossible on such a hot, sticky night. We didn't talk on our way back, not like we did on the trail. But somehow, something changed.

I wasn't exactly truthful with her a few minutes ago. The events I described weren't fabricated, but I may have omitted a few truths. I don't want her to feel ashamed or embarrassed. She has no reason to be, but if I told her she unzipped her dress in front of me, she might not be as calm as she is now.

As soon as the table of women comes into view, I stop and face Meera, which causes her to stop too. She lifts her face, and in the darkness, her gorgeous green eyes meet mine. I want to stare into them for a few more minutes. I want to lean into her, bury my nose in the crook of her neck, and tell her how beautiful she is. I want to ask her what her plans are tomorrow because I want to take her out to dinner.

But I don't. Because I'm a coward. Because Meera is so far out of my league. And to be honest, I'm confused about the way she makes me feel.

Instead, I say, "I should go check on Sophie. It's getting late."

She presses her lips together and nods, her expression unreadable.

My stomach twists. Because I want her to be bummed. I want her to want me to stick around. Hell, I want me to stick around.

We're frozen like this, gazes locked, neither of us moving. And I feel it again. The change between us. She isn't telling me to leave. She isn't saying goodbye. I want to—

"Gabriel Henry. I've been looking for you."

My reaction is to turn at the sound of my name. Though I don't want to, and I know I shouldn't. I know that voice. Fuck, I know that voice. But it's too late. Darlene Daniels is running my way, and before I can react, she launches herself into my arms.

"Oh my God, I didn't know you'd be here. At least not until Sadie told me. You look great. I love your hair." And with that last sentiment, she proceeds to run her fingers through it.

I don't pull back, which is probably why Meera does. Darlene doesn't even notice Meera. Instead, she focuses all her attention on me.

"There's so much. I could literally drag my fingers through this all day," she gushes. Her eyes are bright behind the longest fake lashes I've ever seen.

I set her down, ready to introduce her to Meera, but when Darlene is standing on her own two feet, Meera is nowhere in sight, and my stomach sinks.

"Let's sit by the fire. I'd love to catch up. I just got back from Spain. My mom says to say hello."

I flinch. I've never met her mom. And Darlene and I only dated for a few months, though we didn't see each other much during that time. I knew pretty early on that she and I worked on different wavelengths. She lives in this world where everything is big and bold, like the dress she has on right now. The high waist and the plunging neckline of her white rhinestone dress would look great at a wedding, but it's over the top for a summer barbecue.

"I'm sorry. I was just getting ready to leave. I need to get Sophie home, but please tell your mom I said hello too." I try to let her down easy, but it's futile.

She follows me up the stairs and into the house. She's prattling on about something, but the moment I step into the kitchen, I tune her out, because my heart comes to a screeching halt and all the air is knocked from my lungs like I've just been punched in the chest.

Meera is there, bent at the waist beside the table. And she's hugging Sophie. And Sophie, holy shit, Sophie is hugging her in return. On further inspection, her arms are wrapped so tightly around Meera's waist that it looks like she may be the one doing the hugging. They don't notice me. Not at first. Not until Darlene starts up again.

"I'm letting you take me to Le Bistro Café for dinner next week."

Meera is the first to look up. Her green eyes are wide but duller than before, and her long dark hair hangs over her shoulders, dangling in front of Sophie. Our gazes only meet briefly before she shifts her attention to Darlene. Then she turns back to Sophie.

"Did you hear me?" Darlene whines, nudging my arm.

"Yes." But I have no idea what she's talking about. My entire being is captivated by the two girls in front of me. The way Sophie has so openly embraced a mere stranger, her body pressed so close I can't tell where she ends and Meera starts. The way Meera pulls her close, her arms fitting perfectly around her little waist.

To the average person, this may look like just a hug. But to me, it's interaction I vie for every day. To hold my daughter like this is more than a dream. Something just out of reach. I don't know what Sophie went through before she came to me. I don't know if she experienced abuse. But there was neglect, and her living arrangements were less than ideal. The social worker said communication was the only thing Sophie could control, so we need to be patient with her, that she'll allow us into her life on her terms. And slowly, it's happening. Though it's at a snail's pace, and we have a long way to go.

But this hug. Holy shit. Sophie might hug, but she still likes to keep her distance; she always leaves space between her and the person she's embracing. This, whatever this is, is new for me. It's new for Sophie. If my mom or sister walked in right now, I'd have to pull their jaws off the floor and wipe away tears. And while a sliver of jealousy runs through me at the ache of wanting my daughter to hug me the same way, my heart melts at the sight.

"Good, pick me up at seven, then." Darlene interrupts my thoughts and kisses my cheek.

"Wait, what?" I turn to her, but she's already gone.

I turn back toward my daughter, and Meera is gone too.

"I'm ready to go," Sophie says, a slight smile pressed to her lips.

Now that Jack is out of town, I spend my days balancing my workload with his. Dee stops by my office midweek and drops off a batch of my favorite chocolate chip cookies. We don't have an appointment, but she does this every Wednesday. It's the day she brings her son to physical therapy across the street.

"You know you're my favorite," I say in my most swoon-worthy voice. I flip the lid and snag a cookie, biting into it as I close Jill's file. It's still warm, and it instantly melts in my mouth. I lean back and groan in pleasure.

Dee rolls her eyes and sits across from me, unfazed by my noises. "I hear you're back with Darlene."

I pull myself up and almost choke on the cookie. "What?"

"Word around here travels fast."

"Yeah, I get that. But why is the gossip about Darlene and me? I'm not back with her," I say as I reach for my water.

"That's not what Heidi told me."

"Heidi?" I ask, confused.

She smiles and fluffs her blonde hair. "Heidi cut and colored my hair yesterday. How do you like it?"

"It's gorgeous, just like you are, Dee. But what's this about Darlene?"

Dee winks at me. "Heidi said you and Darlene are going out this weekend. To a fancy French restaurant in Morganville."

I furrow my brows. And then it hits me. The party last weekend. Darlene mentioned something about me taking her somewhere, but I was so fixated on Meera that I tuned her out. Then I forgot all about it. I didn't commit to anything, did I?

"Fuck."

"So it's true?" Dee asks in surprise.

I blow out a long breath, ready to set her straight, when there's a knock on my door.

"Sorry to bother you, but I noticed Dee was here, and I wanted to say hi."

"Grandpa, what are you doing here?" I stand and meet him at the door. "Why aren't you at work?"

He gives me a side hug. "Just dropping off paperwork for Jack."

"Jack?" This is the second time today I'm taken aback.

"He's helping me update my will."

"Grandpa, you know I can—"

"I don't do business with family. Not when it comes to my will. You know this. If I ever get divorced, I'll let you handle that."

I shake my head because my grandpa won't ever get married again, let alone get a divorce.

"How's Bernie holding up?" My grandpa changes the subject by bringing up Dee's Saint Bernard.

Dee pushes out of the chair and makes her way to us. "I think the pain medication is helping. He's more mobile now and follows me and Jeremy when we go outside."

"What's wrong with Bernie?"

"Hip dysplasia. But that's common with bigger dogs like him," my grandpa says. "You should bring him by next week. I have a new doctor, Meera Taylor. She believes in all this holistic mumbo jumbo stuff. Seems to be working, though. That, and we can refill your prescription."

"I'll do that," she says, peeking at her watch. "Want to walk an old lady across the street? I need to pick Jeremy up from the therapist's office."

My grandpa laughs. "You ain't old until you're wearing Life Alert."

My eyes go wide at his words.

"I'm not wearing Life Alert, so don't you go looking at me like that," he grumbles. "Let me grab my keys, and we can head out."

"Your keys are in your hand." I laugh.

He mutters under his breath but holds his arm out for Dee. She loops hers through it, and then they're gone, leaving me to think about Meera again. And Darlene.

"Hey," Ashley calls from across the suite, not bothering to look up from her desk. "Jill is on line one."

I let out a sigh and head back to my desk, pushing away ideas about how to break my dinner plans with Darlene. She was always good at catching me off guard. That, or I never paid enough attention.

"Hi, Jill. I was just about to call you. Bradley's lawyer sent over the paperwork, and it's all signed. You're on the docket for nine on Friday morning."

After we hang up, I clear off my desk and power down my computer. It's still early, but mentally, I'm done for the day. When I tell Ashley she can go home too, she squints at me.

"Did body snatchers take control of your brain? How do I know that's you in there?"

"Leave before I fire you," I say.

"No need to tell me twice."

Her skepticism isn't unwarranted. I'm not the type to leave early, let alone give Ashley paid time off. Even if I'm not actively busy, I find shit to do. And I expect the same from others. But my concentration is shot.

I head down Main Street and stop in front of Betty's. Sophie loves her homemade strawberry shortcake, and it's been a while since I brought any home for her.

"Look at what the cat dragged in," Betty says from behind the counter when I step inside. She gives me a toothy grin that's both genuine and mischievous.

Betty was a client a few years back. Her husband left her while she was barefoot and pregnant and wanted her to sell the bakery so they could split their assets equally. At the time, the bakery was still in its infancy, and her estranged husband didn't think she could keep it afloat after the baby was born. Once we found out he was having an affair, we made sure he couldn't get his hands on it, and here she is. Three years later, the place is thriving, and she's done it completely on her own.

"Hey, Bets." I smile. "You have any of those strawberry—"

"Yup, one strawberry shortcake coming right up." She knows me well. "You're lucky you got here when you did. It's the last one."

"How's Joey?" I ask as she pulls out a long double-layered cake full of strawberries and cream.

"He's a monster. Getting into anything and everything." She laughs.

The chime on the door goes off behind me, and a tall, thin man wanders in and looks around, inspecting the small bakery.

"I'll be with you in just a moment," Betty says as she slides my cake into a box.

"Actually, I'm not here to buy anything. I'm in town visiting, and I'm looking for someone." The man moves closer and pulls out his phone. After a few swipes, he turns it so it's facing Betty. "I'm looking for my wife. Her phone died, and she told me to meet her out front about an hour ago, but I haven't seen her. Do you know if she was here?" he asks.

Betty takes a closer look at the picture. Something feels off about this guy. Something I can't quite put my finger on. The way he moves and speaks feels rehearsed. He sounds like a person on the stand who's prepared their statement so many times they can't rephrase it any other way, so the words come out like they're being read from a script.

With a shake of my head, I pull out my wallet, ready to pay and head home, when my phone vibrates in my pocket.

Betty is in full conversation mode, so I check the name on my screen while I wait for her to take my card. It's Sadie's mom. She's babysitting Grace this week, and if she's calling . . . crap. Grace.

"Hello?"

"Gabe? Oh my God," Barbara says quickly.

"Barbara, is Grace okay? What's wrong?"

"Yes. I mean no. Grace is good. It's Flint. I opened the door so I could check the mail, but when I did, Flint got loose. He ran after a bunny, and then—"

Her loud sobs reverberate from behind the receiver.

"Then a car came out of nowhere and hit him."

My heart stops. Flint is Jack and Sadie's dog. He's a border collie they rescued a few months ago.

"Is he—" I start, but I can't find the words to finish my sentence.

"No. God no. He's okay, but he's limping, and there's so much blood. Grace is asleep, and I didn't know who to call or if there's even an emergency vet in town."

I blow out a long breath and turn to face Betty.

She's staring at me, wide-eyed.

"Barbara, I'll be right over. Just hold tight."

When I click End, Betty is the first to speak. "Is Grace okay?"

I nod. "It's their dog. Flint. I need to—"

"Go, what are you still doing here? Take this in case you get hungry." She shoos me out of the shop while shoving the strawberry shortcake into my hands.

When I'm outside, I call the animal hospital. The phone rings three times before an annoyed Helen answers.

"Helen, it's Gabe. Is Meera there?"

"Oh, Meera. First name basis with the new lady doctor. That's not surprising." She lets out a raspy huff.

"I need Meera. It's an emergency."

"She's in with a patient. I can have her call—"

"Get her on the phone now. A dog was just hit by a car," I bark.

There's silence, and when I'm about to hang up and call again, thinking Helen has decided to set the phone down and ignore me, Meera's soft voice brings my heart rate down a notch.

"Gabe? Helen said someone's dog was hit by a car? What happened?"

"Flint. Sadie's mom just called. I'm almost to my car now. Can I pick you up in five minutes?"

There's a pause, then a muffled commotion, and then Meera is talking again. "I'll be waiting outside."

CHAPTER ELEVEN

Meera

Sadie and Jack don't live far from the animal hospital, but it still takes us a good fifteen minutes to drive across town. It's a quiet ride. No music. No talking. Just the sound of my heart beating and the growl of the engine. Part of me wants to talk to Gabe. Converse with him like a normal human being. But I don't know how.

There's no denying that I'm attracted to him. Good God, I don't want to be. With his looks alone, he's every woman's fantasy. Thick brown hair and a tall, muscular physique. Full, bitable lips and a perpetual five o'clock shadow. It's the perfect amount of facial hair, and I ache to feel each blade as he runs his face across my—I need to stop this nonsense. He's a playboy. A Casanova. Something I have to remember the next time he looks at me. Because those damn eyes get me every time. The way they slice right through me, making me want to forget my own name.

In another life, I might be more confident. I might be bold. Maybe even make the first move. On Saturday, I contemplated it. I wasn't sure what it was I wanted to say, but I ached for the connection between us to continue.

Then that girl showed up. That sexy-as-hell Spanish knockout appeared, and I was jolted back to reality. Gabe's a smooth talker. The way he took care of me when he checked my blood sugar. How he led me to believe he was a true gentleman when he tucked me under the blankets in his room at the bed-and-breakfast. All the while, this tanned goddess was right under my nose.

Nope. I'm not playing that game. It may be painful to let go of the idea of creating something more with him, but I refuse to be the kind of woman who sleeps with another woman's man.

The moment Gabe's tires touch the asphalt of Sadie's driveway, I unbuckle and swing the door open.

"Whoa," Gabe rumbles, sticking a hand out in front of me to hold me back. "Wait until I slow down."

I scoff at him, but I wait the extra second it takes for his truck to come to a complete stop.

Barbara is on the porch, her hands covered in blood. "Meera," she says, sniffling.

I give her a warm smile. "Where is he?"

She steps to the side, and Flint comes into view. He's lying on a towel on the porch. His ears are turned down, and his tan fur is stained red.

I make my way up the steps and squat beside him so he can sniff my hand. "Oh, poor boy. We're going to make you feel better. Can I take a look?" I open the bag I brought and pull out a bottle of water. "Gabe, can you grab the extra towels I left in the car?"

When I turn, Gabe's already jogging up the steps with the towels in hand.

He says nothing as he holds them out to me.

I grab hold of Flint's leg and wash away the blood. Then I gently pat his fur with the dry towel.

The poor guy lets out a whimper, so I pet him behind his ears.

"I need to get him to the hospital. I don't want the laceration on his leg to get infected. Did you see the car that hit him?"

Barbara shakes her head. "It happened so fast. There are so many trees."

"That's okay." I lean down and heave Flint into my arms. "You ready to come with us, boy?"

Gabe takes a step closer, his arms outstretched. "Do you want me to—"

"You worry about driving. I got him."

Inside the animal hospital, Helen meets us at the front desk. "Your room is ready. The CT scan and ultrasound are set up in the back. Let me know when, and I'll run the bloodwork."

I nod and lead Gabe to the exam room. This time, he carries Flint. I'm not about to break my back just to make a point.

"What do you need me to do?" he asks after setting Flint down on the table.

When the dog lets out a long whimper, Gabe shifts his attention back to him, running his hand up and down his chin in slow, soothing strokes.

"Can you call Jack and Sadie? Let them know what happened? I need to clean up and make sure there's no internal bleeding. Once I have some answers, I'll call them back."

He nods but doesn't move.

"You can leave now. I got it from here."

“I’m not leaving,” he says, his brow furrowed and his jaw set. “I’m helping.”

I laugh, mostly at this complete shift in his mood. “That’s not the way it works. You can’t just help. That’s why I have Helen.” Maybe I sound smug, but I don’t care. I’m not here to make him feel good. My job right now is to take care of Flint.

“Yeah, where is Helen now? You can’t open those doors and carry Flint at the same time. You need an extra set of hands.”

As the last word leaves his mouth, the back door of the exam room swings open. “Ready?” Helen asks.

I tighten my lips and square my shoulders. “You can leave.”

CHAPTER TWELVE

Gabe

I've been sitting in the waiting room for an hour when Helen finally steps in. Meera hasn't come out once to give me an update, but she knows I'm here. I made it clear I wasn't going anywhere. Not until we know exactly what's wrong with Flint.

Helen shakes her head, muttering something about irreparable trauma. She almost looks human when she continues. "He'll need the front leg amputated. No need to call your friend. Dr. Taylor already spoke to them and explained the situation. Surgery can take a few hours, but he's in good hands."

I stand, ready to ask if I can see Flint before he goes into surgery, but I'm interrupted when the front door swings open. A tall man with blond hair walks inside. I do a double take, racking my brain for why he looks familiar. And then it dawns on me. It's the man I saw at the bakery a few hours ago.

"Can I help you?" Helen asks, that glimmer of human decency fading once again.

I turn away and pull out my phone to shoot off a quick text to my mom.

Gabe: *I'm at the animal hospital. Jack's dog is going into surgery. He got hit by a car. I might be here for a few hours. Is it all right if Sophie eats dinner with you?*

As I stick my phone back into my pocket, I spin back toward the reception desk, where Helen is telling the man that Dr. Taylor is in surgery and that she'll be unavailable for a few hours, but she'd be more than happy to take a message for him.

I smirk at the last part, because even if the guy left a message, Helen would not be happy to take it. Nor would the message find its way to Meera.

The man shakes his head and turns back to the door. When he opens it, he catches me watching. He must recognize me too because he nods and says, "Hope the dog is okay." Then he slips out into the parking lot.

Two hours later, I've paced so much, I've practically worn a hole in the linoleum floor. I don't know what kind of doctor Meera is, but I hope she knows what she's doing.

Finally, when I can't take it any longer, I inch my way down the hall. I was basically raised here. When my mom was working late or in class, I'd follow my grandpa from room to room, acting as his helper. Not much has changed here since then. Not even the outdated oak picture frames that line the walls.

I know I shouldn't enter the surgical room, but tell that to the side of my brain that actually gives a fuck. I march for the door and snatch hold of the handle, but before I can do anything, the door swings open, and I'm forced to jump back so it doesn't hit me.

Meera stands at the threshold. Her eyes are bloodshot, and her cheeks are hollow. She blows out a long breath before she notices me. Then she shifts gears and affects one of her signature glares. "Why are you still here? I told you to leave."

I shake my head. "And I told you I wasn't leaving Flint. Is he okay? How'd it go?"

Her shoulders relax a little, but she closes her eyes in exhaustion.

"Gabe." She says my name like it's a thorn on her tongue. "I'm tired. And I'm hungry. It's been a long day. You should go." She heads to the exam room we were in earlier and flips on the light.

"Is Helen still here?"

"She left after she helped me move Flint to the back. He'll have to stay the night for observation. Maybe tomorrow too. I don't know yet." With her back to me, she rummages in the drawer under the countertop in the corner of the room.

"Who's going to stay with him?"

She stops, turns, and pinches the bridge of her nose. "I am. Does it look like there's anyone else here?"

"Meera, I just want to—"

"You want to, what? You want to help? You want to stay and watch Flint so I can sleep? You want to feed me so my blood sugar doesn't tank?"

My eyes go wide. "You need food, don't you?"

She lets out a loud huff. "I need a lot of things right now, Gabe. But most of all, I need you to leave."

I'm too stunned to move. I don't understand Meera's irritation. I want to fix this. And I don't want to leave when she's so upset. With a huff, I put my hands on my head and spin toward the opposite wall, racking my brain for ways I can get her to understand that I only want to help. Across the exam room, a white canvas bag hanging on the wall catches my attention. A rainbow of pom-poms cascades across the top. Behind the rainbow is a duplicate rainbow, sparkling in the same shades of glitter. A double rainbow. This is what Sophie was making. This is the project she insisted on finishing before we could leave Jack's house.

"Sophie made that," I breathe, pointing.

"Yes. She wanted me to have it."

"Why?" I ask.

She narrows her eyes. "Why not?"

"Why did she give it to you?" I ask again, my voice a little harsher than I intend it to be.

Sophie never gives away her art projects. Not even to me. She insists they're not good enough, not perfect, no matter how many times I tell her they're beautiful. She stores all of her crafts in a tub under her bed or she rips them up, depending on her mood. On very rare occasions, she's left pictures she's drawn while she's at my mom's house, but only when my mom insists she wants to display them on the refrigerator like the proud grandmother she is. But this is different.

"She said she heard about the Rainbow Bridge. The mythical overpass that takes animals to heaven," she says, her tone matching mine and her eyes defiant. But when she continues, she lowers her voice and her tone turns sad. "Like the bridge she wished her mom could cross back to her."

My chest tightens, like all the oxygen is being squeezed out of my lungs.

Then Meera drops her head. "I'm sorry," she murmurs. "For your loss."

"I didn't lose anything. Her mom isn't dead."

She lifts her chin in a jerky motion, and confusion spirals in her irises.

"She's a deadbeat. Left Sophie on my front step like something straight out of a movie. And then she came back a month later and took her from my mom. Just up and vanished." My voice quavers, but I can't stop. It's no secret what happened to my daughter, but I'm not usually the one telling the story. My insides burn as the words pour out of me. It's the picture, the craft, that sends me over the edge.

"You know how we found her?" I ask, but I don't give Meera time to respond. I'm a volcano, ready to erupt. "I hired a private investigator. He found her an hour away. An hour fucking away. In an abandoned building. Sophie opened the door wearing nothing but a T-shirt. Not even a goddamn pair of underwear. Her mom was strung out on the floor. Told the private investigator she'd sell Sophie for a score."

"Gabe," Meera says. The tension in her shoulders eases, and her expression softens.

"No. I don't want your sympathy. And my daughter doesn't need your sympathy." I run my hands through my hair and tug so hard my scalp burns. "I don't understand. Three years. Three years, and out of the blue she gives you this?"

"Gabe," Meera says again, the tone far more gentle than I've ever heard from her.

I know I'm being unreasonable. Taking this out on Meera wasn't my intention. I'm just angry. How does she come into town and get my daughter to hand over a piece of her heart in a matter of days? I've been trying for three fucking years.

"Gabe . . ." Meera's voice grows louder now. The tender tone is gone, and her eyes go wide. Her lips are pressed together tight as she nods at something behind me.

I turn, and my heart stops beating.

Sophie is standing in the doorway. Her body is rigid, and she's holding a piece of paper.

"Sophie," I say, but she doesn't let me finish. The paper falls from her hand, and she bolts in the opposite direction.

"Shit. Sophie. Stop." I chase after her, but she's quick, and by the time I'm at the front entrance, she's gone.

"What was that all about?" my mom asks from the counter at the front desk. She's got a brown paper bag hanging from her arm.

"I don't have time for this. I need to find Sophie." And then I throw open the door and leave.

CHAPTER THIRTEEN

Meera

Gabe storms out, and silence fills the room. I wait, unmoving, until the bell over the front door chimes and I know he's gone. Then I drag myself toward the lobby to lock up, but not before I pick up the paper Sophie dropped.

It's a sketch of a veterinarian with long brown hair and a white lab coat over blue scrubs. A dog sits to her right, wearing a blue cast on its front leg. The detail she added catches me by surprise. The buttons on the lab coat, the green eyes mixed with a sea blue. The blended shades of beige, tan, and brown for the dog's fur. Even the paw that peeks out of the cast is etched with precision.

Still soaking in the details, I head for the front door, but the sight of a stranger startles me, and I jump, slapping one hand to my chest.

"Oh, I'm sorry. I didn't mean to scare you," she says. "Are you Dr. Taylor?"

"Yes," I say to the beautiful woman with auburn hair standing before me. Immediately, I notice the similarities between her and Gabe, and even Lydia and Sophie. The same tanned skin, the same oval blue eyes. The dimple in the right cheek. "You must be Gabe's mom. You look just like him."

"Oh, I hope not." She laughs. "I like to think Lydia and I look more alike." She extends her arm. "My name is Evelyn. I brought dinner for you two. Figured you'd be hungry. But it looks like I was a bit too late." She gives me a crooked smile.

"That wasn't necessary."

"No, but Lydia said you barely eat, and Gabe mentioned the surgery. And, of course, Sophie wanted to come by and give you that." Her eyes drop to the paper still in my hands.

"Oh. Yeah, I . . ."

"Honey, you don't have to explain a thing. If Sophie wants to draw a picture for you, you're already a rock star in my book. Gabe? He just doesn't know how to express himself the way he should. He's a bit delayed when it comes to emotions. When he's overwhelmed, anger tends to take over. But he knows when he's wrong. And if I know my son, he'll apologize for his outburst sooner rather than later."

"He has nothing to apologize for," I say with a slight shake of the head.

She tilts her head. "Don't you take anything less than an apology, you hear me? My son knows better." She takes my hand and leads me to the front counter, where she drops the brown bag. "I have orange chicken, beef and broccoli, and a vegetarian delight. Wasn't sure what you liked."

"Oh, no, it's okay. I'm fine."

"Lydia said you'd be stubborn. She likes you, by the way." She pulls out three boxes, and one by one, she unfolds them. "She hasn't been this excited about working here since she was a teenager. She might even switch her major next semester."

I watch as she opens the last box, then stabs a spork into each one. "Teaching is a great profession, don't get me wrong, but her heart has always been with animals. She just lost her spunk somewhere along the way. Personally, I think it was Helen." She laughs.

Standing beside this woman as she goes on like we're friends, I'm at a loss for how to respond. I'm not even sure what's happening. The food smells delicious, and my stomach grumbles loud enough for the entire town to hear.

"Here, eat." Evelyn hands me a plate and then pulls one out for herself. "Gabe hasn't had it easy. He didn't want kids. Not at first." She's giving me far more information about her son than she probably should. "And not because *he* didn't want them, but because he was afraid he'd end up like his dad. He was scared he didn't have it in him to take care of anyone other than himself."

"You don't have to explain. None of this is—"

"You're a gorgeous young lady," she interrupts. "I can see why both of my kids are smitten with you. And my granddaughter. Oh my. I feel so old when I say that." She waves a hand in the air. "And I like you too. You're clearly great for this family. But I want you to know that Gabe is not the ticking time bomb he's portraying himself to be. He has a good heart." She presses her hand to her chest, like she's driving home that point. "The poor boy became a lawyer to help women like me face scumbag husbands like his own father. I couldn't shield him from everything. For years, I wanted nothing more than to erase those memories for him, but I'm so glad life didn't work out that way. Because it prepared him for Sophie." She shakes her head and then catches my eye.

"His dad came in and out of our lives for years, and when he knew he couldn't get a rise out of me anymore, he started taking it out on Gabe. When Gabe was twelve years old, after we hadn't seen or heard from the man in three years, he had the audacity to tell our son it was his fault we divorced. All because Gabe didn't want to visit him. Because he was tired of being an afterthought. And did *that* set off an inferno. The next thing I knew, he lawyered up and wanted custody. Said I was keeping his son from him."

"What happened?" I ask, invested despite my earlier apprehension.

"Once he realized they were going to appoint a guardian ad litem for Gabe, he pulled the plug."

"What's a guardian ad litem?" I ask. I take a bite of the orange chicken and then wash it down with a swig from my water bottle.

"A lawyer for minors. Someone who represents the child independently from either parent, to look out for their best interest. It went on like that for years. He'd show up out of the blue and treat us like trash. Like he was entitled to whatever he wanted because he shared DNA with Gabe. But my boy is a tough cookie."

She pauses to take a bite and chews thoughtfully, then continues. "Did you know Sophie didn't come to us until she was five? The poor girl was malnourished and wouldn't speak. Partially because she hadn't been exposed to enough oral language, but also because it was the only thing she could control. What Gabe said in there, about Sophie answering the door in just her T-shirt. It's true. They showed us pictures of the place. They had one sleeping bag and a trash bag full of clothes. No furniture. No food. No electricity."

My stomach sinks. I can't imagine what that must have been like. I think back to how I lived out of my car. But that was my choice. And I was an adult.

"Breanna is an addict. She and Gabe dated on and off in high school. Nothing serious. Neither of them had expectations beyond that. Gabe planned to join the Marines after he graduated, and he was somebody to fill her time. She was a sweet girl back then. But there was too much going on in that house of hers. And then she got swallowed up by life. Couldn't handle the pressure society placed on her. She left town, but she showed up when Gabe got out of the Marine Corps. She didn't stay long, though. And no one heard from her, not even her parents, until she was banging on Gabe's door, telling him he was Sophie's dad and she needed money. She left that sweet girl here and disappeared." Evelyn shakes her head, a sad frown marring her face. "But a month later, Breanna was at *my* door. She looked terrible. Too skinny and had track marks all over her arms. Told me she needed Sophie back. I tried to convince her to stay. I offered her a warm meal, and when I walked out of the room to grab plates, she disappeared. Took Sophie with her."

Evelyn breathes out a long, steady breath. "You have no idea how hard that was. To know that child was about to endure more trauma all because I turned my back."

My heart shatters at this. "You can't blame yourself. You couldn't have known."

With a warm hand on mine, she gives me a sad smile. "I don't blame myself. Not anymore. But it was hard. I watched my son lose his mind. In the month Sophie was with us, I witnessed a transformation in him I never could have imagined. He has always been a good boy. Don't get me wrong. But he had his moments. He liked to go out and have a good time, if you catch my drift. When Sophie came to live with him, it was like he was reborn. He went from being a bachelor to being a father overnight." She removes her hand from mine and stands, folding her now empty plate. Then she heads to the garbage can.

"After Breanna took Sophie, he reverted back to his old ways, only worse. As a mom, it was hard to watch."

I stand and fold the boxes back up. "But he has Sophie again," I remind her.

"That he does. But what he just heard? That his daughter wants her mom to find her? That had to have hurt his heart. I know it hurt mine."

I bite my lip and study my sneakers. "I didn't know." The hurt he must be feeling. The inability to help his daughter. To decipher those feelings. The thought of all of it makes my heart ache.

With a nudge to my shoulder, Evelyn says, "Now don't go blaming *yourself*. Gabe was reacting. But if you ask me, that picture was progress. I've never seen her want to give something away like that." She looks at me for a long moment, as if deciding something. "Sophie really verbalized that about her mom?"

I nod.

Evelyn gives a wry smile and then wraps her arms around me. It takes me by surprise, but the warmth of her embrace is settling, so I hug her back.

After I help her pack the leftover food and utensils in the brown paper bag, I ask, "Where is Breanna now?" I swallow nervously, dreading the response I know she'll give me.

She presses her lips together and scrunches her nose. "We have no idea," she says. "She went to rehab for three months after we got Sophie back. But she checked herself out, and we haven't seen her since."

The next morning, Helen carries in two large iced coffees. She places one in front of me and asks, "How's Flint holding up?"

"Is this for me?" My eyes go wide as I clutch the plastic cup, afraid it might be a trick and she'll take it back.

"Yeah, but if you tell anyone I did this, I'll deny it," she says without looking up, her expression wooden.

I smile as brightly as my tired muscles will let me and take a sip of the much-needed caffeine. "He's good. I just checked on him. We'll have to change his bandages soon."

She throws her bag under the desk and boots up the computer just as Lydia and Dr. Coleman walk in.

"Good morning, everyone. It's a beautiful day out there today, isn't it?" Dr. Coleman cheers. "Let's adjust the schedule today, shall we? Lydia, Dr. Thompson will be here shortly. Give him all of Meera's patients."

Helen grimaces and places her hands on her hips. "I am not working with that mouth breather. He's prescribed the wrong dosage of medication at least three times in the last week."

"You're taking the day off too," Dr. Coleman cuts her off, his brows raised. "Both of you."

"But—" Helen starts.

"You had a long night, and I need you in tip-top shape for tomorrow."

She and I look at one another in confusion. She's probably thinking the same thing I am. I want to be here. I need to be here for my patients.

"Yesterday, I was reminded that I'm not getting any younger, and I don't want to waste another day missing out on life. So I need you all rested and ready for tomorrow."

"Grandpa," Lydia breathes. "What are you trying to say?"

He laughs. "I'm retiring. Tomorrow is my last day."

"What?" She gasps. "Are you for real?"

"Yes, I'm *for real.*" He chuckles. "Like I said, I'm not getting any younger."

"What are you going to do?" she asks, reaching for his arm.

"I'll sleep in late. Read the newspaper on the back porch. And travel. Always wanted to go on an Alaskan cruise. Maybe I'll even sleep in late."

"You already said that." Lydia giggles. "But you won't sleep late. It's not in your DNA." Then she sobers, her expression tightening. "But that's not what I meant. What are you going to do about the hospital? What will happen—"

"You'll all be okay without me," he says, turning from the desk to wipe away what I can only assume is a tear.

I shift my weight, digesting the information before finally opening my mouth. "That's great news, Dr. Coleman—"

"Edgar," he corrects me.

"Edgar." I nod in acquiescence. "But what I think Lydia is trying to say is, what will happen to the animal hospital once you retire? And I don't want to sound selfish, because I appreciate the opportunity you've given me here, but what will this mean for my contract? I've only been here two weeks, and we agreed on a year."

"And am I getting paid for today, or will this be considered a sick day?" Helen scowls.

"Oh. I forgot about that. I have an announcement to make tomorrow. We're having a party." Edgar turns to Lydia. "Your mom is planning a small retirement shindig. We're having it at the Tipsy Brew Garage. Just family and friends. But everything is going to be fine. And Meera"—Dr. Coleman gives me a toothy grin—"you'll get to finish out your contract. I promise you that. And maybe you'll even stay a bit longer." He winks at me.

Helen clears her throat.

"Yes, Helen. You'll get paid for today. Go now before I change my mind. But I need one quick—"

But Helen doesn't wait for him to finish that sentence. She's already out the door.

He looks at me and laughs. "I should have asked the favor before I confirmed that she could leave. I guess it's you, then. We ran out of Carprofen, and our next shipment doesn't come in until Monday. Dr. Stevens said they had plenty. He's pulling some for us and said we can pick it up this morning."

"I'd love to, but my car is out of commission. I think the battery is dead."

"Is it here? We can jump it. I have cables in my trunk," he says, fishing for his keys.

"It's at my apartment. In the back lot."

"Why don't you take my car, then, and we'll get yours situated later?" he says, tossing me his keys.

"Wrong keys," I say, catching them midair. "I think these are the hospital keys."

Dr. Coleman's face pales. "Crap. I must have left them at home."

Lydia cackles. "Grandpa." She puts her hands on her knees and sucks in a breath before she can continue. "You drove here. Check your bag."

He does as he's instructed, hefting his work bag onto the counter and digging through it. It takes him a while, but he smiles when he finally pulls them out.

Harbour Animal Hospital is bigger than Morganville, but it's farther from the heart of town center. There are only a few buildings nearby and absolutely no cars in the parking lot. For a second, I wonder if anyone is inside.

A closed sign hangs on the door, listing their updated nightly hours. But below it a piece of copy paper is taped to the glass. *Text for Medication Pickup.*

I follow the instructions, and a moment later, a thin woman with shallow cheeks rounds the corner and peeks through the glass. She looks skittish, but her shoulders relax when she sees me, though she doesn't open the door.

"Hi," I call, "I'm here to pick up the Carprofen for Dr. Coleman. I work at Morganville Animal Hospital."

She nods and unlocks the door, then waves me in.

"Dr. Stevens told me someone would be by. Let me grab it for you." Her voice is shaky, and she pulls at her sleeves as she heads toward the counter.

I follow behind, taking in the lobby. "I love the pictures on the wall." I laugh. "They're the same ones we have."

She looks at the painting I'm pointing at and grins. "I'm pretty sure all animal hospitals have these."

"How long have you been here?" I ask. I still don't know many people in town, but that needs to change, so I might as well make small talk.

She pulls a small brown paper bag out of a cabinet and checks the contents as she responds. "About a year."

"I hear you guys decided to go to nights only."

The woman nods and hands me the bag. Her eyes are small but friendly when she makes eye contact. "Small town. Not enough clients to keep us open during the day."

"Well, it will be nice to work with you guys. I'm Meera, by the way."

She tilts her head and furrows her brow as she works her thin brown hair into a ponytail. "Work with us?"

"We're closing our after-hours emergency room. This way we can work together, so to speak. You take nights, we do days."

"Dr. Coleman is shutting down his emergency room?" she asks, her tone filled with surprise.

"At night. We'll still be an ER during the day. But yeah, he's ready to retire, and he figured with you all focusing on nights, we should focus on days."

She laughs. "Wow, I never thought he would retire."

"You know him?" I ask, moving the bag from one hand to the other.

"I did. I mean, years ago." She lifts her sleeve to check the time on her watch, but she's careful as she inches it up. "I'm sorry. I need to get going. I have a meeting to get to, and I'm already running late."

"Oh. Sure. I'll get out of your way." I head to the door, and when she follows behind, I remember there is no car in the parking lot.

"Do you need a lift somewhere?" I go for cheery because the last thing I want is to come across as condescending.

She scans the parking lot before flicking her wrist again. "I don't want to be an inconvenience."

"No, not at all. I'm heading home after this, so I'm not in a hurry to get anywhere."

"It's not far. But I would really appreciate it since I'm running late. If you don't mind, that is. I just bought a car, but they're putting new tires on it, and it won't be ready until tomorrow."

With a smile, I lead her to Dr. Coleman's car.

"I'm Bre, by the way. And again, I really appreciate this."

Bre was right. I didn't have to go far. I drove maybe two miles before she asked me to pull over in front of a large brick municipal building in downtown Harbour Village.

Once she's out of the car, I reach into the back seat and retrieve the stack of envelopes and papers I moved from the passenger seat to make room for her.

My breath catches when the subject of the top page catches my eye. I don't mean to look at it, and it's none of my business, but right there, in bold print, are the words *Prostate Cancer. Stage four.* One word in particular screams at me: *Terminal.*

It's the same cancer that took my grandpa's life.

My stomach tightens. This explains why Dr. Coleman is retiring.

At home, I open the curtains and take full advantage of the morning light that comes from the east. I try to push out all thoughts of Dr. Coleman and cancer because it isn't any of my business, no matter how much it gnaws at me.

Instead, I pull out my tool belt, fasten it around my waist, and get to work pulling the old oak trim from the walls and door frames. I hammer the nails in sideways and stack the trim against the wall closest to the door. I've only got three or four pieces left when there's a knock at my door. The only visitors I've had so far have been Sadie and Gabe, but Sadie is still in Hawaii, and after last night, I doubt it will be Gabe, though his mom did mention he would likely apologize fairly quickly. The thought makes my heart rate accelerate.

But it's not Gabe.

Shock ripples through me when I pull the door open and come face-to-face with the man standing on the other side.

"Tom."

"Hi, Meera. Or should I say Dr. Taylor?"

My feet are rooted to the spot and my mouth goes dry. He watches me, unsmiling, probably waiting to see what I'll do. But I tip my chin higher and hold strong. Tom wants me to ask him why he's here. He wants me to invite him in. When I don't, his lips tighten and scrunch until they're barely visible.

"I should have figured you'd be here, living near Sadie and Jack. And you took your grandparents' name, I see." He glares at me as he pushes his free hand into his pants pocket while he clutches a manilla folder in the other. His blond hair is perfectly manicured. High and tight, gelled, and not a hair out of place. To someone who doesn't know him or the kind of cruelty he's capable of, they'd see a good-looking guy with a resemblance to Ryan Gosling. He hasn't changed one bit.

When I don't respond, he inches his way closer. "Damn, Meera, you look good. You've lost weight."

I tighten my hand on the doorknob, but I don't attempt to close it. He's too quick for that. I learned long ago that if I want a fighting chance, I need to wait him out.

"Aren't you going to ask your husband to come inside? It's been, what, three years since you've seen me?" He says this without taking his eyes off me. He's daring me to shift my gaze, to submit to him.

Instead, I take on his challenge, keeping my focus squarely on him. "Four years," I correct him. "Not since I found you screwing Lizzie for the third time. How is she, by the way?" I keep my tone flat as the words roll off my tongue. I've never stood up to Tom before. I've cried and I've pleaded, but I've never purposely caused unnecessary friction between us. But I'm stronger now. Braver than I was four years ago.

He cocks a brow and smirks. "Has it really been that long? Sometimes it feels like yesterday." He shakes his head.

Lizzie was the young blonde Tom hired to manage our restaurant while I was pregnant. He said we needed the help, and she was the perfect face for our brand. She was also perfect in bed, according to Tom the last time I found him screwing her.

"We went our separate ways."

“That’s too bad. She was good for you.”

“What’s good is the way you smell.” Tom’s voice deepens.

My throat tightens and my knuckles hurt from how hard I’m clutching the doorknob. I want to tell him to leave. I want to push him away. But I’m frozen, brought back in time to when I was pregnant. To when Tom took me by my throat and lifted me onto the kitchen counter. His hands firmly wrapped around my airway. His faraway stare as he mouthed the words “You smell so good.” His hands tightening until tears tracked down my cheeks and I couldn’t breathe.

“What’s this?” Tom says, pulling me back to the present. “A tool belt? Looks hot. The fixer-upper thing works on you. Is that what you’re doing in there?”

Tom finally shifts his gaze away from me and cranes his neck to get a better view of the inside of my apartment. I’m not sure if it’s intentional or if he really did lose interest in me, but I breathe out a sigh of relief and loosen my grip around the doorknob.

But the second I do, he takes advantage of the momentary drop in my shield and pushes his way inside. “Hot damn, you’re doing pretty good for yourself, aren’t you? I figured you might be struggling. But here you are. Dr. Taylor.” He saunters toward the open kitchen and stops when he reaches the island. He slaps the Formica countertop and runs a finger along the edge. “It’s not like what we have in California, though, is it?” He laughs and then spins to face me, propping himself against the countertop, his elbows bent behind him.

My eye twitches and irritation bubbles up inside me at his near constant condescending remarks. “Why are you here?” I finally ask, unable to hold it in any longer.

“I came to see my wife. Isn’t that a good enough reason?” He holds his free hand out in my direction, as if I’m a prize to claim.

"No. You wouldn't be here if you didn't need something. But even that confuses me. I don't have anything to give you." My gaze shifts to the manilla envelope.

Tom's smile fades and his eyes grow cold. "You left me. High and dry. Just up and vanished."

"You didn't give me any other choice."

"What the hell is that supposed to mean? You always had a choice. You chose to marry me and sign your name next to mine on the deed for our condo. You chose to open a restaurant with me. And then you fucking left, leaving me with expenses I couldn't possibly take care of on my own." He heaves himself away from the countertop and steps forward.

For a split second, I think about the hammer hanging on my hip. My hand, now free from the door handle, finds its way to the smooth steel hammerhead.

Tom watches my movement, a scowl marring his face. "You left, and everything went to shit. Did you ever think about what you were doing to me? How your absence would affect our business?"

"Tom," I warn, but he doesn't listen.

He takes another step closer.

"You think because you're a fucking woman, you can run away from your responsibilities and there won't be consequences?" he asks, his tone hollow. His eyes are dark and blazing, the coldness instantly igniting.

"Tom," I urge, my voice softer this time. The same useless tone from my past.

He's too close now. Too angry.

My stomach twists and my heart speeds up.

"You think because you lost our baby, your grief trumped mine?"

In that instant, and of its own volition, my hand slips off the hammer and makes contact with Tom's face. The loud smack surprises us both.

"You fucking bitch," he spits.

With his fingers wrapped tightly around my wrist, he yanks me toward him so hard I fall into his chest.

I squeeze my eyes shut. There's no turning back now. So I brace myself for what happens next. I clench my jaw and hold my breath, waiting for the inevitable. But Tom doesn't hit me. He doesn't pin me beneath him. He doesn't do anything except . . . release me.

When I wrench my eyelids open, Tom is tumbling to the floor, and the contents of the folder are scattering around him.

"What the fuck?" He moans.

"Didn't anyone ever teach you to keep your hands to yourself?"

"Gabe," I gasp, my voice shaky. My face flames with embarrassment as I turn toward him. I'm not sure what he heard or when he walked in, but I'm suddenly mortified.

"I'm sor—"

"Sorry?" He cuts me off. "Don't ever take responsibility for the actions of someone else. Especially an asshole like this," he thunders. His arm is extended in front of me as if to protect me from Tom, who is just now gathering his wits.

"Who the fuck are you?" Tom demands. "Who the fuck is he?" he shouts, this time at me. His nose is bleeding, but he ignores it. He scrambles to gather the papers and shoves them back into his folder before he gets to his feet and takes a step back. "Do people just walk into other people's homes around here?"

Gabe tips forward, pushing me back gently with his forearm, as if he's going to move closer to Tom. But I grasp his sleeve to stop him before he has a chance. This is my mess. Not his.

"Tom, you need to leave."

"Not before you sign this paperwork," he demands. He shoves the folder past Gabe, who stands a head taller than him.

Gabe's eyes never leave me as I take the folder and flip it open. "What is it?"

"Divorce papers. It's about time, wouldn't you agree?" Tom wipes at his face, finally acknowledging the blood below his nose. "Shit, my nose better not be broken."

While he dabs at his skin and pulls his hand away, checking for blood, I scan the first page. It looks like something he printed himself. I flip through a few more pages before the name of our restaurant catches my eye. "What's this?" I pull it out and wave it in the air.

"It's a bill of sale. For the restaurant."

"I see that, but what does it mean?"

"It says you agree to give it to me."

Gabe snatches the paper from my hand, along with the folder. "You should have your lawyer look that over before you sign anything," he says to me.

"Her lawyer? She doesn't need a goddamn lawyer. She left. Abandoned everything. This is a formality. I don't have time for this shit." Tom's face grows red. "And who the fuck are you, anyway?" he growls, puffing his chest.

"I'll look this over," I acquiesce. "I'll call you tomorrow once—"

Gabe cuts me short when he slides his hand into mine. He laces our fingers and squeezes. "I'm her boyfriend. And I said she needs her lawyer to look over those papers."

"Boyfriend," he snorts. "Now that's funny."

Tom goes on, but his words become a jumbled mess when I'm suddenly lip to lip with Gabe. One second, Tom is complaining. And in the next, Gabe has his hands in my hair, and he's pulling me up to meet him as he bends forward. At first, he brushes his mouth against mine gently, but when I grasp his forearms, realizing what's happening—when we both realize what's happening—he presses harder, forcing my lips to part with his teeth. Though force may be an exaggeration when I'm a willing participant.

"Awesome, and now you're a slut too," Tom snarls.

CHAPTER FOURTEEN

Gabe

The words slice through the air like razor blades. Everything in me wants to punch him in the face again. I pull back, but Meera squeezes my arm. We lose breaths simultaneously. Maybe it's from the kiss. Or maybe it's because of Tom. But when I look down, Meera is gripping the front of my shirt and swaying.

"My bag," she whispers. "I need my bag." The words are barely audible, but I hear her loud and clear.

Quickly, I steady her and lead her to the couch. Tom moves out of my way, though he doesn't show the slightest bit of concern. It doesn't surprise me. He's a douche. He's too wrapped up in his own world to care about anyone but himself.

"You need to get the fuck out of here," I say, not bothering to take my eyes off Meera.

"Just sign the damn paperwork, Meera. Clearly, you've moved on too. We don't need this tether between us anymore."

"Like I said"—I finally tear my gaze from Meera so I can glare at him—"she'll have her lawyer look at it. Leave your number on the table." I gesture to it with a lift of my chin. "And I'll make sure to pass it along."

I turn back to get Meera's bag, but Tom stands in my way. When I move toward him, ready to barrel through him if I have to, he puts his hands up. "Okay. Okay." He pulls out his wallet and digs inside before retrieving a small black business card. "I'm in town for the weekend. My flight leaves Sunday." Tom tosses the card onto the counter next to Meera's black Accu-Chek bag.

I don't wait for the door to close before I unzip the bag and pull out the juice.

"Drink," I say after stabbing the plastic container with the straw and placing it in Meera's trembling hand.

She takes three or four slow sips at first and then sucks down the rest in one gulp.

When she finishes, I take the juice box and set it on the table. Then I sit next to her. And I sink into the cushions.

And for the first time, she graces me with a laugh. Maybe not the *first* time. Because the moment I laid eyes on her when she walked into the Tipsy Brew Garage with Sadie three years ago, when Jack lifted her off the ground, she laughed. And again, as the girls I went to school with welcomed her into their group. And at the wedding. Okay, I've seen Meera laugh. *And* the way her smile lights up a room. But since she's been here, all I've seen is a woman who's worn down by the world. Except for when she drank too much at Sadie's. When her eyes shone and her shoulders were relaxed. But I've never witnessed anything more beautiful than this, in this moment, as she laughs at the way I plunge into the cushion.

A snort escapes, and she instantly covers her face. "Oh my God. I'm so sorry. This couch is the worst. There's nothing under that cushion."

I narrow my eyes, but my lips tug anyway. Fuck, she's beautiful.

"For real, you have to get up. Sit on this side." She pats the cushion to her right.

But I don't move. My ass continues to sink downward.

She laughs again, but this time she gets to her feet and takes my hand, offering to pull me up. Her smile is so big it reaches her eyes.

I want to pull her down on top of me. I want to tell her how pretty she looks right now.

But I don't. Instead, I let her lift me out of this death trap. When I'm on solid ground again, I lift the cushion. Yup. Nothing but a hole the size of my ass. I shake my head and turn back toward Meera. Our eyes catch for a second, and her smile slowly slips away.

"Thank you," she says, "for all of that." She waves at the door and the juice box. "But I could have handled it."

"I know, but I'm glad I got here when I did. I wouldn't want to lie to the police."

Her brow creases in confusion, and though her laugh is my new favorite thing, her confusion is adorable.

"We'd have to hide the body, and I'm not good at lying. Never have been."

Meera throws her head back and guffaws. "Why are you even here?"

"Oh, crap." I run to the door and open it, then look both ways. No sign of Tom. "Still here." A sigh of relief escapes me. "I brought a peace offering." I pick the paper bag up off the floor where I set it when I noticed the door was ajar and hold it out.

Meera gives me a side-eye.

"Food. And an apology."

"Is that Chinese?"

"It is," I enunciate. "Do you not like Chinese?" I drop my arm, suddenly worried she might be a vegetarian or allergic to MSG.

She shakes her head. "Is this a Henry family ritual?"

It's my turn to give her the side-eye.

"Your mom. She brought Chinese with her yesterday." A smile reappears as she moves toward the kitchen. "Bring it over. What do you have?"

She pulls two paper plates down from a shelf and lays them on a distressed white kitchen table. Then she grabs two water bottles from the fridge.

"My mom brought you Chinese?"

"She brought *you* Chinese. And me by default, I guess." Meera tosses a few napkins next to the plates and points at the table, motioning for me to set the food down. "How is Sophie?"

I drop the bag on the distressed surface, and instantly, Meera is opening each carton and smelling its contents. When she sees the orange chicken, she sticks a fork into the container and begins scooping it onto her plate. Maybe she's avoiding having to talk about the kiss. Maybe it's me.

"Yeah." I heave out a long breath. "That's why I'm here. I need to apologize. I overreacted," I say, dropping into the seat across from Meera.

"I didn't know. About Sophie. Your mom told me she doesn't open up very much. That picture, though, is beautiful. She's very artistic."

"She is." I nod. "What else did my mom tell you?"

She lifts her head and meets my gaze. "That you would come by to say you were sorry."

I can't help but laugh at that. "I'm sure she did." I pick up a carton and pour some beef and broccoli onto my plate, avoiding eye contact while I get this out. "Listen, what I said yesterday, all of it, I don't know what came over me. Between the picture and . . ." I pause, my mind a twisted mess of words I know I need to say. I planned it all out in my head, but now that I'm here, I can't get them to materialize.

"Me," Meera says, her tone firm. "I was sort of a bitch. I'm sorry. I was tired and hungry, and I pushed you. Sophie's your daughter. You have every right to be protective of her." She reaches for the rice and dumps a small pile onto her plate.

"Did you know Sophie comes to see me almost every day? She brings Charlie. At first, I really thought Charlie was swallowing Legos. But after you said Sophie didn't play with them, it got me thinking."

She twirls her fork on the plate, not paying any attention to the food.

"I thought maybe she was just lonely. Or bored. She doesn't have any other kids to play with. You work. She lives right behind the animal hospital. I figured she was intrigued by all the animals we see. But now I get it. I mean, sort of." She looks away. "When my parents died, I wanted to run away. I wanted to hide. I hated when people told me they were sorry about what happened. After the funeral, all anyone saw was the sad girl who lost her parents. Like I lost my identity. My thoughts and interests were of no consequence. It wasn't until I met Sadie that I felt whole again. She didn't know my past. She didn't have expectations of how I should act. She just accepted me for me."

With that, her shoulders slump, like a weight's been lifted. She reaches for her water bottle and takes a sip, then places it back on the table.

Without second-guessing myself, without reading into the situation between us, I do something completely out of my norm. I rest my hand on top of hers on the tabletop, looping my thumb under her palm. "I didn't know she was visiting you. But thank you. And you're right. She doesn't have friends. I wish she did. But she's a bit of a loner. She doesn't care to play. She'd rather stick with arts and crafts and books."

When I finish, I examine our hands. The way mine engulfs hers. The rougher, darker skin contrasting with her light complexion. Meera hasn't pulled away, so I ask, "How old were you when your parents passed away?"

"Thirteen," she says. "They were coming home from a wedding, and a drunk driver hit them head-on. They were pronounced dead at the scene."

I squeeze her hand, and to my surprise, she strokes her thumb along my skin. "Sadie said you lived with your grandma?" I go on. It's been so long since I've had a meaningful conversation with someone. That, and right now, I want nothing more than to know who Meera really is.

She nods. "And my grandfather. They're both gone now. Sadie never met my grandpa. He was sick when I moved in with them. He knew he didn't have much time left, but he still insisted on spending every minute of his good days teaching me how to use these tools." She drops her gaze to her lap. To the tool belt she has wrapped around her waist. Though she still doesn't pull her hand away.

"He knew my grandma would smother me with love but worried that I wouldn't survive without knowing how to hang cabinet doors." She lets out a small chuckle, tipping her head toward her doorless cabinets.

"He sounds like a smart man. Everyone should know how to hang cabinets. What about your grandma?"

"My whole life story, huh?" She huffs, but there's a hint of a smile playing on her lips. "If you must know, I think my grandma died of a broken heart. She was the matriarch of our family, but after her only daughter died, and then my grandpa . . ." She swallows thickly and pushes the food around on her plate with her free hand. "I miss them every day."

Silence slips between us, though it's far from awkward. It's like a magnetic pull that only we can feel. I could sit here all night, observing her, studying her, and I'd be happy. But something still weighs her down. I can see it in her face. She puts on a great façade, acting like she has everything put together. Maybe that's how she got here. Maybe she always had to be the strong one. But she should have people who support her, who hold her up when she hurts. She shouldn't have to carry the weight of the world on her shoulders.

A bead of sweat trickles down Meera's neck and slips between the swell of her breasts just visible above her tank top. Another follows quickly behind, dragging my attention along with it.

She fans herself. "Is it warm in here, or is it just me?"

I shake my head. "It's definitely gotten warmer." I release her hand and stand. Her thermostat is mounted against the newly painted white wall across from us. "It's set for seventy, but it says it's eighty degrees in here. Where's your air conditioner?"

Meera stands and slides her chair under the table. "Over here."

Down the short hallway, there's a pair of trifold closet doors. When she pulls them open, dust bunnies fly out and circulate between us. The air conditioner and furnace are old. They were probably installed when the building was first constructed.

"It's not running. Sometimes they just need a new filter." I pull at the one that's currently wedged inside, but it snags, and a wave of dust billows out, the particles swirling. When it finally comes loose, the aluminum mesh practically disintegrates before us. "This can't be good." I hold up a half-intact piece of cardboard and mesh.

Meera rubs her face with her hand. "Just my luck. I didn't even think to look at it."

"I'll run down to Moe's Hardware. It's only a block or two away." I check the time, then pull up the search engine on my phone. "Looks like they just closed."

"Already? It's only seven thirty."

"Small town. Everything closes early. Temperatures should drop soon. If we open all the windows, you might catch a crosswind. Do you have any fans?"

She tightens her lips, which causes her cheeks to lift. Something I've come to realize she does when she doesn't want to admit defeat.

"Let's start with the windows," I say.

CHAPTER FIFTEEN

Meera

Gabriel Henry has impeccable timing. I've been in Morganville for two weeks, and while, when I first arrived, I'd hoped not to run into him, it seems as if he's unavoidable. Though I'm not complaining. Not after he punched Tom square in the nose. And that kiss. We'll have to talk about it at some point. Especially the part where he told Tom that he was my boyfriend. That kind of feels like it might blow up in my face with the way my luck goes.

But right now, I'll let him open my windows, because it's too hot to think about anything else.

"Do you have a flathead? The windows are painted shut." Gabe holds his hand out, likely already knowing the answer.

I pull a screwdriver from my tool belt and lay it in his hand.

Then he gets to work. He starts at the top, his muscles flexing as he scrapes and digs layer upon layer of old paint from the trim. Standing behind him, I get a good view of his taut muscles glistening with sweat.

"I think I got it," he huffs, and then he hands the screwdriver back to me. He pushes the top of the windowpane, and it rattles loudly—a scraping of wood against wood. It comes loose, and with a little effort, he pushes it all the way up, exposing a weather-beaten screen.

"One down, a million more to go." He laughs.

We go on like this for a while. There are four windows in the living room, two in the kitchen, and four more in my bedroom. When Gabe pushes the last one open, we're both drenched in sweat.

"It feels cooler already," I lie.

He gives me a sideways glance with a mischievous tip of his lips. He inches closer, and before I know it, he's hovering over me and his arms are looped around me.

I don't have much time to react, but my heart thumps wildly. And then my tool belt falls from my waist and into Gabe's hands.

"That should cool you down," he whispers, tilting his head so close to me that his nose brushes against my ear. The gentle pressure of his flesh connecting with mine causes my body to wilt.

I hold my breath. God, why am I holding my breath? He's just Gabe. This intensely attractive man who happens to also smell delicious. Even when he's soaked in sweat, his signature evergreen scent still floods my senses.

And then, just when I think he might kiss me again—damn, I wish he'd kiss me—he drops the tool belt to the floor. The loud thump pulls a startled gasp from me.

He breathes out a soft laugh and squats and grasps my legs. Then he hoists me over his shoulder.

"What are you doing?" I shout, suddenly panicked. This is not what I was envisioning that moment turning into.

"Cooling you down." He grips my thighs tighter, his fingers digging into my flesh.

"How is this cooling me down?" I'm upside down, and my head is against Gabe's back.

"I don't know. But it's fun. And you could use a little fun." He does a quarter turn and then drops me onto my bed.

I breathe out a sigh when I flop down onto my new white cotton sheets, relieved that the frame didn't give out. Then I laugh because I don't know what just happened.

Gabe hovers over me, smiling. Like a full-on smile with teeth. He's got the whitest teeth I've ever seen. And then there's the dimple. A small fleck that only comes out when he's genuinely happy.

My smile slips, but I reach for him and clutch at his neck, surprising myself with the bold move. This is a bad idea, but I can't seem to stop. I want to touch him. I want him to touch me. I want his lips on mine more than I want oxygen to fill my lungs. And if I don't do it now, I don't know if I ever will.

He climbs onto the mattress, straddling my body, as if he's reading my mind. Inches above me, he watches me with an intensity that burns right through me. Then his smile fades too. With one hand, he tips my chin up and runs his thumb along my jaw. Then his fingertips slowly slide down my throat and across my collarbone. His eyes, however, stay glued to mine until my chest heaves at his touch. That's when his gaze shifts lower and he whispers my name.

"Meera." His voice is thick and gravelly.

My body liquefies at the need behind the single word. If I was hot before, I'm melting into a puddle now. This is an awful idea. I know it is. But I've always been the good girl. I've always done the right thing.

This doesn't have to be as bad as I've made it out to be. It can be a one-time thing. And then we can go our separate ways.

Gabe grips my hip and tugs, then lowers his head and presses his lips to my neck first. They're soft and wet and warm.

His rough stubble scrapes against my chest, and a small moan escapes my mouth. I can't believe this is happening. Gabe in my bed. His lips are on my skin. And I like it. I more than like it. I run my hand through his thick hair and hold it tight when he brings a hand to my thigh, right under the edge of my cotton shorts. He drags his lips up my neck and over my jaw, but when our lips are millimeters apart, he stills.

"Did you hear that?"

"What?" I breathe, not wanting him to stop.

A soft bang comes from the kitchen. The front door.

"Oh crap." I go rigid. "That's probably your mom," I say and wiggle out from under him.

"My mom?"

I run my palms over my hair to smooth it and watch as Gabe adjusts himself. "I texted Lydia and Helen when you were prying open window number two. About fans. Lydia said your mom has a bunch. And then your mom messaged me and asked for my address."

The knocking starts again, this time louder.

I turn and rush to the door, regret washing over me. But I'm not sure where that regret is rooted. Is it because we were interrupted, or because we almost took things further than I was prepared for? I'm almost thirty, yet I'm still bound by the idea that sex comes after dating. Not before or instead of.

I don't want to date Gabe.

And then there's the hot Spanish girl from Sadie's party. He's a casual dater. And that's not me.

When I pull the door open, Evelyn and Sophie stand on the other side, holding box fans.

"Thank you *so much*. You have no idea how much I appreciate this," I say to Evelyn as I take the small white box fan from Sophie.

Gabe reaches for the larger fan after Evelyn steps inside. "Yeah, thanks. Perfect timing."

I shoot Gabe a look, but he doesn't bother to make eye contact with any of us.

"It's no trouble. I have another one in the car. Gabe, can you run down and get it when you're done plugging those in? Whew," she breathes out, tugging at the front of her shirt. "It is hot in here. Do you live here all on your own?" She looks around the half-finished room, sizing it up. I can't blame her. I'd do the same thing if I walked in on a newly painted apartment with no carpet and a mess of tools scattered about.

"I do. It's under renovation. Sorry about the mess." I plug the small fan into the wall near a pair of windows in the living room and turn it on high. Then I head to the kitchen and pull out a notepad and pen from a drawer.

"Under renovation? That doesn't sound like Tanner."

"You know Tanner?" I ask, looking up. I turn to Sophie, who's following me. "Did you get a chance to visit Flint today?"

She nods but doesn't speak.

"Oh honey, everybody knows Tanner. That's why I'm concerned about you being up here by yourself," Evelyn continues. "Do you have pepper spray?"

"She'll be okay," Gabe assures his mom as he strides into the room and drops a can of pepper spray onto the table.

I turn back to Sophie. "How was he doing?"

"He was sleepy. I got to pet him. I think he liked it. Will he be okay without his leg? How will he walk?"

Evelyn and Gabe enter the kitchen, both intent on her.

I pull out a barstool and pat it, motioning for Sophie to sit, and then I begin drawing a dog with three legs.

"Dogs have incredible strength. They learn to shift their weight across their other three legs. This here is what we hope Flint will look like once he's all healed up and walking again." I use my pencil to point to the three legs holding the weight of a dog so it's standing as if it had all four.

"You and I only have two legs. If something happened to one of ours, we'd have to do the same thing."

Sophie gives me a quizzical look.

"Come here." I take her hand and lead her off the stool. Gabe and Evelyn are both propped against the cabinets near the stove, giving us room to pass them. "Let's say something happened to my leg and I couldn't walk on it. I'd have to readjust my weight." I drag her to the middle of the living room and bring one foot off the floor. "Try it with me. Lift one leg. Can you walk?"

Sophie mimics me, picking one foot up and bending her knee so her foot is behind her. She hops toward me on one foot, smiling, and for a second, I think I see a fleck of a dimple that matches Gabe's.

"Like this?" she says, holding her arms out for balance. "Will Flint have to hop?"

"Oh no. Lucky for Flint, he has three other legs to help him out. In the beginning, he'll probably fall a lot. But with practice, it will get easier each day. He'll be running around before you know it."

Sophie hops all the way to the counter and climbs onto the stool again. Then she picks up the pencil and draws on a blank piece of paper.

"I love the open shelving. Are you going to keep the doors off or rehang them?" Evelyn asks.

"Don't mind her. She's a bit of a designer." Gabe chuckles.

"Oh," I say. "I'm not sure. I was going to paint the cabinets and rehang the doors, but I kind of like this look too. It gives the place some personality."

"It absolutely does. Especially if you painted the shelves. Green would make the place pop. Now that I think of it, green is your color. You haven't bought yourself anything to wear for tomorrow night, have you?"

"Tomorrow night?" Gabe asks.

"Grandpa didn't tell you? We're having a small retirement party for him at the Tipsy Brew Garage. He chose the location, not me." She stops and pulls his half-tucked shirt out of the waistband of his shorts like he's a small child. "He said all you, and I quote, 'young'uns' would want to stay and have some fun after he got too tired and went home."

A twinge of jealousy hits me in the center of my stomach at the way Gabe and Evelyn interact. It makes me think of my mom and how we used to talk to each other. How she'd slip my hair between her fingers and guide it back behind my ear while asking me about my day.

"Mm-hmm. Green is your color. Wouldn't you agree, Gabe?"

"I like green," Sophie pipes up, pulling her focus from her drawing.

My chest squeezes with affection at Sophie's approval of the color. "No, I didn't buy anything. I wasn't sure what to wear."

"Oh good. Lydia has the perfect dress for you. She said she doesn't have the legs to pull it off. But with your height, you'll be a knockout in it for sure. I'll drop it off tomorrow afternoon."

"Oh no, I couldn't," I insist.

Evelyn cuts me off. "Yes, you can. And as for you." She points to Gabe. "I bought you a new shirt. I'll drop it by your office after I bring Meera her dress."

"I have to be in court early. I can pick it up on our way home. It's getting late, anyway, and Sophie needs a shower."

"No, I don't. I showered yesterday," Sophie argues. She's listening to every word, but her hand keeps moving.

"I can bring Sophie home with me, right, sweetie?" Evelyn says.

"Yup."

"Finish your dinner. That's what you were doing before we interrupted you, right?" Evelyn raises her brows at her son.

Heat rises in my cheeks at her words, at the thought of what she really interrupted.

Gabe's quick to catch my eye, but he's careful not to draw attention to himself. "We finished a while ago. I was helping her with the windows. But we're all set now. Come on Sophie, you ready?"

She jumps down from the stool, and before I know it, they're gone. It's not until I'm turning off the lights that I notice the paper she left behind. I pick it up, slipping it between my fingers. It's a detailed sketch of me. I'm standing on one leg with what looks to be Flint, with three legs, standing just the way I showed her in my drawing.

I wake to the sound of birds singing. Or fighting. I'm not entirely sure. Either way, they're loud. Even over the blades of the fan slicing through the air. From my bedroom, I can't see them, so I shuffle to my living room and pull back the new curtains. Two beautiful tan doves skitter to the far end of the ledge, and then they're gone. I would have loved to watch them as I drank my coffee, but I'll take this as a sign that I should just forgo the caffeine.

Instead, I take a quick shower, throw on a pair of clean scrubs, finger comb my hair, and apply a thin layer of mascara to my lashes. I'm collecting my things, getting ready to leave, when out of the corner of my eye, I see the manilla envelope Tom left on my table yesterday. With my air-conditioning going out and the discussion over tonight's party, I'd forgotten all about his unpleasant visit and the divorce papers.

I slide the envelope off the table and slip it under my arm, and then I head for the door.

Outside, even in the early morning hours, the air is thick with humidity and the sun paints the horizon in soft shades of pink and purple amid an orange backdrop. People pass, some with a clear purpose as they scurry by, while others meander the streets like they have all the time in the world. Kind of like the elderly couple in front of me, walking hand in hand as they make their way through downtown Morganville. I'm not in a hurry, but I'm a fast walker by nature. I'm debating whether to slip around them or force myself to slow my pace when they stop in the middle of the sidewalk. I skid to a stop to avoid colliding with them and turn, curious about what's caught their attention. The words *Betty's Bakery* in curly white lettering on a large window catch my eye. And when the older man holds the door for his wife, the scent of cinnamon rushes out. My mouth waters. I can't resist a good cinnamon roll, so I follow them inside.

The gooey treats dripping with white frosting in the display case jump out at me right away. I have time to kill before work, so maybe I'll grab a cinnamon roll for Gabe too. I really should talk to him about my ex and that kiss.

When it's my turn to order, the short blonde behind the counter points a long finger in my direction. "You're that girl." Her voice is high and accusatory.

I raise my brows and turn to look over my left shoulder, then my right. But other than the older couple, who have stepped to the side of the display case, I'm the only patron in the shop.

I point a finger at myself. "Me?"

"Yes. A man came in looking for you the other day. Said he was looking for his wife. Showed me your picture on his phone and everything."

I blow out a breath, ignoring the dread in the pit of my stomach. "Was he dressed in designer clothes? Blond hair?"

"That's him. He found you?" Her face pales.

I nod.

"Maybe this is none of my business, but I wouldn't feel right if I didn't tell you." Her eyebrows slant down, and she works her jaw back and forth. "When I was locking up, I saw him again. He was . . ." She bites her lip and lets out a loud breath. "He was walking with another woman."

I press my lips together, that dread inside twisting me into knots. But I mentally shake it off. Because Tom and I are not together anymore. His affairs are none of my concern.

"I can't believe I'm about to say this." She frowns and wrings her hands, but then she pulls her shoulders back. "I know how it feels to be married to a man like that. At first, I didn't think anything of it. Because it could have been his sister. His cousin. A friend. But then I heard them fighting about a wedding." She clenches her jaw but continues. "And she was pregnant. Very pregnant."

I swallow thickly. The last of her words hit me like a punch to the gut. I place a hand over my own stomach, unable to stop a flash of memory from when we were together, but I quickly move it, hoping she didn't notice.

"Thank you. But he's not my husband anymore." I remember the envelope in my hand and shake it in front of me. "Divorce."

The woman's eyes go soft, and there's genuine relief in her expression. "Oh good. I was so worried. I'm divorced myself. Do you have a lawyer? If you don't, I have the perfect person. He'll take good care of you. And"—she lifts her brows—"he's easy on the eyes."

She scoops two oversized cinnamon rolls into a box and then places it in a bag. After she hands it to me, she holds out a business card. "His name is Gabriel Henry. His office is just down the street."

The second I step out onto the sidewalk with my pair of warm cinnamon rolls, my phone vibrates in my hand. Sadie's name flashes across the screen. I swipe my finger to activate the call, but before I drag the phone to my ear, movement ahead of me catches my eye. About a block away, Gabe crosses the street. A young blonde is at his side, dressed in a tiny black skirt and a lacy black top to match, revealing more skin than I've seen outside of a swimsuit.

She's wearing what must be six-inch heels, showing off a pair of killer long legs. And she's hanging on Gabe's arm.

I suck in a breath and hold it. I shouldn't care. This is exactly why I didn't want to get involved. Why I was relieved that Evelyn interrupted us last night. If I'm feeling like this now, then I can only imagine how I'd feel if we had gone further. I let myself get too emotionally attached, and the letdown is always more than I can handle.

I release a breath and spin on my heel. I will not let Gabe do this to me.

"Meera. Are you there?" Sadie's voice echoes through the receiver.

CHAPTER SIXTEEN

Gabe

Leaving Meera's last night was harder than I thought it would be. Not only because I'm attracted to her, but catching Tom there, trying to hurt her, was enough for me to want to camp out on her deck and make sure Mr. Up to No Good didn't return. The nerve of that condescending asshole putting his hands on her.

Sure, telling Tom that I was her boyfriend was unnecessary, but I wasn't thinking rationally. The moment I saw his hand on her wrist, my vision went red and I was blinded by a bright haze that brought back memories of my dad and how he treated my mom. How he'd wrap his fingers around her arms, demanding she do as she was told, shouting at her not to question his authority. Degrading her and isolating her so that even my own grandparents couldn't call her without having to speak to him first.

For years, he made my mom believe that he was the only thing good in her life. And all the while, he was cheating and telling her that it was her fault. That she wasn't enough to keep him happy.

I've met a lot of assholes to know one when I see one. They carry the same characteristics. Condescending words. Demands for attention. The desire to isolate their so-called loved ones. And the need to control. If there was a school for assholes, Tom would surely be an alumnus.

I wanted to show that good for nothing piece of shit that Meera had moved on. So I kissed her. I wanted him to see her being treated the way she should have been all along. But I acted without restraint. Meera didn't need me swooping in and pretending to be her boyfriend.

I'm making my way down the sidewalk, lost in thought and briefcase in hand, when I hear my name float out from behind me. I turn, already knowing who the voice belongs to. Jill rushes toward me. She's wearing a short black skirt and a tiny black top that's more appropriate for a strip club than court. And she's wearing the heels to match.

"Whoa, careful there. Don't break an ankle in those," I say, surprised to see her. "I thought we were meeting at the courthouse."

She clasps my arm and gives me a crooked smile. "I was just walking. Is it a crime to want to walk to court?"

Her eyes are hazy, and there's a hint of whiskey on her breath. "You live half an hour away," I say, eyeing her heels.

"Okay, you got me. I met someone last night. I'm allowed to have fun if *he's* having fun," she says, referring to her soon-to-be ex.

"True. But you can't walk into court like that. Here, take this." I shuck off my blazer, then help Jill slide her arms through it. "I'll call my assistant and have her run something over. We aren't the first people on the docket, so we might have some time."

Two hours later, I have a few missed text messages from Jack and my mom. I open my mom's first in case something's wrong at home.

Mom: *Hey sweetie. I took Sophie shopping and found her a gorgeous dress that'll match your shirt. We'll meet you at Tipsy Brew tonight. Don't be late.*

Mom: *Also, we stopped at your place and picked up some of her clothes. Sophie wants to sleep over tonight. I promised to take her out for breakfast tomorrow.*

I laugh at my mom's subtle way of telling me I have the night to myself and to have fun. Then I close out my mom's messages and click open Jack's.

Jack: *Home. Call me when you get this.*

Just as I'm about to do that, an incoming ping alerts me that I have a voice mail.

Darlene's sultry voice comes over the line. *Gabe. I just heard about your grandpa's retirement party. I can reschedule our reservation at Le Bistro Café for another night.* And that's it. The voice mail ends abruptly.

I sigh with relief. I'd completely forgotten about the dinner I accidentally agreed to.

I cross over Main Street, and my phone pings again. This time it's a voice mail from Jack.

Call me.

My stomach drops. Jack doesn't leave voice mails. He texts. Shit. I hope Flint's okay. I tap his contact and put the phone to my ear.

"Gabe. Where are you?"

"Just finished with Jill. Is Flint okay?"

"Yeah. I think so. We just got home. Sadie is on her way to pick him up. Are you on the way back to the office?"

"Not yet. I wanted to make a quick stop, but—"

"Get here. Quick."

When I open the door to our second-floor law office, I'm met with a side of Ashley I've never seen before. Her lips are curled down and her eyes are slanted. She gives me what I can only guess is an apologetic expression, but she doesn't speak. She just points toward Jack's office.

Before I open my mouth to greet him, Jack, his face red from too much sun, looks up from the file in front of him and pushes out of his chair. "I have bad news and worse news. Which do you want first?"

I chuckle, because I have no fucking clue what has Jack's panties in a wad. "I'll take the bad news for one hundred, Alex."

He clenches his jaw and works it back and forth before he finally speaks. "Your grandpa. He stopped by to drop off some paperwork while I was gone. This"—he waves a small stack of papers in the air—"is his last will and testament. He has stage four prostate cancer."

The air grows thick, and my vision goes blurry as that word, *cancer*, ricochets through me.

"I'm sorry, man. I don't know what to say," he continues.

I swallow hard, unable to make sense of his words. My grandpa? Cancer? He can't have cancer. He's the strongest man I know. He survived the jungles of Vietnam. Made it out of two major surgeries after he took a bullet to the chest and another to the neck while saving a woman from her mentally unstable husband. He's worked day in and day out to provide for his family for decades. And now, at seventy-two, he's supposed to enjoy retirement. It's finally time for him to wake up late and travel.

"I saw him the other day. He didn't say anything to me."

Jack swipes the case file off his desk. "I don't think he's told anyone yet. But when Ashley told me about his retirement party when I called to check in this morning, I knew something was up. These papers." He waves the file. "These are for the animal hospital. He was going to leave it all to you. But when I called him this afternoon to clarify some things, he was confused. He said he wanted Lydia to take over and that it should all be in her name."

I drag my hand down my face and heave a groan. My grandpa knows I can't take over the animal hospital. I already took over his property. All twenty acres of it. House and all. And I have my own business to run. When I'm not working, I have Sophie, so I'm more than grateful he changed his mind. Lydia knows more about the hospital than I ever will.

"The worse news?"

Jack drops his chin and shakes his head. "Breanna. She's back."

My heart comes to a screeching halt. "What?" I ask, slack jawed. Breanna's been missing for the last couple of years. Not even her parents have seen her. And now she's back?

"She's got a lawyer. They're petitioning the court for visitation." He rubs the back of his neck. "They know it'll have to be supervised, but she's asking for you to consider doing this outside of the court system."

I'm rooted to the spot, my body so heavy it takes everything in me to remain upright. Breanna tried selling her own daughter to get high. She's the reason Sophie won't open up. Why she struggles to communicate.

"Does it say where she lives? There has to be an address, right?" Everything in me screams to seek her out, to give her a piece of my mind.

He shakes his head. "All I have is her attorney's information. Jeff Turner. He asked me to give him a call so we can try to work out the details next week."

"Is that the hotshot over in Savannah?"

"You're thinking of his dad. This guy has a practice in Harbour Village. If it was the old man, I have no doubt he'd be pressing for full custody. He'll do just about anything to make a buck. But I think Jeff's smart trying to come to an agreement outside of court."

I puff out my cheeks and blow a long-winded breath.

Jack finally sits and laces his fingers on his desktop. "What do you want to do?"

"With Breanna? Fuck. She doesn't deserve the right to see her daughter. Not after what she put her through. No judge in his right mind will allow someone like her to gain their rights back after that kind of neglect and then abandonment."

Jack watches me. I know him well enough to know he's doing his best not to pity me. He won't tell me what he thinks I should do. He won't even offer advice. He'll let me call all the shots.

I change the subject because this is all bullshit. "Does my mom know? About my grandpa?"

"I don't know."

Jack leaves shortly after, promising to meet me at Tipsy Brew later tonight.

Ashley leaves me alone for the day, which I'm thankful for. I try to call my mom half a dozen times, but she doesn't answer. It's not until I'm about to leave that my phone pings with an incoming text.

Mom: *Sorry, sweetie. We've been running around all day picking up decorations. Just got home. Changing now. I'll see you soon. Did you ever get Meera's AC working? I meant to ask earlier, but it slipped my mind.*

Shit. It slipped my mind too. I check the time.

"Ashley, go home. I'm locking up for the night," I shout from my office.

"You don't have to tell me twice," she says.

When she's gone, I race out the door and text Meera to see if she's home. I head over to Moe's Hardware and buy a two-pack of high-efficiency fiberglass filters and then jog to her building.

She hasn't responded to my text, but maybe she's in the shower or getting ready for tonight. When no one answers, I knock harder while simultaneously hoping she isn't in there. With the heat and humidity at an all-time high, it's got to be even hotter in her apartment than it was last night.

I knock one last time and then shoot off another message.

Me: *I have a new filter for your furnace. I hope you aren't inside. It's too hot to be in there if your AC isn't working. Please tell me you're okay and didn't pass out from heatstroke.*

After I click Send, my messages go from delivered to read. Then a set of blue dots appear, indicating she's typing out a response. But then they disappear. When five minutes pass and I don't get a response, I pick up the filters and head back to my car.

CHAPTER SEVENTEEN

Meera

My eyes go wide as I pull the zipper over my hips and straight up to my bra line. The dress fits perfectly. On the hanger, it was cute, though maybe a bit overdramatic. It's definitely more fitting for a twentysomething like Lydia, with lots of sequins and tiny gold shoulder straps. I haven't worn a dress in years, so I was apprehensive to put it on, but as I examine my reflection in the mirror, I'm shocked at how good I look. It's short, but thankfully not too short, ending just a few inches above my knees.

If I wasn't borrowing this, there is no way I would have even bothered trying it on. Even when I did wear dresses, the act of shopping gave me so much anxiety that I always bought the first casual black dress that fit.

I smile and check out my backside in the bathroom mirror, and for the first time, I truly feel confident. I guess the saying is true. If a person looks good, they feel good, because I feel like a million bucks in this thing.

I open the door to the bathroom and step into the dimly lit hallway barefoot, carrying my heels in one hand and my purse and phone in the other. My phone pings, and Gabe's name appears on the screen. I consider telling him where I am. My fingers even type out a few of the words. But I stop and delete the message, then slide my phone into my purse. If he knew where I was, he'd probably offer to pick me up, and I don't want him to. He's thoughtful and sweet. I'll give him that. But I don't want to sit in a car with him while he's playing hero again.

I do a quick scan of the animal hospital to make sure I haven't forgotten to put anything away. Then I slip on my heels and lock up. The sun casts shadows as it begins its descend over the horizon. Streetlights flicker, and local shop owners close their businesses for the night. Dark clouds lower, bringing with them the threat of rain.

CHAPTER EIGHTEEN

Gabe

Three long oak beams run the length of the ceiling inside Morganville's longest-standing but newly rebranded bar, the Tipsy Brew Garage. Strings of black pendant lights dangle from the wood in various lengths, casting shadows across the wide-open space in an attempt to create a more modern look. A sort of cowboy-meets-New York appeal that falls flat and looks more like the set of *Cheers*.

It's crowded with people I've known since childhood, but I spot my mom easily at the far end of the bar where she's talking to a waitress who doesn't look old enough to serve alcohol.

Mom gives me a wave and points toward the table in the corner where Sophie sits alone on a bench. She's cracking open peanut shells and popping them, one by one, into her mouth. She's wearing a forest-green dress with sequins and rhinestones. Her long brown hair is tied back with two small braids and lots of curls. She looks cute and sophisticated, and the sight of her makes me realize I've never seen her in a dress before now.

"You look beautiful," I say, dropping to the bench beside her. "Did you have fun with Grandma today?" I trace the sleeve of her dress gently. "She said you picked out the dress."

She doesn't look up. Instead, she nods and pops another peanut into her mouth. "I'm hungry."

"What do you want? I'll order something."

"No need. We have more than enough food coming out soon. Pizza, beef, chicken. You name it." My mom leans in and kisses my cheek. "You look good."

"You match Dr. Taylor," Sophie says, crunching into another peanut.

I give my mom a sideways glance. "Don't think I don't know what you're doing."

She tries to suppress a smile, but it only makes her cheeks lift higher. "Have you seen your grandfather?" she asks, not-so-slyly changing the subject. "He's late. To his own party."

"No. He probably got caught in the rain. It's coming down good."

I'm itching to ask her if she knows about his cancer, but I don't want to talk about it here. Not with so many people around. Especially if it's news to her when I bring it up. So I ask her about the animal hospital instead. "How long have you known he was retiring? And did you know he was leaving the hospital to Lydia?"

She presses her lips together. "He told me last weekend. After Meera showed up. He said everything was falling into place and he wanted to retire before it got too late. But I didn't know he was leaving it to your sister. That makes me feel so much better. I thought he was going to sell it."

"Does that mean she's changing her major?"

My mom beams. "Thanks to Meera."

"What—"

"Hey, you look good in green," Justin says, giving me a pat on the back and cutting off my question to my mom. Justin's got at least six inches on me. He's lean and has a head full of gray hair that's combed over to the right. Thick white stubble covers his jaw.

He towers over my petite mom as he gives her a kiss on her cheek. "And you," he whispers, resting a hand on the small of her back, "look gorgeous in black. How did I get so lucky?"

My mom brushes her palm over his jaw and turns his face to meet hers. "Flattery will get you everywhere," she says, and then she kisses him.

"So what did I miss?" he asks, taking half a step back but keeping his hand on my mom's back.

"You're early, believe it or not. I haven't seen Dad, but Gabe says he's not selling the business." Mom clasps her hands over her chest. "It'll stay in the family. Isn't that great?"

Justin raises a brow as he stuffs one hand into his pants pocket. "You?"

"No. Lydia."

"Hmm. Really?"

"Yes, really." My mom swats him on the arm. "This is what she's always dreamed of. I'm so happy that Meera reminded her of that."

"I'm going to grab a drink. You want anything?" I say, needing an excuse to ease out of the conversation.

"Can't. I'm on call tonight," Justin responds.

"I'm okay too. Thanks, sweetie." She cranes her neck, looking at something behind me. "You should ask Meera, though. She's over by the bar."

I peer over my shoulder, and the world around me slows. Meera is walking toward the bar, turned mostly away from me. If my mom hadn't pointed her out, I might not have recognized her. Since she came to town, I've only seen her with her hair pulled back, but tonight it hangs in loose curls that fall well past her midback. A dark emerald-green dress hugs her figure, shining as the overhead lights reflect off the sequins.

She inches her way around a table full of young guys, and I can't help but scan every inch of her back all the way to her ass, and then down her legs.

But a jab to my ribs brings me back to reality, and everything suddenly speeds back up.

"Go ask her before someone else does," my mom says just as several guys in the group Meera just avoided take notice of her.

Two of them get up from their table and follow in her wake.

Without hesitating, I push my way through the bystanders and round the other side of the table the guys occupy. I slap my hands on the bar just as Mack, the bartender, angles toward Meera.

"She'll have a gin and tonic. Actually, make it two."

Meera and Mack look up in unison. Neither of them looks happy. Neither do the two boys behind her who grind their jaws and curse under their breath.

"Since when do you drink gin and tonic?" Meera asks as soon as I inch my way closer. The annoyance in her voice takes me by surprise. After last night, I thought she'd be happy to see me. She's the one who made the first move when she pulled me on top of her and forced my lips to her neck. They'd almost made their way to her mouth before my mom's sudden intrusion. Good God, I wished I'd tasted her.

"Since today," I say, trying not to sound like a complete tool.

Mack reaches for two highball glasses and fills them with ice.

"Did you get my message? About the filters? They're out in my truck. Maybe after the party I can swing by and put one of them in?"

Meera scrutinizes me, as if examining every one of my words like she's looking for the deeper meaning. "Thanks. I can do it myself. I've changed filters before."

"I wasn't trying to—"

Meera cuts me off. "You have a bit of a messiah complex, don't you?"

I squint at her. "A messiah complex?" I grind out the words.

"Yeah. Pretending to be my boyfriend and fixing my pipes. And let's not forget about Jack and Sadie's party, where you just knew I needed to walk off the alcohol. And now you want to put a filter in my air conditioner when all I have to do is slip it in there by myself."

Her words come out fast and full of fire. Almost as if they've been brewing inside her all day.

"I was just trying to help. I'm definitely no messiah."

Mack lets out a snicker as he sets our drinks in front of us.

I ignore him because Mack's a good kid. He's a bit older than my sister and lives down the street from my mom. Since Justin has always worked long hours, Mack helped my mom with yard work for years when he was a teenager. And it was no easy feat because my mom has a huge yard and loves to garden, just as my grandma always did.

Meera and I remain silent, watching each other. I don't want to be the first to look away, and from the determination I see in her eyes, she doesn't either.

But then her attention is drawn to something over my shoulder. Her jaw drops and she examines the wooden bar top for half a second. "Thanks for the drink." She snaps up her glass and bolts.

"Gabe, there you are."

That voice. I suck in a harsh breath and close my eyes, hoping that when I open them, I'll realize I imagined the sound.

It doesn't work.

"Surprise." Darlene squeezes between two people and slips in front of me. Then she throws her arms around my neck. "That French café would have been so much nicer, but I know you couldn't miss tonight." She leans in, her focus locked in on my mouth, but before she can make contact, I turn my head, and her lips graze my ear.

"Darlene," I say a bit harsher than I intend.

She smiles, ignoring my tone. "You look wonderful. And smell good too." She wipes at my collar and then turns and waves. "Oh, Sadie's here. I'll be right back. I want to talk to her about Hawaii. Grab me a dry martini, would you?"

When she's gone, I scan the room for Meera. But she's nowhere in sight. Not even a glint of her green dress catches my eye.

After letting out a deep exhale, I rub a hand down my forehead and temple. I feel a migraine coming on. This can't be happening. Not tonight. I grab my drink and take a sip from the tiny yellow straw.

"What are you drinking?" Jack pats me on the shoulder and laughs. "Looks kind of dainty."

"That, my sweet husband, is a gin and tonic."

Sadie is behind him, trapped between a crowd of people pushing their way through to the bar.

"Isn't that Meera's drink of choice?" Jack side-eyes me.

"It sure is," Sadie replies for me. Her brows raised as she scrutinizes me.

"Darlene was making her way to you." I try to change the subject. "How did she know about tonight, anyway?"

Sadie deflates. "I dodged her at the entrance. She's over there chatting with Jacob and Leila." She points to a side table, where a handful of our friends are settling. "I may have let it slip about tonight. I *tried* to tell her you couldn't make it to dinner tonight, since *you* never did."

I grimace, knowing all too well that I'd forgotten.

"But you know Darlene. She took it as an invite."

"How do I fix this? I have too much going on and this is just—"

"I know, Jack told me." Sadie nods at her husband, who's wandered off to order drinks.

"Breanna hasn't shown up, though, right? Have you seen her?"

I shake my head and take another ridiculously small sip from my drink, wishing it was a shot of whiskey.

"I can't begin to imagine what that poor girl has gone through. But you'll do the right thing." She grabs hold of my arm and squeezes. "By the way, where is Sophie? Is she here tonight?"

"Yeah, she's over there. With my mom and Justin." I point across the crowd.

"I'm going to go say hi before I get too drunk. My mom is here for one more night, and I fully intend to take advantage of it." Sadie grabs a beer from Jack's hand. "Oh, Meera's over there too." She winks at me.

I lift my chin and peer over the crowd, and that's when I see her. Meera, leaning over Sophie. Smiling at something my daughter has to say.

"But to answer your question," Sadie says, "you have to put your big boy pants on and tell it like it is. Be honest with her." And then she's gone, weaving through the crowd, pulling Jack along with her.

For a moment, as the words sink in, I don't know whether she's talking about Darlene or Meera.

Loud cheers explode across the bar when my grandpa finally shows up to his own retirement party. The bar is packed, with more than half of the patrons being our friends and family. Someone in the crowd chants, "Speech. Speech. Speech."

And before long, everyone, including the other half of the bar, joins in. "Speech. Speech. Speech."

My grandpa is old school. He believes in posture, precision, and articulation. And he always takes into consideration the audience. So when the music dies down and he speaks, I immediately notice his sunken shoulders and tear-rimmed eyes.

"Today isn't about me. It's about this community." He coughs and then clears his throat. "It's about you all entrusting me with your pets for the last four decades. I'm not leaving for good. I'll still be around. It's just time for this old man to enjoy his last days on this planet doing something else. Maybe I'll take up skydiving or mountain climbing."

That gets chuckles from his audience. Lydia, who's sitting next to my mom, is grinning. My mom wipes a tear from her eye. Helen is there too, with the other doctor on staff.

Grandpa clears his throat. "I wanted to thank you all. You've allowed me to do what I love—take care of your pets."

He pulls out a handkerchief and dabs at an eye. "I've been thinking about retiring for a while. But not until I knew your pets would be in good hands. You're family, and family takes care of one another. Two weeks ago, we were blessed with another doctor, and it was clear from the start that she was who I've been waiting for. Now we have two incredible doctors that are more than capable of bringing the hospital into the modern world."

He sniffles as he digs for something inside his pocket. He dips his chin and tries his other pocket, but he can't seem to find what he's looking for.

The half of the crowd that isn't here to celebrate with us loses interest, and the noise level in here ramps up again as they go back to their conversations. Grandpa is scanning our group, struggling to regain his composure like he forgot what it was he planned to say, so I make my way to him, ready to jump in to ease the pressure.

When he notices me, his eyes clear, and he stands a little straighter.

"Oh yes. Like I was saying," he drawls. "Without further ado, I want to introduce you to the new faces of Morganville Animal Hospital. Dr. Meera Taylor and Dr. Daniel Thompson."

My eyes dart toward Meera, who is wide-eyed, probably due to the unwanted attention. The other doctor grabs Meera by the arm and tugs her along with him up to where Grandpa is standing.

"These two doctors, with the very best veterinarian technician Georgia has ever seen"—he winks at Helen—"will ensure your pets remain in your family for as long as their health allows them. They'll take good care of you all."

His audience breaks out into applause, but my grandpa raises his hands in an attempt to quiet them.

"One more thing. Morganville Animal Hospital was grown with the love and the support of my own father, may he rest in peace. And so, it is my wish to keep it in the family. Please join me in congratulating my-my—" he stutters. He's gone pale, and the lines on his face are more pronounced.

I hand him a glass of water, and after he's taken a long sip, he continues.

"Please congratulate my granddaughter, Lydia. The new manager of Morganville Animal Hospital."

"I'm already your business manager," Lydia yells out from across the room.

"You are not *my* business manager anymore. You are *your own* manager. That is, unless you hire someone new."

Lydia's mouth drops open. "Are you saying . . ."

He nods.

And then she's running to him, and the people surrounding us cheer.

A hand rests on my lower back and a warm breath hits my neck. "Do you want to get out of here?"

I don't need to turn around to know who it is. I puff out a long breath, steadying myself, and then face her. Her jet-black hair lies straight down her back. Her tight black dress barely contains her breasts. She's beautiful, I'll give her that. But Darlene isn't my type. Sadie's right. I have to be honest. It's the only way.

"Darlene. I'm sorry. I—"

"We don't have to leave yet. I just thought maybe we could go somewhere alone. You know, catch up on old times." She drags her hand up my abdomen and over my pecs. Before she can touch my face, I grab her wrist, but I let go when an image of Tom clutching Meera's arms tightly flashes before my eyes. There is no way I'm going to be that person.

"Darlene. No. I'm sorry. I'm not interested in catching up. I never meant to give you the wrong idea."

She drops her attention to a spot near the top button of my shirt and pushes her lips into a pout.

"You're a great person. And I enjoy hanging out with you." I grind my molars when I stretch the truth too far. "But I think we're better off as friends. You need more than what I can give you."

She lifts her chin. "Don't get me wrong. I was hoping for more. But there's no reason we can't have some fun. You look good. And I look good." That hand is on me again, and she scrapes her fingers down my torso and around my waist until her palm is planted on my ass. She squeezes and licks her lips. "You're wound up tight. Let me loosen you up."

I close my eyes. This woman is telling me that I need to have fun. Isn't that what I told Meera the other day?

I grab hold of Darlene's hand and pull it away gently. "You don't want just fun. And neither do I. There are plenty of guys here who would love nothing more than to take you out to a nice dinner, I'm sure." I nod at the table full of men on the other side of the room. "But don't be casual about it. Make them work for it. Unless all you want is fun."

CHAPTER NINETEEN

Meera

I watch Lydia as she throws back a shot of tequila. She's wearing a tiny baby-blue dress that only she can pull off. It's shorter than the one she loaned me, but it's tasteful for a girl her age. Actually, now that I think of it, I'm not even sure how old she is.

"Lydia." I tap her on the shoulder. "Are you old enough to drink legally?"

She tips her head back and guffaws. "I'm twenty-one. No one here would serve me if I wasn't. The bartender? That's Mack. His parents own this place. They live down the street from us. Mack would never serve me if I was underage. Trust me, I've tried."

She drags her attention back to Mack, dipping her chin. Her eyes are laser focused as they travel down his backside when he turns to serve another customer. And I follow Mack's movements as he not-so-subtly keeps her within arm's reach. The way he grins at her with his eyes and not his mouth. I let myself smile. I'm envious. At her youth. At her innocence. How she wants something that's so clearly within her reach but is too nervous to go for it. I bet she has butterflies in her stomach right now. Butterflies are the best.

"Do you want one? The girls and I are taking turns ordering rounds," Lydia shouts over the twang of a country song I'm not familiar with.

"Oh no. I'm drinking water for the rest of the night. You girls have fun."

Out of nowhere, Helen materializes beside us and throws down two twenty-dollar bills. "This round is on me. What are we drinking?"

Lydia bounces on her heels, and with her elbows close to her sides and her hands in front of her chest, she claps. "I knew I loved you, Helen."

"We're celebrating," Helen says, a hint of her usual surliness breaking through. "One shot, and then I have to leave. Pick your poison."

I sigh, knowing I'm not getting out of this one. No one in their right mind tells Helen no. And being encouraged to join in on a round of shots by our cranky vet tech? This is a once-in-a-lifetime moment, I'm sure. My plan was to have one drink tonight so I don't have to have to worry about my blood sugar. But Lydia's excitement is contagious, so I say, "Okay, if we're doing this, then it has to be whiskey."

"Ugh. You're just like my brother. He always picks whiskey," Lydia says. "Jim Beam."

"Your brother doesn't know good whiskey. Buffalo Trace," I counter. "But this is it. I can't drink anymore."

Mack fills three shot glasses with amber liquor and smiles at Lydia when he slides them over.

The three of us clink glasses and toss them back. The robust flavor of the bourbon warms my throat and heats me up further as it makes its way to my belly. When I slap my glass to the bar and straighten, my attention is drawn to Gabe. He's on the other side of the restaurant. That girl is still with him, with her sleek black hair draped down her back and her barely there dress inching up her thighs. Her hands are on his . . . ass.

I look away. My stomach tightens, then rolls. I'm not jealous. It's got to be the whiskey. I haven't had a shot like this in ages.

"All right, ladies. Have a good night. Don't do anything I wouldn't do." Helen waves and takes off for the exit. I watch her, the paradox of a woman so intriguing sometimes. When she reaches the door, Dr. Thompson is there. He holds it open and smiles at her, then follows out behind her. I shake my head. No. It has to be a coincidence. Helen is always complaining about him.

"Meera, hot damn, you look good tonight."

I startle, the sound of my name pulling me from my thoughts.

Lydia spins in her seat and looks just as shocked as I do.

"Wow. I mean, wow."

It's Tom. Of course it's Tom.

"What are you doing here?" I say, the air whooshing from my lungs. I pull at the hem of my dress when his perusal of my body continues south.

"I was just about to ask you the same thing. This isn't our type of hangout, is it?" He laughs. "I'm staying down the street at the hotel off Hillside. I came by for a drink."

He steps closer, and I stiffen. A smug smile spreads across his face at my response. He knows he's making me uncomfortable. "Who's your friend?" He eyes Lydia, who's watching him with a curious frown.

When I don't respond, she throws her hand out. "I'm Lydia."

"Nice to meet you, Lydia. I'm Tom, Meera's husband." The instant the words leave his mouth, my stomach plummets to the floor.

Lydia's eyes go wide, but before she can respond, I interject.

"Ex. Ex-husband."

"That's not the way the court sees it. Not until you sign those papers. If you don't want to, then maybe we can take off. Go have some fun. Like old times. Hell, we can have some fun even if you do sign them." He slips two fingers between the strap of my dress and my shoulder and tugs on it.

I tense. I don't want Lydia to see this, but I don't want to step away from the bar with him and give her the wrong idea either. And Tom knows it. He's using it to his advantage. He pushes closer, and I shuffle back, but I'm trapped between him and the bar.

"Where are the papers?" he murmurs over the music, his face inches from mine. One of his hands is still on my shoulder, but the other one skates down my thigh to the edge of my dress.

He presses his fingertips into my skin and slides them under the material.

My stomach churns, and suddenly the whiskey isn't sitting well. I close my eyes to fight off the nausea.

"Hey, buddy," a gravelly voice booms, "remember me?"

I peel my eyelids open just in time to catch the sight of Gabe smashing Tom in the nose for the second time in two days.

"Whoa." Lydia yelps and jumps to her feet. She wobbles but holds herself upright with the help of the blond bartender.

"What the shit, man?" Tom cries out. He doesn't return the hit. Instead, he holds his nose and steps back as the crowd shifts and all attention is drawn to the guys.

"Gabe. You can't go around hitting my customers," Mack growls.

"It won't happen again. My apologies," Gabe says to the bartender, who undoubtedly doesn't care. His focus is still on Tom. "I told you to leave her alone. Hasn't anyone ever taught you how to treat a lady?"

"I just want those fucking divorce papers. The bitch left me high and dry and up to my eyeballs in debt. I just want to move on with my life. Is that too much to ask?"

"I told you she'll have her lawyer look them over. He'll be back in the office on Monday. Until then, you might want to leave her alone. Unless you want to spend the weekend in lockup. The cell at the police station probably isn't as nice as your hotel, but they'll still serve you a hot breakfast."

Tom and Gabe appraise each other as the crowd resumes what they were doing. Some go back to their tables and point while others wait their turn to order drinks.

"Tom." I finally break the standoff. "You should leave. I'll call you Monday."

"I can't wait until then. I'm leaving Sunday."

"Tom." I sigh.

"If it means getting you out of town, I'll make sure we get them looked at tomorrow," Gabe says.

When Tom fades into the crowd, I glare at Gabe, my blood boiling. "Messiah complex," I snap.

Lydia snorts. "She's right, brother. You do have a messiah complex."

"Go back to drinking," he mumbles to his sister. But his eyes never leave mine. They're intense, his irises igniting and the flames burning hot.

I need to breathe. I need to get away from him. So I push through the crowd and head toward the bathroom. But Gabe is at my heels, pushing through the door behind me and locking it behind us.

"What are you doing? You can't be in here," I shout.

"Messiah complex? That douche was about to take advantage of you. Forgive me for wanting to help."

Gabe's voice is raised, but I'm louder.

"I could have handled myself."

"How? By letting him feel you up under your fucking dress? Is that how you take care of problems? That would have showed him, all right."

I slap him. My hand actually makes contact with his skin. And it's hard.

"Oh my God. I'm sorry. I—" I clutch the offending hand in front of my chest, a wave of shame washing over me.

Gabe only watches me. He doesn't bring his hand to his face. He doesn't yell. "That. That's what you should have done when that asshole touched you. And I told you not to be sorry. I was an ass. I deserved it."

The door behind him rattles. "Hurry up in there."

He turns to leave, but I reach out to him. This time my hand lands softly on his arm.

"Wait." There's desperation in my voice.

Turning back to me, he growls, "Never let a piece of shit like that touch you again. Your response should be an instant knee to the balls. Knee to the fucking balls. You hear me?" His chest rises and falls, and he closes his eyes. "And yeah, maybe I do have a messiah complex."

When his eyes flick back open, my heart pounds against my ribs. The way he looks at me, like I'm the only one he sees, sets me on fire. I hate that look. It makes me feel things I shouldn't want to feel. Why does he have to say that stuff?

"I like helping people. I'm good at it," he mutters.

"Hurry up. There's a line," a girl yells from the other side of the door.

Shaking his head, he turns to leave for the second time.

I want to reach out again. To tell him to wait. To spend just a few more moments alone with him. But I don't. Because the voice on the other side of the door sounds all too familiar.

When Gabe steps out, the gorgeous girl with black hair is standing against the wall with her mouth wide open. Sadie stands next to her, wearing a matching expression.

"What the fuck? Are you two—"

"Are we what?" Gabe cuts her off. He's still angry, and it's partly my fault. I try to slip by because this isn't what it looks like and I don't want to get involved.

"Is she the reason you don't want to date?" she demands in a huff.

"It's not that I don't want to date. It's just, I don't want to date you," Gabe says as I turn the corner.

At their words, a wave of heat courses through me.

"Meera." Sadie is at my heels, tugging on my arm.

I face her, knowing the lecture is coming. She's going to tell me that I'm foolish. That I shouldn't get involved. But when our eyes meet, Sadie does the most unexpected thing. She squeals.

"Were you two doing what I think you were doing?" She grabs my hand with both of hers and squeezes. "Please tell me you were."

Her words shock me. She sounds giddy at the prospect of what didn't go down in the bathroom.

I shake my head. "No. It's not what it looked like."

She deflates and her beautiful smile melts into a frown. "Why not? You two would be so good together."

I tilt my head and scowl at her. "You told me not to get involved. You said he was a womanizer."

Now Sadie's scowling back, and her brows are slanted over her eyes. But in the next moment, they pop back up. "That was three years ago.

Oh my God. And he had you in the bathroom that time too." She laughs. "What is it with you two and this bathroom?"

I tug my arm from her grasp and turn. Gabe is still talking to that girl, and I don't want to be here when they walk by.

"Meera, wait. I'm sorry." Her heels click loudly on the floor as she scurries to catch up to me. "But for real. Gabe is a completely different man now."

I keep walking. I need to leave. The bar is packed, and while I know I should say goodbye to everyone, I just don't have the energy. I'll find Lydia and make sure she's okay. But after that, I'm leaving.

CHAPTER TWENTY

Gabe

I don't try all that hard to placate Darlene. She really isn't my problem. We aren't dating. I made it crystal clear earlier. And right now, nothing I say will make her feel better. I know how it must have looked when I exited that bathroom, but I really don't give a shit. When she storms off, I slump against the wall in the hallway and try to regain my bearings.

That's when Sadie rounds the corner, a glum expression on her face.

"Okay, I don't know what happened while Jack and I were in Hawaii, but whatever it was, you need to fix it."

I'm about to tell her nothing happened. That she's reading too much into something that never existed, but a loud crash startles us.

Without waiting for Sadie, I jog around the corner with my heart in my throat and images of Tom hurting Meera flipping through my mind. Near the bar, Meera is extending a hand to Lydia, who's cackling from where she's sprawled on the ground.

With a huff, I slide my arms under Lydia's and lift. When I settle her on her feet, her eyes are closed, and she's still laughing.

"Lydia, grab my hand," Meera urges. "I'll get you some water."

"I don't need no water. Make it another round of whiskey. My brother likes whiskey." She slurs her words, and when she blinks her eyes open, she finally notices me. "Oh, hey, Gabe, you made it to the party." She laughs again and stumbles backward.

Meera catches her in time.

"Party's over," I mumble, helping Meera steady her on a barstool. "Mack, how much did she drink?"

He cringes and rubs the back of his neck. "She and the girls were doing shots. I told them they should slow down, but they insisted they were celebrating."

I scan the crowd around us, but none of "the girls" are here.

"She's been drinking water the last half hour. Her friends left. She said you'd take her home," Mack continues as he cracks a beer open and serves a man on the other side of the bar.

"I'm tired," Lydia says with a yawn.

"Come on, I got you. You can sleep at my place tonight so you don't wake Mom and Dad."

I lift Lydia off the stool, and instantly, she pales. Her eyes go wide and her cheeks puff out.

I take a quick step backward, but it's futile.

Lydia expels far more than her tiny frame looks like it can hold.

Most of it lands on me. But when I look up, I see that Meera was also in the splash zone. Her face twists, but she doesn't complain. Instead, she grabs a stack of napkins and wipes Lydia's mouth.

"All right, time to leave," I say and haul Lydia over my shoulder like I used to when she was a kid.

Lydia groans but doesn't put up a fight.

Meera grabs my arms and blocks my exit. She throws her hands over Lydia's ass. "You're giving everyone a show. You can't carry her like that. Her dress is too short."

"Then cover her ass and walk with me," I demand.

We make our way through the crowd with Meera leading the way backward with her hands on Lydia's ass. My lips lift in spite of the ridiculousness of the last five minutes. Most women would have complained. Most would have been appalled at what just happened. But Meera? I doubt she even notices the vomit sliding down her chest.

Someone opens the door for us, and I tell Meera to turn to the right. My truck is around back.

"Thanks," I say after I buckle Lydia into the back seat. "Hopefully she stays asleep and doesn't throw up again. Do you want me to drop you off at home?" The rain stopped, but I don't want Meera walking alone, even if she only lives a few blocks away.

"How far do you live?" she asks.

"Just past Jack and Sadie's house. You're on the way."

Lydia groans in the back seat, and both Meera and I cringe as we watch each other and hold our breath for a moment, fearing the worst.

"Yeah," she says when Lydia settles again, "I'll grab something clean for her to change into."

We hop in the truck and in minutes, I'm pulling up to the back of Meera's apartment building.

"The filter is in the back, if you still want it."

"I'll be back down in two minutes," she says, reaching between the front seats for the bag with the filters in it. Her dress inches up, and I allow my eyes to wander over her backside.

When she slams the door to the truck, Lydia wakes up.

"Where are we? I need fresh air." She groans. "Why did you let me drink so much?"

I laugh, the sound apparently making her revert back to my bratty little sister who tells me she hates me.

A minute later, Meera opens the passenger door and heaves herself inside. "Wrong size," she says. Then she buckles her seat belt.

I raise an eyebrow.

"They don't fit." She holds up the bag of filters. "And my room is like a sauna. I'll help you with Lydia. Pretty sure she wouldn't want you helping her change. And I can't sleep in that place another night."

I press my lips together to hide my smile as I shift into drive, but it's impossible not to like the idea of Meera coming home with me.

When we pull up in front of my place, a large two-story cypress wood–framed house with a wraparound porch, Meera lets out a gasp. Then she shifts in her seat so she's facing me. "Why are we here?"

"Because I live here." I laugh.

"You can't live here." She tilts her head and stares at me in disbelief. "This is the bed-and-breakfast."

Truth is, I knew she'd be surprised. It's why I didn't say anything. She stayed here the night of Sadie and Jack's wedding, along with a few other out-of-town guests. At the time, I'd just moved in. The place hadn't hosted guests since my grandma was alive, but I opened it back up for Jack and Sadie.

They begged, and I relented.

That was the one and only time I've had guests. The private investigator found Sophie, and within a week, I had her back. I couldn't possibly juggle my career and fatherhood while operating a bed-and-breakfast out of my home.

"It *was* the bed-and-breakfast," I correct her, holding my keys out to her.

"Go unlock it. I'll grab sleeping beauty."

Lydia's out cold, so I lift her over my shoulder and carry her inside.

Meera is waiting on the porch and follows me in so she can shut the door and lock up behind me. When I drop Lydia onto the bed in one of the spare rooms on the main floor, she barely moves.

"Could you bring me a towel? I'll clean her up," Meera says.

I snag a towel and a garbage can from the attached bathroom. "Just in case." Then I close the door, leaving the two of them alone.

A shower is nonnegotiable. I smell terrible. So I hustle to my bathroom and get to work cleaning off.

After I towel off and throw on a pair of running shorts and a cut-off T-shirt, I go in search of Meera. I find her standing next to the stove. She doesn't see me at first, so I take the opportunity to watch her. She's barefoot and still in that tiny-ass green dress. Her long legs stretch as she pushes up onto her toes to reach for the cabinet above her head. The sight has my groin taking interest, so I mentally chide it, telling it to calm the fuck down.

The sound of the kettle whistling startles me, which then startles Meera.

"Oh my God, you scared me," she says, spinning away from the cabinets. "I made myself at home. I hope you don't mind."

Her hair is tangled, and there's still a chunk of something dried on her chest.

"Do you drink tea?" she asks.

I nod. "That's why I have a kettle. Why don't I finish this so you can shower?" Carefully, I peel the food from her chest with my thumb and finger.

She freezes at my touch, her eyes fixed on me, but when I show her what's in my hand, she squeezes her eyes tight. "That's so gross."

"Use the bathroom in my room. The only other full bath down here is attached to the room Lydia's in, and the rooms upstairs are being remodeled. There are towels in the cabinet next to the tub, and I'm sure I have a spare toothbrush under the sink somewhere."

"You don't mind?" she asks, fidgeting with the hem of her dress.

"I'd prefer it." I laugh.

When Meera emerges from my bedroom, her hair is wet and uncombed and she's wearing one of my old T-shirts from college. A navy-blue shirt with *Emory* written across the chest.

"Please don't say anything. I'm mortified." She covers her face with both hands. "I was in such a rush to grab something for Lydia, I forgot to pull out clothes for myself. This was on your dresser. I hope that's okay."

"It looks better on you," I admit.

She dips her chin and blushes.

"How do you like it? Cream? Sugar? Cream and sugar?"

"Black," she says.

I fill two mugs and hand one to her. "Do you want to sit outside?"

"Sure," she says with a shrug and steps closer.

I slide the back door open and flick on a switch, causing the overhead light to brighten the deck.

When I set my mug on an old iron table and turn to offer to take Meera's while she gets comfortable, I realize she hasn't followed me out. She's still at the back door. Her lips are parted and her eyes are wide as she scans the yard.

"It's breathtaking," she whispers.

I can't help but stare, thinking the same thing. Though I'm not referring to the land that lies to the south. The meadows of wildflowers.

The pond in the middle. And the trail that wraps around the property with overgrown bushes and trees. They're all visible in the light of the almost full moon.

"This land is yours?" she breathes, her attention still fixed on the view. She steps to the edge of the deck and points. "Back there . . . is that where we were walking during Jack and Sadie's party? Is that the same pond?"

I nod, still taking her in, thankful she's not paying any attention to me.

"It's incredible." Her voice is soft.

"Do you want to go down there?"

She turns to me, an excitement in her eyes I've never seen before. "Can we? Do you think Lydia will be all right?"

"She'll be fine. But fair warning—I haven't had much time to maintain the grounds lately. And with the rain tonight, there'll be a ton of mud and bugs."

She isn't listening. She's floating down the stairs on bare feet.

"Hey, wait. Let me grab you a pair of my boots."

She nods, but her feet don't stop moving.

When I come back outside, she waves at me wildly. "Shh. Look over there. It's a swan."

"Put these on," I say.

"Shh," she says again, not bothering to look at the footwear I'm holding out to her.

I crouch beside her and tap her left leg. She lifts it up and rests her hand on my back as I slip my oversized boot onto her foot. I repeat this for the right leg before I stand straight and tell her that swans don't live around here.

"Then what do you call that?" she asks. Her smile stretches from ear to ear.

I shift my attention to the pond and freeze. "Holy shit, it is a swan. Two of them."

We stand in silence and watch as they float in the murky water. The peaceful moment with Meera sends a warmth I'm not sure I've ever felt radiating through me. It starts in my stomach and then travels to my chest. I try to hold back a smile, but it's impossible when I'm this close to her.

After a few moments of silence where Meera watches the swans and I watch Meera, she surprises me by grasping my arm and leading me toward the trail. "Does this go around the entire property?"

"Yes. If we go that way"—I point toward the property line to the far right—"we'll end up by the bench. If we go the other way, we'll eventually get there, but it'll take a lot longer, and that path hasn't been maintained in years. It's been on my list of things to take care of since I moved in, but the whole process has taken longer than I imagined."

Meera tugs me toward the maintained path, sidestepping the larger puddles but trudging through the thick mud as a result.

"Tell me about all of this," she says, dropping my arm and falling into step next to me. "It belonged to your grandparents?"

"It did. I pretty much grew up out here. My mom was a typical single mom for most of my childhood. We lived here with my grandparents before she met Justin so she could work and finish her degree. My grandma looked after me. I'd come out here every day after school and help in the garden. She put me in charge of creating this path. That's why it's not very straight."

Meera tilts her chin, focusing on the mud and gravel below our feet as we travel across the uneven earth.

"I had way too much energy as a kid, so my grandma literally made me dig a path around the property to keep me busy. It took me an entire summer, but this is the end result."

"That's impressive," she says. "I didn't take you for a gardener, though."

"Ha, that's what you took from that? Not that I carved out almost a mile of earth as a child? But yes, I garden. Or I used to. My grandma turned this place into a bed-and-breakfast when I was in middle school, and by then she'd hired people to help. So it's been a while since I've gotten my hands dirty. When she passed away, my grandpa let everything go. He was never really involved with it in the first place. It was kind of like my grandma's private not-so-little hideaway. After she passed away, my grandpa put it on the market."

"Let me guess. Your messiah complex got in the way, and you bought him out?"

I chuckle. "Is it that obvious?"

She grins. "It's noble. And if I had the money, I would have done the same thing. So," she continues, "you don't use it as a bed-and-breakfast anymore?"

I shake my head. "Once I took over, Sadie begged me to open it up for her wedding, but that was the last time this place had any guests. One day I'll open it back up. That's why I'm remodeling the upstairs."

"I hope you do. It's so magical."

My breath escapes me at her words. "That's *exactly* what my grandma used to say. Do you see those oak trees over there?" I point across the pond. "With the Spanish moss? My grandma used to hang lanterns out there. She'd take me out there around sunset and read to me under the trees. She always wanted a gazebo, but she and my grandpa never got around to building one. That's the first thing I want to do once I get the land cleaned up. Or maybe a pergola."

"That sounds nice." Meera's tone is dreamy, almost like she's imagining herself under one of those trees, the tone such a juxtaposition to the rigid way she usually speaks to me.

"It was. Though she was resolute in her belief that magic only comes from hard work."

"My kind of lady." She smiles, though the expression quickly fades, and she goes back to examining the ground in front of us. "So. The girl at the bar. Is she an ex-girlfriend?"

"Darlene," I huff, "isn't really what I'd call an ex-girlfriend."

"Oh," Meera replies, her voice quiet and full of disappointment, the implication obvious.

"That's not what I meant. We never slept together. We only dated. Though that's not entirely accurate. I tried dating her a while back. Thought that maybe I was ready to settle down, so I gave the whole dating thing a try." I don't add that *she's* the real reason I thought about settling down. That her presence that night at Tipsy Brew gave me that once-in-a-lifetime feeling I imagine people getting when they just know they've met their person. But with the chaos that unfolded afterward—my mom dragging me out of that bar, telling me they'd found Sophie—I chalked those feelings up to my gut telling me to grow up.

Instead, I keep it simple. "Darlene wasn't my type."

"She's gorgeous. I'm surprised she isn't your type."

"We're two very different people."

"Ah, so she's nice?"

"Funny," I growl, though I can't help the chuckle that slips out after it.

"So, blondes, then." It's a statement. She doesn't look at me as she says it, and she doesn't slow her pace.

"Blondes? No."

Meera huffs a snort and shakes her head.

"Why would you think blondes are my type? Because I wasn't interested in Darlene?"

She shakes her head, but her demeanor changes immediately. I see it in her rigid posture and in the steps she takes. The way her stride lengthens like she's uncomfortable.

"I was going to bring over the paperwork Tom left. To see if you'd look at it for me and maybe offer some advice."

"And?" I ask, confused about how blondes fit into all this.

She bites her lip. "You had your hands full with a very sexy blonde."

"*What*?" I cough out. At first, I'm baffled, but then it hits me. "Jill." I laugh. "She's Jack's client. I took her to finalize her divorce. Are you telling me that you saw us and you didn't stop me?"

"Why would I do that?"

"You were coming to see me." I chuckle.

But she doesn't seem to find it funny. She keeps moving, attention locked on the path, lost in thought. Or maybe she's avoiding my gaze. And then it dawns on me. She's thinking about me. Matching me up to all these women. She's been avoiding me because she's seen me with Jill and Darlene, both out of context, and thinks I'm dating them. That I'm still that womanizer Sadie told her to avoid.

"Ask me," I say, matching her step, my eyes locked on her face.

Her forehead creases. "Ask you?"

"Ask me what my type is."

"Gabe." Her forehead relaxes a little. "It's none of my business. Honestly."

I stop in my tracks, stubbornly holding my ground. Meera peers at me over her shoulder and stops too when she notices that I'm no longer beside her. When she turns to face me, she's biting her lip again.

"Ask me," I say for the third time, this time with a little more bite.

"You're impossible, you know that?" She blows out a reluctant breath but finally gives in. "Okay. What's your type, Gabe?"

"You." The word comes out quick and clipped because I want her to know the truth. Honesty. That's what she needs. And that's what I want.

In response, her lips part and her eyes widen. But as shocked as she looks, she's quick to recover. "You have this grumpy nice-guy thing going on. I'm sorry for saying you have a messiah complex. But you're not *my* type."

CHAPTER TWENTY-ONE

Meera

The minute the words leave my mouth, Gabe's body deflates. But he's a big boy; he'll get over it. Just because I misread the situation between him and that blonde doesn't mean he's my type. I have too much on my plate right now, anyway. The last thing I need is a broken heart because of a stupid feeling I have in my woman parts.

"I deserved that," he says in a deep growl that I can't seem to get enough of.

Turning, I continue along the path, and he catches up again, but the air between us changes.

"So what is your type?"

I contemplate his question and consider the responses I can give him. But tall, dark, and handsome is cliché. And someone nice and easy to get along with screams snooze-fest. Gabe is all those things, and he doesn't beat around the bush. So I don't lie to him or sugarcoat things. "A man who doesn't expect me to take care of him or give up my dreams." And then I add, "Who doesn't expect me to have his baby."

Crap. I mentally kick myself for that last part. There was no reason to add it.

There's silence again. I hate silence. Although I don't mind when it's quiet, I hate the awkwardness that settles in. I should say something. Change the subject. But my chest is tight and my throat is dry.

Gabe's warm hand slips into mine, surprising me.

"It sounds like you're willing to settle." His voice is low but unwavering as he pulls me to a stop.

The bench is barely a hundred feet away, but we stay put on the path.

"Settle?" I challenge, turning to him. "I call it knowing what I don't want."

"Call me crazy, but I don't recall hearing what you *do* want. Tom's an ass. I don't understand why it's taken you this long to divorce him. You deserve to be happy."

"Happy? Everyone deserves to be happy. But not everyone gets a redo in life. We don't all get to right our wrongs." My voice is pitched. I know this. I don't mean for it to be, but every nerve ending in my body is on fire, and my anger is dangerously close to bubbling to the surface. I don't want to be angry, but without that emotion to cling to, I'll self-destruct.

"Meera. From where I stand, you have no wrongs to right. Tom's the one who put his hands on you. In the two interactions I've had with him, it's clear that he treats you like crap. You can't seriously blame yourself for that."

I swallow hard and drop my chin. Gabe has no idea. No one does. I want to yank my hand back, but he tightens his grip, almost like he can read my thoughts. Without my permission, tremors rack my body and my heart begins to race. I'm not sure if it's because of what I'm feeling or if it's because Gabe won't back down.

"Meera—"

"I was pregnant." The words tumble out. Though I know I should stop, a wave of instant relief washes over me when Gabe catches my eye, so I continue.

"Chloe. Her name was Chloe. I went into labor. I'd made it nine months. Nine months of morning sickness. Nine months of reading and singing to her. Waiting to hold her. I'd heard her heartbeat. Felt every kick to the rib. But then . . . I never got to hear her cry. I never saw her eyes. I don't even know what color they were." I inhale a shaky breath. "I told them I fell down the stairs. That I missed my footing. Since I had vertigo, no one thought twice about it. The doctor said she had significant brain damage, and her spinal cord—" I stop short when I taste the salty tears that fall to my lips.

Gabe releases my hand and wipes at my cheeks with his thumbs. Then he dips his chin so I'm forced to look at him and says, "Keep going."

I shake my head. I don't know what I thought would happen tonight, but this isn't it. I haven't talked about Chloe. Not since that night.

"Please," Gabe pleads. "I want to know."

I exhale. And then I surprise myself when I open my mouth. "The week before I went into labor, Tom had been drinking. More than usual. I don't remember what set him off, but I remember feeling like I deserved it. I was scared. All I could think of was survival. Not how to save my baby. It was the first time he'd actually hit me. He'd grab my wrists. He'd shake me. But he hadn't ever hit me before that night.

When it was over, I didn't go to the police. I didn't go to the hospital. I didn't do anything."

"Meera," Gabe says.

I turn away, blocking out the soft tone of his voice.

"I can't divorce Tom. It's the one thing he can't control. And it's the only thing still connecting me to Chloe." I hang my head and close my eyes, pulling in a long breath and holding it in my lungs.

Gabe's silent for a long moment. Though I can feel him watching me. Finally, he says, "You're punishing yourself while you punish him. You know that, right?"

I ignore him. He's right. Of course he is, but I won't admit that out loud.

When I don't respond, Gabe tries another tactic. "How do I fix this for you?"

My mouth drops, and I snap my eyes to his. For half a second, I almost think he's serious. But when I see his expression, I let out a teary guffaw and give him a small shove. "Seriously?"

"Mr. Messiah, right?" he asks with an arch of his brows.

I shake my head and take a step forward, ready to move on from this conversation.

He reaches for my hand again and slides his fingers between mine. They're warm and soft, and I send myself a mental kick in the ass for enjoying it.

"I've never told anyone. Not even Sadie."

"I'm sorry you had to go through that. Especially alone." The gentle tone of his voice soothes me in a way nothing ever has.

"Why is Tom actually here? I looked into it. In California, all he has to do is prove he tried to locate you. He can argue that you abandoned the marriage and ask them to grant a divorce."

We reach the bench, but there's mud surrounding it. On tiptoe, I step through it on my toes and sit, careful to pull my shirt down over my ass so I don't get splinters from the worn wood.

"I haven't looked through the paperwork yet, but probably because we own a restaurant, and that's his payday."

"A restaurant?"

I nod. "When my grandma passed away, she left me a lot of money. I invested it in a restaurant because that was Tom's dream. That, and our condo. I was young and I didn't know any better."

"So you're punishing him by not giving him a divorce, but you let him bask in the glory of a house and restaurant that you paid for?"

"Condo," I correct him. "I know. It sounds ridiculous now. But if Tom knew where I was back then, he would have convinced me to come back. He has to have everything his way. He has to keep up appearances. And I wasn't strong enough to face him. So I left. But I think he's here because his girlfriend is pregnant. He probably wants to get remarried."

Gabe swats at a bug in the air. "*What*?"

I launch into the story the girl from the bakery told me, fidgeting with the hem of my T-shirt the whole time, only working up the nerve to look at him when I'm finished.

And when I do, his eyes are wide. "I'm going to take a stab in the dark here, but he's probably so adamant about you signing those papers because he wants sole ownership of that restaurant and condo."

"Yeah." I've already come to that conclusion.

"What do you want now? You know I'm a lawyer, right? And a pretty damn good one at that."

"So I've heard." I try to smile, but my lips don't make it very far.

Gabe swats at another bug. This time, he smacks his leg. "The mosquitos are terrible out here. We should go back. But I'm serious. I can read through the documents. If there are any hidden agendas, I'll find them."

We stand and navigate carefully through the mud again, but this time, my boot slides. Gabe tries to reach for me, but it's already too late. A slimy slickness coats my arms and legs as I land in the black sludge.

A manic laugh escapes me. A loud crackling sound. I can't stop. And I can't move. I'm on all fours now, and I know without a doubt this shirt is not covering my ass, but I can't do anything about it. All I can do is hope Gabe is enjoying the show.

Before I can drop to my ass and give in to my predicament completely, he grasps my waist with both hands. He hauls me toward him, but I'm dead weight. I laugh even harder as I watch his feet shift in the mud next to my knee.

And then it happens.

He topples over me, and his hands slide through the thick goop.

A snort escapes my nose, and the laughing rachets up a notch. My cheeks hurt. I don't think I've laughed this hard in years.

When he plants a foot in the mud, attempting to get back up, he's grinning. But there's no laughter on his part. So I rise up to my knees, and using as much upper-body strength as I can muster, I push him back. Naturally, I go with him as one of my knees slides forward.

Finally, a small laugh bubbles up from him, and my heart goes still. It's deep and sexy and everything I suddenly crave. When he rolls over, his face speckled with mud, our eyes lock, and everything I said earlier about him not being my type escapes me.

And then I act. Quickly. Before I can change my mind. Before we're interrupted again. I don't want to think of other women. Or Tom. I just want to live in this moment.

I straddle him, my knees sinking in the mud. And then I angle forward and kiss him. My lips burn the second they land on his. A sensation so addicting I go back for more. And he's just as hungry for it as I am. He loops his arms around my midsection and draws me in hard. Like *he* needs more of it. More of *me t*o help put out the flame.

He slides his hands up my sides and around my face and cups my jaw with his muddy fingers. His cool touch against my hot skin is like gasoline on a smoldering fire. I want more of this. More of his mouth. More of his hands. More of him. My heart is pounding out of my chest. My face feels fuzzy, and I know I'm about to lose myself in him. I want to lose myself.

When our lips part, my breaths are shaky and shallow. My eyes are closed, but when I open them, Gabe's face is only inches from me, his pupils almost eclipsing his cobalt irises. It's both intimidating and intimate. Like he's staring at the scars on my soul, but he's silently telling me he wants to see them all, wants to know every part of me.

He moves one hand to my thigh and slides the other to the back of my neck. It's caked in mud, and the texture is rough, but it brings a welcoming sensation to my core.

I moan into his mouth as he tugs me closer, tightening his hold on my leg, which causes me to bite down on his lip.

He groans in return, and then he inches that hand higher. He pauses when he reaches the hem of my shirt, his shirt, where the cotton meets my skin. Then he slips his fingers underneath and traces the band of my underwear.

The way he brushes his fingers back and forth across my sensitive flesh makes goose bumps erupt over every inch of me. I like it. Maybe too much. I squeeze my legs—a reaction I couldn't stop even if I wanted to.

That sets off a low growl deep inside Gabe, and I like that too. I like that I have just as much as an effect on him as he has on me.

He digs his fingers into the flesh of my hips, the mud now crumbling between us. Then he rocks against me.

His erection rubs against the thin material between us, the friction spurring me to sit up high and rock into him. Once. Twice. Three times before I close my eyes and arch my back in pleasure, all the while clamping my lips tight to stay quiet.

With his fingers tangled in my hair, Gabe pulls me back to him, drawing my face to his.

"Meera." He whispers my name into my open mouth, rubbing his nose along mine. His breath is hot on my lips, half melting me and half breathing life into me.

But instead of speeding up, he slows down. He loosens his grip on my hair and trails a rough finger down my face until it reaches my mouth.

"Meera," he breathes again, this time with more urgency. A ridge forms between his brows, and then he presses his lips together. "You don't want this."

I nod and pant, "One time."

"Meera," he says again, his voice desperate like my own. My name on his lips adds kindling to the raging inferno in my core.

"Stop talking," I say, dragging his hands back to my hips.

Heat pulses through me. I shift my weight, and Gabe shifts with me.

Under my shirt, his fingers trail up the length of my back and stop at the strap of my bra. And then he slides his fingers across the material, the same way he did with my panties. As if testing the waters. Waiting to see if I'll protest. If I'll stop him from going too far.

But I won't. I want to feel his skin on mine. So I help him. I lay one more lingering kiss on his lips before lifting myself up. I straddle him again, but now, one knee is pressing into the mud as I position myself so I won't fall.

Gabe watches me, his eyes twin flames in the moonlight.

Slowly, I grasp the hem of my shirt and drag it over my head.

Gabe releases a gasp. His chest rises sharply, and his eyes go wide, his fingers digging into my hips. "Fuck, Meera."

The way he says my name, with so much need, so much reverence, makes me somehow weak *and* more powerful than I've ever felt before. I grasp his hand and bring it to my black lace bra. The material is so thin his touch makes my nipples harden further. Biting his lower lip and dropping his gaze to my chest, he drags his hand down and across my breast, then back up before he hooks his finger under the lace. The heat from his fingertips on my tender skin sends my insides soaring. It's been so damn long since I've been touched. Since I've felt like this.

"Meer," he says my name again, shortening it to fit his mouth, but I don't hear what comes next because a moan escapes me as he brushes my nipple again, this time with nothing between us.

He unclasps my bra, and before I know it, he's sliding the straps down my arms. He moves slowly. Methodically. Watching my face the whole time, looking for signs that what he's doing is okay.

Gabe exhales. "Goddamn, you're beautiful." He drops his attention to my exposed breasts.

And I let him. I want him to touch me, but I also like the way he assesses me, studies me. As if I'm a prize he's just won. His gaze shifts back to my face, so I seize the opportunity and impatiently guide his hands back to my chest. One hand on each breast.

I've imagined Gabe being forceful. A man who takes charge. A brute with his hands. But he's the opposite. He's slow. Uncertain. Careful.

While he hesitates, I run my hands through his hair and drag my body closer to his face. Finally, he responds by pressing a kiss to the skin between my breasts.

I moan again and pull at his hair. He turns his head, and very slowly, his lips inch their way to the lower curve of my left breast. He teases it with his mouth while he drags his fingers across the other nipple. His teeth nip and tug, and I'm a puddle in his lap.

"Fuck, you're perfect. You're absolutely perfect," he says, coming up for air.

"Stop talking," I say again.

It's my turn to touch him now that there's room between us. I slide my hand down the length of his erection. The friction causes him to pulse.

He growls. "I like how your body responds to my voice."

I drop my head back in pleasure. I want to deny it. I want to be in control. But he's right. His voice alone might take me over the edge. Maybe that's why I don't argue.

"I want you, Meera," he murmurs against the sensitive skin of my breast, peering up at me. "But not if I'm not your type."

I bite my lip and watch him, our eyes locked.

He nips at my breast. "Tell me I'm your type. Tell me this is what you want. I promise this—"

But he doesn't get to finish his sentence because suddenly I'm leaping to my feet. I scream and scramble to hide myself with my hands, but I slide on the slippery ground and fall back into the mud.

Laughing, Gabe pulls me to my feet. Full-blown laughing. With tears in his eyes and everything.

"What the fuck is that?" I point at a creature with glowing eyes a few yards away. "You have monsters out here?"

"Monsters?" He cackles. "It's a raccoon. Don't you have raccoons in California?"

At the mention of racoon, the furry creature runs back across the path toward the bushes. I jump again, but this time, Gabe secures me in his arms.

"A raccoon? That thing looks like a man-eating vampire with four legs."

"Come on," Gabe says, pointlessly wiping at the mud that now covers my arms. "Let's get washed off." He presses his shirt to my bare breasts and grasps my hand.

CHAPTER TWENTY-TWO

Meera

When we get back to Gabe's house, Lydia is standing in the kitchen, a bottle of water in her hand. She turns at the sound of the door opening, and her mouth drops open.

"Oh my God, what happened to you?"

She's staring at me. At the dried mud caked across my body.

I don't think she's even aware that I'm basically naked because the mud coating me is so thick.

Before either of us can respond, her face goes pale. She covers her mouth and then runs to the bathroom.

When the door slams behind her, I release a breath. "Oh, thank God."

Gabe looks me over and grins. "Follow me."

He leads me into his master bathroom, only releasing my hand so he can turn on the shower.

"Here's a clean towel and a new shirt. I can't help you with a bra, but you can wear a pair of my boxers if you want."

I look at him as steam fills the room, only then realizing that he doesn't plan on joining me. But my libido is still on fire, and I refuse to let a raccoon ruin my night. I want this. I deserve this. This is happening because I know damn well I won't have the courage later.

I drop the muddy T-shirt and shimmy out of my panties.

Gabe tries to school his expression, but it's futile. His eyes go wide and his jaw clenches tight.

"Meer," he says. His voice is so soft it draws goose bumps down my spine.

He was right. It does incredible things. I want him to keep talking.

"I want one time." My words ping-pong through the air as I step into the shower. I keep my gaze locked with his as the water runs down my naked body, taking the mud with it and exposing me to him completely.

Gabe keeps his focus on me too. Not on my body, but on my eyes. Like he's doing absolutely everything he can not to drop his gaze, and it's driving me insane.

I want him to look. I want him to touch me like he did outside. I want his hands on my body and his mouth on my lips.

"You're dangerous," he growls. He tears his shirt off over his head and drags his hands to the band of his shorts.

When they drop to the floor, heat pools in my belly. I've never seen a body quite like his before. His chest is all muscle. His six-pack has a six-pack. His waist tapers to a slim waistline, and then, holy fuck—

My breath catches when my eyes land on his massive erection.

He steps forward, slipping beneath the heavy stream of water, and I commit his every move to memory.

I turn around to give him more space, but he tugs at my hips, pressing his chest to my back and his male parts to my ass. Then he threads my wet hair through his fingers, pulling it away from my neck.

"You surprise me," he whispers, his lips brushing the shell of my ear.

"This doesn't change anything. You're still not my type." I'm breathless when the words escape my mouth.

"I didn't take you for a liar." His words are nothing more than a low rumble. He lays both hands flat against my abdomen and then drags them up until he's cupping my breasts. Then he presses his mouth to my neck, right below my ear, while kneading the flesh around my nipples.

My breaths come out quick, and I close my eyes, taking in every sensation. The thickness of his hands. The heat from his fingertips as they trace circles against my skin. But just as quickly as it starts, it stops.

"It's too bad I'm not your type. Because there are things I'd do if I were."

What the hell? What kind of man just stops when there's a naked woman giving him full permission to go forward?

When I spin to glare at him, he's grinning. He's teasing me. He's fucking teasing me right now.

I don't want to be teased. I don't want this to stop. I want more. It feels as if I'm having an out-of-body experience. Tom was the last man I was with. And before him, there was only one other. A nobody I had sex with after I graduated from high school. I've never taken the initiative. I've never been so bold.

"First, tell me I'm your type," he demands.

Fine. If this is what he wants to hear, I'll tell him anything.

"You," I say. "You're my—"

He slams his mouth to mine before I get to finish. It's forceful and rough, and holy fuck, he tastes good.

Our tongues tangle while his hands explore my body. Mine do their fair share of exploring too, but I'm so lost in sensation that I'm not entirely sure what I'm doing.

When his hands return to my breasts, I inhale sharply.

At my reaction, he drops his lips to one breast, keeping hold of the other with a practiced hand. And then he draws me into his mouth. Sparks rocket through my center when his teeth scrape against one nipple while he rubs the other peak between his fingers, pinching and pulling and twisting.

Water cascades down his face, only making him look more ravenous as he slides his hand down toward my navel.

Straightening, he brings his lips to mine again. "Turn around," he moans into my mouth. He guides me so my ass is flush with his groin, then slides his hands even lower, smoothing the warm water against my curves.

"How long, Meera?" he whispers. "How long has it been?" He scrapes his teeth against the skin at the crook of my neck.

He's got me by the waist, my hips locked firmly against him.

"Too long," I respond. My voice hitches and my chest pulses with desire. I ache for his hand to drift lower.

"How long?" he asks again, his lips at my ear and a desperate edge in his voice. His fingers trail down my thighs, teasingly slow.

"I don't know. Years. Three at least. Maybe four."

He stops, his fingers searing my skin. "Meer."

"I told you to stop talking," I say, my voice cracking. "Keep going."

Gabe bites down on my shoulder and pulls me even tighter against him.

"Spread your legs," he grunts.

My knees almost buckle at his demand. At any other time, his bossy tone might piss me off, but right now, I can't get enough of it.

When I widen my stance, he leans forward and presses his nose against the sensitive skin just behind my ear.

I close my eyes, relishing the feel of his hand hovering over my center, anticipating his touch.

And then it happens. He slips one finger down my folds.

For a second, we're both holding our breath. Then he slips his fingers inside, causing my whole world to crumble around me.

"You feel . . ." he says, but he doesn't finish his sentence.

His fingers move faster, and I'm doing everything I can not to fall apart. I slap my palms against the wall to hold myself up while I ride his hand.

Gabe laughs. "Slow the fuck down, Meera. I'm not going anywhere."

"Stop talking."

"Then slow down. I want to enjoy this," he says.

And for once, I do too.

I wake to a sliver of sunshine streaming through Gabe's bedroom curtains. It's the same bedroom I woke up in three years ago. And while I'm wrapped in his white cotton sheets in much the same way, this time, I remember everything. Every last satisfying moment. We didn't have sex, because Gabe didn't have any condoms, but what he did to me, taking me to places I've never gone before, was better than any sex I've ever had. He was relentless and generous, with absolutely no resemblance to the selfish man I imagined he would be.

When the mattress shifts, I roll over and find a very disheveled man peeling back his eyelids. He blinks a few times and then smiles. His hair crisscrosses in every direction in a way I never thought I'd find sexy, and I wonder if this is how he wakes every morning or if it's a result of us.

"Did you sleep well?" he asks, his voice rough from disuse.

I nod, but I can't muster any more of a response as panic sets in. Shit. What did I do?

"Get out of your head," he growls. "You enjoyed yourself. I enjoyed myself." He drops a kiss to my forehead and sits up. "I'll make some coffee and check on Lydia."

Lydia. I'd completely forgotten about Lydia.

Gabe gets up and pulls a shirt from his dresser. "You can throw this on." He tosses it on the bed, then disappears, leaving me to freak the fuck out alone.

I'm midpanic when a phone vibrates on Gabe's nightstand. The word *Her* flashes across the screen. *Her*. Not even a name. And then I remember why Gabe and I didn't do this sooner.

Fuck, fuck, fuck.

CHAPTER TWENTY-THREE

Gabe

I don't regret a goddamn thing. Meera wanted me to touch her, so that's what I did. She wanted me to bring her pleasure, and I brought her mind-altering, explosive euphoria. Her words, not mine. And now she's going to hole herself up in my bedroom like what I did wasn't the best damn thing that's ever happened to her. Nope. That's not going to work for me.

I start the coffee and then head to the spare bedroom to check on Lydia. She has one arm hanging off the bed and a pillow over her head. She's going to wake up with a hangover from hell, so I go back to the kitchen and pull out the ingredients for my famous breakfast biscuit.

The sausage is just about finished when Meera finally materializes. She's wearing the shirt I gave her and looking hot as fuck in it, but I don't say that. Instead, I hand her a cup of coffee. "Don't overthink this."

I want to smack her on the ass, but something tells me she isn't that type of girl. But then again, she tore apart all my preconceived notions last night.

Meera gives me a noncommittal smile in response and takes the coffee, but not before placing a phone on the counter. "It smells good in here."

"Making my famous hangover breakfast sandwich. Eggs, sausage, cheese, and a buttery biscuit. Grab a plate."

"It's okay. I'm not really hungry," she mumbles from behind her mug.

"Grab a damn plate. You're eating," I say, not the least bit apologetic about my tone.

For once, she obeys.

I fold a piece of cheese in half and lay it flat on both sides of the biscuit. When the sausage is ready, I toss that on top, along with scrambled eggs, and then hand the plate back to Meera. Our eyes meet for a second, but she's quick to look away.

I don't know what happened between her screaming my name last night and waking up this morning, but I don't like this one bit.

"Don't mind the mess," I say to lighten the mood. "You know what it's like living in the middle of a renovation. I'm just a lot slower at it than you are. Never seems to be enough time in the day."

"It's beautiful," she says, scanning the kitchen. "The whole thing. Especially the windows. They're the same as the ones in your bedroom. Do all the bedrooms have them?"

"Yup. My grandma fought my grandpa tooth and nail for them. Told him she'd leave him if he didn't put them in for her." I make my way to the kitchen table and sit across from Meera.

She laughs. "What happened?"

"The windows were installed a week later."

Meera takes a bite of the sandwich, then she closes her eyes and hums in delight. It might just be the most beautiful sound I've ever heard.

"Are you changing out the trim?" she asks, pointing at the white casings on the floor.

I nod. "Giving the house an upgrade. My grandma would be pissed if I let it go to shit."

Shifting in her seat, she scans what she can see from the table. "So you're retrimming the entire house?"

"Eventually."

"Does your grandpa miss it? There's got to be a million memories boarded up in these walls."

I shake my head. "He couldn't get out of here fast enough. Hasn't been here in two years, at least." I sigh. "He's ornery. Very set in his ways. I'm sure you can see it at the animal hospital." I set my sandwich on my plate and take a sip of coffee, looking around the room, trying to see it from Meera's perspective. "He likes things the way they are. The way they've always been. But my grandma, she liked to keep up with the times. Hence the windows. My grandpa doesn't do anything without thinking things through. Unless something drastic happens, and then he's ready to make life-altering decisions without thinking them through. The day after my grandma's funeral, he decided he wanted to sell it." *Kind of like his retirement and his cancer.*

"I'm sorry," Meera replies with soft eyes.

"Sorry about what?" Lydia asks, her voice low and sluggish. "Oh my God, is that what I think it is?" She heads straight to the stove and builds a sandwich for herself.

"About your grandpa," Meera says, undeterred.

I squint at her, but she's too busy enjoying her coffee to notice.

"I'd want to retire too. Do all the things I never had a chance to do. Do you know how long he has?"

I'm taken aback by her words. Does she know about my grandpa? Does Lydia?

The confused frown Lydia wears as she takes a seat next to me gives me the answer right away.

"What? What do you mean?" she asks.

Meera's eyes widen, and her focus shifts to me, but before I can get a word out, my mom and Sophie are walking through the front door.

"Good morning," she sings out. "We brought donuts."

The room goes silent.

And Meera's eyes, now swimming with panic, grow even larger.

"How you two feeling this morning?" she asks, stepping into the kitchen. "Oh. Meera, what a surprise." She grins as she drops a box of donuts on the table.

When no one acknowledges her, she scrunches her nose. "What?"

"Yeah, what?" Sophie says, stepping out from my mom's shadow.

Shit.

That's all it took for Meera to turn into a damn ghost. She squirmed for a bit, because I was too shocked to pipe up myself and ask my mom what she knows about Grandpa. But after about ten minutes of squabbling and tears the size of golf balls, I take Meera outside and sit her down on the porch swing. I can't do tears, and from the looks of it, neither can Meera.

"I swear, I thought everyone knew. I thought that's why he decided to retire."

"Probably was," I say, pressing my weight into the seat next to her. "It needs to sink in. They'll be okay. After they yell at him for not telling them."

But how did she know?

We sit quietly, listening to the birds chatter and the leaves on the maple nearby rustle in the wind for a moment before I turn to look at her and let out a chuckle.

Her nostrils flare in response. "What?"

"You dodged a bullet. No one asked you about your clothes."

She rolls her eyes, but her lips twist in a wry smile. She swats at my arm. "Yeah, about that. I need you to take me home. I have to shower and replace that filter."

I let out a breathy laugh. "Another shower? I thought I took care of that last night. Or are you ready for round two?"

Meera's eyes grow until they're the size of saucers. Then she whips around, checking that we're still alone.

"Tell anyone, and I'll deny it. And I said *one time. One time.*"

"Honey, that's what they all say."

"Ugh, this is why I didn't want to in the first place." She balls her fists in her lap. "I don't sleep around. And I sure as hell don't sleep with men who are seeing other people."

She's agitated. I should stop, but there's a hint of disgust in her tone, and I suddenly feel attacked.

"It was metaphorical. I was just sayin'."

"Say all you want. Can you just take me home? I'd hate to take up any more of your time. What with all those women who keep coming back for more."

When she stands, she cusses and presses her finger to her lips.

Shit. She's probably got a splinter. This piece of crap wooden swing needs to be sanded and refinished. I make a mental note to add it to my list of things to get done around here.

Standing, I pull her hand away from her mouth. She fights me on it for a second, but when I turn and tuck her hips behind me, she gives up and allows me to inspect her finger.

"I see it. Let me grab a pair of tweezers. It'll be out in no time."

She doesn't respond. Her lips are pursed and her eyes are like daggers.

"Meer, you're going to have to spell this out for me, because I don't understand what's wrong. I'm sorry if the remark I made upset you. The only women in my life are those three inside my house right now."

"It's honestly none of my business."

"Spit it out," I growl.

"Gabe," she says, her body deflating.

"If you're referring to that girl at the bar yesterday, I told her I wasn't interested. You were right there. You heard me."

She shakes her head. "You don't need to explain. I told you this was a one-time thing."

Dammit. I open my mouth, ready to tell her she can shove that one-time thing in the fucking garbage, because one time won't be enough. But my mom opens the door, preventing me from going any further.

She looks from me to Meera, and then to where I've got my hands wrapped around hers. I can only imagine what she's thinking. But rather than the smile I expect from her, worry creases across her forehead. She holds out a phone. My phone.

"Have you spoken to her?"

"Spoken to who?" I ask more harshly than I mean to.

"Her." My mom's tone is quiet, but there's no mistaking the meaning behind that word.

Meera pulls her arm back, and this time I don't stop her.

"You have five missed calls from her."

I let out a deep breath. "No. I haven't. I'm surprised she still has my fucking phone number."

"Language," she says as she shuffles closer and hands me my phone. "Why do you think she's calling?"

"She wants visitation."

"*What*?" she almost shouts, her voice panicked.

"She hired a lawyer. She wants supervised visitation, but she wants to keep it out of court. Jack wanted me to think about how I want to proceed before he calls her lawyer back."

"When was this?"

"Yesterday morning."

"So you've been sitting on this for the last twenty-four hours without telling any of us?"

"What was there to say? Hey Mom, Breanna's back. She wants to see her daughter. Oh yeah, and Grandpa has cancer too."

"Gabriel," she warns.

"I'm sorry. But I don't know what to do. Do you think I should call Sophie's therapist and see what she recommends?"

"I'll call her after lunch. But in the meantime, you need to fix whatever that was." She points to Meera, who is wandering, barefoot, in my backyard. "Lydia said you two came in covered in mud last night, and she was half naked." Finally, a hint of a smile graces her lips, but it drops again after a second. "That and her ex-husband is in town and you punched him in the nose."

"Of course she'd remember something like that. Only drunk girl in the world with the fucking memory of an elephant."

"Gabriel." She glowers. "Fix it. I'll take Sophie to the library before they close so she can check out new books."

My mom leaves, taking Lydia and Sophie with her, and I'm standing on the back patio alone. Meera is pacing back and forth between the pink and white pentas and overgrown wildflowers snaking their way across the path. She makes her way from one end to the other, stopping just long enough to look at a few flowers. But then she's moving again, and from here, it looks like her lips are moving. Though if she's speaking, she's doing it quietly.

I make my way down the stairs, barefoot like Meera. When I get close, she turns. Her face is pulled tight, but there's also softness there.

"I told you not to get in your head. What happened last night—"

"Won't happen again," she murmurs solemnly.

"Won't happen again," I repeat. "Now let me see your finger." I grab her hand because I know she won't willingly show me herself. "Let's head inside. The tweezers are in my bathroom."

"Was that about Sophie's mom?" she asks, following me back up the stairs.

I nod, knowing full well Meera saw my phone this morning. She saw *Her* scrawled across the front and probably made assumptions. But none of that matters now. She's making it more than clear that she isn't interested in taking this anywhere else.

"She's back in town. Wants visitation. But also wants to keep it out of court."

Inside, I guide her to sit on the bed and rummage through the drawer in my bathroom, looking for the tweezers.

"Are you going to let her?"

"I don't know," I say honestly without stopping my search. "I don't really know what to do."

Meera doesn't respond. She doesn't offer words of encouragement. Doesn't tell me she's sorry I have to deal with this. She just sits silently.

When I find the tweezers, I return and kneel beside her. For an instant, her bare thigh is a centimeter from my face. But when she notices, she crosses that leg over the other, thus moving away from me, but the action only hikes her shirt up even more.

She lets out a ragged but defeated breath, and I laugh in response.

"Finger," I say.

She sticks her hand out, finger extended, and I find the tiny sliver.

I quickly but carefully pluck out the piece of wood.

And then I drive her home.

CHAPTER TWENTY-FOUR

Meera

"All the fun stuff happens when I'm not around," Sadie huffs on the other end of the line. "Jack said he thought he saw Tom when we were coming back into the bar, but I told him he was crazy. Tom would have said hi to us, right?"

I'm standing in front of my fan, waiting for the room to cool down. After Gabe dropped me off, I threw on a pair of shorts and ran across the street for a new correctly sized filter for my furnace. While I was tinkering with it, I missed a call from Sadie, so I decided to call her back before plunging into a cold shower.

"It wasn't fun. It was mortifying. Lydia was right there. And Gabe. He hauled off and punched him, like it's something he does every day." I throw a hand in the air, even though she can't see me. "Where were you, anyway?" Because how could they have missed the spectacle at the bar? Every eye in the place was on us.

"If you must know, we went out back and had a quickie."

"Sadie," I gasp, more astonished than anything.

"What? I'm ovulating. We were hoping to make baby number two in Hawaii, but I didn't start ovulating till yesterday. And my mom was at the house with Grace, so it wasn't like we had many choices."

"You thought having sex in public was the next best alternative?" I laugh into the phone.

"Girl, you have no idea what you're missing out on. You don't know how hot it is when you're the one calling the shots." Her voice is light and airy, like it was during our college days, when things were simpler. "You should have seen Jack's face when I pulled him into the alley. It was all-consuming. There better be two embryos in this uterus with what we did.

"But enough about me. Why is Tom here in the first place? What does he have to gain by showing up unannounced? He couldn't handle this from California?"

I sigh. It's now or never. I have to tell her. I should have told her years ago. And I should have leaned on her for support rather than going it alone. So I lay it all out there. I tell her about the restaurant. About Chloe. Sadie knew about the baby, of course, but I tell her the other things, including the guilt I've harbored over Chloe's death.

"Oh, honey, I had no idea," she says, sniffling. "And I get why you didn't tell me sooner. You were barely surviving while I was the oblivious asshole planning a wedding." She makes light of the situation, which I appreciate. It's a thin line, and she knows I hate being pitied.

Then I tell her about the pregnant woman Tom was seen with in town. The idea that he's going to be a father before I become a mom sinks in then, sending nausea swirling in my stomach.

"He's such a dick. I'm surprised he didn't knock someone up sooner. But girl, take a step back and look at the bigger picture. You're here now. You aren't surviving anymore. You're thriving. Signing those divorce papers won't erase Chloe's memory. And I agree with Gabe. He needs to go through the documents before you sign. I wouldn't put it past that slimeball to pull a fast one. Now go wash your face, because we have pressing matters to discuss, and I think it'll cheer you up."

She's already lightened my mood, so I follow her directions. I run water over my tear-streaked face and then dry it before pressing my ear back to the phone.

"Word on the street is you went home with Gabe," she chirps.

My heart plummets. "Word on the street?" I squeak.

"Small town. What can I say?" She laughs. "So? Is the rumor mill true?"

I pull in a deep breath, then let it out slowly, buying myself a minute. "I did, but not for the reasons you think. You saw Lydia last night. I helped him get her home, and since my AC isn't working, I stayed at his place."

"Damn, girl. You may be the first person to have broken his golden rule."

"Golden rule?"

Sadie clears her throat and does her best impression of Gabe, deep, raspy voice and all. "No woman shall enter my domain. Not to Netflix and chill, not to eat dinner, and most certainly not to spend the night." She giggles and then adds, "Okay, so maybe he isn't quite so archaic, but you catch my drift. Of course his mom, Lydia, and Sophie are exceptions. And if he hosts a party, but that hasn't happened yet. He keeps to himself quite a bit."

"It wasn't like that," I say, cringing at the lie. So I add, "At first. Anyway, Lydia—"

"Wait, back up. Did I hear you correctly? You better start spilling the details."

I tell Sadie about last night. Most of it. Keeping the toe-curling orgasms to myself. "But this morning, I panicked. This isn't like me. I don't do that kind of stuff."

"I've got news for you. It is you. Because you did it. And wasn't it freeing? Gabe really is a great guy. A bit moody at times, but if I were to fix you up with somebody, it'd be him."

"Sadie," I groan, but she cuts me short.

"I'm serious. He had a rough go of things for a while. When I moved out here, he was a different man. I heard all kinds of stories, but they all stemmed from that woman. Sophie's mom. That night, after the whole bathroom debacle, Gabe's mom showed up. That's the night he got the news that Sophie was safe. It took a few more days for child protective services to get her back to him, but he did a complete one-eighty. Stopped drinking. Stopped going out. It's pretty amazing, if you ask me."

Sadie continues, but I tune her out. Gabe's mom came to get him that night? The realization reverberates through my body. The tall woman with auburn hair. The woman he left with was his mom?

I shake my head. It doesn't matter. It's in the past.

"Can we not talk about Gabe?" I sigh. "I have more important issues to deal with."

"More important than Gabe's fine ass?" She chuckles. Then there's a commotion on her end of the line, and, voice muffled, she says, "No, sweetie, your ass is way hotter."

"Is that Jack? Oh my God, did he hear our entire conversation?" I jump to my feet and pace from one end of my living room to the other.

"Just the tail end. But he knows girl code. Right, sweetie?"

"As long as you agree that my ass is hotter," he mumbles in the background.

"Put me on speaker," I demand. "Am I on speaker?"

"Yes ma'am," she says.

"You are both sworn to secrecy. I mean it. That was a one-time thing. I don't need it getting out that I fooled around with my boss's grandson."

"Your secret is safe with me, Meera Beara," Jack promises, his voice is warm and sincere.

"Thank you," I say, choking back emotion at the nickname.

He and Sadie started calling me that the night I found out I was pregnant. I was a junior at San Francisco State, and I was terrified of the idea of being a mom. I still felt like a kid myself.

When I held out the pregnancy stick Sadie had forced Jack to buy at the gas station off campus, that's when they'd said it. Maybe it was Sadie who said it first. Or maybe it was Jack. But the next thing I knew, the two of them were pulling me into a warm embrace. "Meera Beara, you're going to be a mom."

Somewhere along the way, Tom decided it was best that we get married and that I drop out of school. So I did.

But that's in the past. So I push the emotions back down and clear my throat.

"Hey, while I have you on the phone, any chance you're free sometime this afternoon? Do you think you can take a look at my car?" I ask. "I think my battery is dead. Could you give it a jump?" I worry as the words leave my mouth. I hate being a nuisance, but I also hate that if I don't ask for help, I'll be stuck inside all weekend. I want to get out and explore my new town.

"Sure thing. Give me an hour, and I'll run by," Jack says.

After an hour, I haven't heard a word from Jack. Instead, from my window, I watch a familiar black truck pull into the back parking lot of my building.

What in the actual fuck? I grit my teeth, ready to spit out a text, when an incoming alert beats me to it.

Jack: *Sorry. Sadie made me do it.*

My friends are traitors.

Fingers flying, I type out a quick reply. *You used to be my favorite.*

The door to the truck opens, and Gabe steps out. His dark hair is artfully tousled in a *my hair was almost ripped out from the roots as I delivered the best damn orgasm known to man* way. I doubt he even bothered with a comb, but I'm not about to complain because I'm fully aware my fingers were probably the last thing that raked through that sexy mess.

He's wearing a pair of dark jeans and a black T-shirt that shows off his broad, muscular chest. This man could wear a potato sack, and he'd still, by far, be the sexiest man I've ever laid eyes on. When he catches sight of me in the window, he gives me a nod.

Steeling my spine, I let out a long breath. I can do this. Last night was great. I got exactly what I wanted. I just wish I didn't want more.

CHAPTER TWENTY-FIVE

Gabe

Two words. Fuck me.

How in the hell did I allow Sadie and Jack to rope me into helping Meera again? I'm the last person she wants to see. That's made crystal clear by the sour expression she's wearing when she steps outside.

I try to ignore the power she has over me, but when she walks by, her long-ass legs on display, I have to restrain myself. She's wearing worn denim shorts that no doubt show off her ass the second she bends over and a pretty little pink tank top. Her hair is pulled into a giant mess of a knot on the top of her head and bound by a matching pink bandanna, just like the flowers in her apartment.

Just as well. She's too roses-and-sunshine for me.

Outside, the air is hot and sticky, and there is absolutely no wind to cool us down.

I lift the hood to my truck and turn so I can do the same to Meera's car, but she's beaten me to it. She watches me, wordlessly waiting for me to continue. I throw the jumper cables on my battery and then brush past her, doing my best not to lean toward her as I clamp them onto her battery. But she's so damn close and impossible to ignore.

When I finish, I head back to my car and turn the key in the ignition. I wait a second and then bark out for her to do the same.

"Are you starting it?" I yell when I don't hear her engine turn over.

When nothing happens, I jump down from my truck and dip my head into Meera's vehicle. "Did it do anything?"

"It was clicking. That means I need a new battery, doesn't it?" She rubs the side of her face in defeat. "Don't worry about it. I'll call my insurance company on Monday."

I shake my head. "No. We'll deal with this now."

"It's no big deal," she says. "I can wait until—"

"You don't need your insurance company for this. Out of the car. Now."

I slam the hood to Meera's little white sedan and wait for her, but she doesn't move from the driver's seat.

"Let's go. Auto shop closes soon. If you get your ass out of the car and into my truck, we can make it before they turn out their lights."

"Gabe."

Ignoring her, I round the hood of my truck and open the passenger side door for her.

She lets out a huff, but she does as I instruct, and before long, we're on our way to the damn auto shop.

We ride in silence as we pass Betty's Bakery and the animal hospital and the long stretch of shops that occupy downtown Morganville. When we turn off Main and onto Murphy Road, an abundance of greenery adorns either side of the street.

"It's beautiful," Meera muses, her attention fixed on the passing scenery.

"Just wait," I reply.

She rolls down her window, letting in the humid summer air, and then sticks her head out. "Oh my God. It's gorgeous."

"Most people think of Savanah when they think about oak trees and Spanish moss. But there are more trees in a square mile right here than there are in all of Savanah. It's our hidden gem."

When she pulls her head back in the cab and relaxes back, I clear my throat. "You ready to talk now? About Tom?"

She inhales, that moment of tranquility instantly broken as her body goes taut. "What do you mean?"

"The divorce papers. I went through them after you left. He wants everything."

She exhales, and her shoulders drop. "He can have it all. I don't want it. That was his dream, not mine."

I grind my jaw and squeeze the steering wheel tighter. "He's not asking you to give it to him."

Finally, she turns to me, her brows creased in confusion.

"He's demanding you pay him to take it. Says he's been financially burdened by your absence and that your abandonment left him in debt."

Scanning the street ahead, I allow the words to sink in for a moment before I continue.

"He threw in an itemized report, detailing the costs of the condo and the restaurant over the last four years. He's demanding you pay him two million dollars."

Her eyes go wide. "Can he do that?"

"No, he can't demand anything. But if you sign those papers, you'll be liable for it. I don't know if he's ready to go to court over this, but with such a large amount of money on the table, I wouldn't be surprised. I did some digging. Looks like the restaurant, Spice Life, right?" I glance over for confirmation. When she nods, her attention once again out the window, I go on. "Contradictory to what he's claiming, it seems to be booming right now. Doesn't mean he hasn't sunk his money into it to keep it alive, though. And after four years, he can definitely claim you abandoned it. Still, two million is a hefty request. But I don't know why he'd think you'd have that kind of money to fork over."

Her lips are tight and puckered, causing her cheeks to lift to her eyes. But she isn't smiling. "I may sort of have two million in the bank."

I stomp on my brakes *and then* look in my rearview mirror. No one is behind me, thank fucking God. "*You what*?"

She bites her bottom lip, her focus darting around the cab of my truck before she looks me in the eye. "I have two million in the bank."

"I heard that part. But I don't understand. Your apartment. You said you lived out of your car."

"Pull over. You can't stop in the middle of the street." She drags her hand over her brows.

I accelerate, then pull over to the shoulder. Once I come to a stop, I turn off the engine and shift in my seat. "You realize he's already entitled to half that money, right? You were married, so half of your assets—"

"We have a prenup. My grandma made us sign it before we got married. She didn't like him, and she made it very clear she didn't trust him from the start. That money, it's insurance money from my parents' accident." She runs her hands up and down her legs, her chin tucked and her shoulders slumped.

"This whole time I thought I was the one in control. That by disappearing, I was preventing him from moving on. But the joke was on me."

I press a hand over hers on her thigh. "Don't do that. Don't second-guess yourself."

"This is why he waited so long to find me. That money's in a trust. It becomes available next month. When I turn thirty."

"Fuck. Meera. That's a lot of money. And he knows about it?"

She nods. "That's the exact amount of my inheritance, minus the interest it's accrued over the years."

"Shit," I say.

"It's fine. I'll figure it out. Maybe he'll settle for half?" She sounds almost hopeful.

Dammit. He's not worth it. People like him never settle. He'll never be happy. He'll only come back for more.

"No the fuck you won't. You're not giving him a goddamn penny. He isn't hurting. That restaurant is bringing him profits. And the condo is estimated to appraise at three-quarters of a million alone. He's going to have to fight you for that money."

"That money doesn't hold any real value in my life, though. I don't want to go to court. I don't want to drag this out any longer than necessary. Maybe it's a good thing he finally found me. Maybe it's time I make peace with my past."

"Peace? You don't have to hand over your money to that dirtbag to be at peace. In typical cases, he'd have to buy *you* out if he wanted to maintain rights. Or you would have to agree to sell and split your assets. But in this case, he'd have to prove you abandoned everything for personal gain and that he had to take a hardship of some kind. But from where I stand, you've gained nothing and he's lost nothing."

Meera shifts her fingers under my hand, so I tighten my hold. "You can donate that money to a good cause if it doesn't hold any value to you. Give it to a women's shelter, a homeless shelter, to victims of domestic violence. Any fucking organization. But don't let that prick have it."

She tips her chin up and meets my gaze, pain etched in her expression.

"You don't have to do this alone," I say. "You'll have me and Jack and Sadie."

She's quiet for a moment. But then a small half smile lifts her cheek, so I continue. "And Lydia and my grandpa. They all love you."

"I just don't want—"

"You won't be inconveniencing anyone. You're going to have to learn that it's okay to lean on others. I think you've been on your own for far too long. You've forgotten what it's like to be cared for."

Her hand moves from below mine again, but this time, she curls it around my fingers. She doesn't say anything. She doesn't have to. She only gazes out the window. So I take that as a sign to get back on the road. I keep my hand pressed to hers the whole way, and by the time I pull up to Marv's Auto and Repair, I'm no longer sure where she ends and I start.

CHAPTER TWENTY-SIX

Meera

"Start it up," Gabe calls from under the hood of my car, wiping his hands together.

I slip into my seat and turn the key. The engine roars without any hesitation, and I let out a sigh of relief.

"Perfect," I breathe, thankful to finally have my car back in working condition.

"Dr. Taylor. Dr. Taylor," a familiar little voice chants, pulling my attention to the large black SUV pulling up next to me with the windows rolled down. Sophie pokes her head out, waving a piece of paper at me.

Smiling, I climb out of my seat just as Gabe slams the hood of my car.

"Sophie, you don't have to call me Dr. Taylor all the time. You can call me Meera. What do you have there?" I ask.

The little girl unbuckles and leans out the window so far, the top half of her body is floating in midair. "It's a picture for you. We went to the library, and I checked out a book about a dog that only had three legs. It said sometimes a dog needs something to keep his mind off his missing leg, so Grandma let me pick out a stuffy for Flint. Then she took me over there so we could give it to him. He liked it."

The words tumble out of her mouth so quickly I have a hard time following her.

"This is a picture of Flint playing with his new toy."

Smiling, I take the drawing she holds out. The joy radiating from Sophie makes my heart clench. I've never seen her so animated.

"This is amazing. You captured so many details. And it looks like Flint loves your toy. Is that a stuffed fire hydrant?"

She nods vigorously, her grin growing wider.

"Hey, Soph, what do you got there?" Gabe asks as he squeezes between the cars, wiping his hands on a towel.

"It's Flint," she squeals. "Grandma took me to see him today." She drags her focus back to me. "You were right. He was already running around on his other three legs. He fell a few times, but he got right back up like it didn't even bother him."

Gabe's focus drops to the paper, the corners of his eyes creasing and his lips curling upward.

"That's impressive, Soph. You keep this shit up, and your work will be displayed in art galleries around the world before you're driving." He ruffles her hair.

She giggles and ducks back into the car, swatting his hand away.

"So, Jack and Sadie were home, huh?" Gabe asks his mom, but his eyes land on me.

"Yeah, I sent Jack a message asking if we could stop by, and he said they'd be home all day."

"So he wasn't out shopping with Sadie?"

"Oh no. They were just hanging out at the house."

"I'm sure they were." He chuckles.

"We just came by to see how you two were doing. Sophie wanted to drop off the picture and to invite Meera for dinner," Evelyn says from the front seat.

Opening my mouth, I suck in a breath, ready to make up an excuse about already having plans—I can't just join them for a family dinner, can I?—but Gabe speaks up first.

"That's a great idea, isn't it?" He cocks a brow in my direction. "We haven't eaten all day, and I'm starving."

"Actually—"

"What's on the menu?" He maneuvers around me, placing his hand on my hip as he passes by.

The subtle touch draws heat to my chest, reminding me that, without a doubt, dinner is a bad idea. Anything with this man is a bad idea. *Especially* dinner with his family.

"I've got stew in the Crock-Pot, so it'll be ready when you get there. Justin will be home soon, and Grandpa said he'll be by as soon as he wraps up his game of golf."

"Sounds good. We'll head over there in a few minutes." He leans in and kisses his mom on the cheek.

After Evelyn's SUV disappears down the street, I turn to Gabe.

"Are you kidding me?"

A smug grin splits his face. "You were halfway between running and sprinting your way out of that. I couldn't possibly sit back and watch you break Sophie's sweet little heart."

I gape at the mention of Sophie. "That's not fair. It's a family dinner. I can't crash a family dinner night. And it's your job as her dad to explain that to her."

He laughs. "No one is crashing anything. My mom invited you. And you're hungry. Don't think I didn't hear your stomach growling over there."

I cringe. He's right. It's been grumbling for the last hour. But the thought of eating with Gabe and his family—*and* my boss—gives me the most unfathomable anxiety known to man.

"It's dinner. You eat and then you leave. Simple."

Sophie opens the door the second we pull into the driveway, a grin plastered to her face, as if she's been waiting by the window since she got home.

"This is such a bad idea," I whisper, more to myself than to Gabe.

But he hears me anyway. "Stop worrying so much. The worst that'll happen is you'll have fun."

With a frustrated huff, I open my door and jump down from Gabe's oversized black truck.

He makes his way around and grabs the bag of fresh bread from my hand. "If they could trade me in for you, they'd do it in a heartbeat."

"Stop," I growl.

"I'm serious. My mom said you're the reason my grandpa finally decided to retire, aside from obvious reasons. And not only are you a kick-ass doctor, but you convinced Lydia to change her major back to veterinarian science."

I shake my head. He's wrong. But he's got a way with words, and it's nice to hear the compliment, even if it is coming from him.

When we make it up the stairs, Sophie props the door open for us. "Dinner is ready. We were just waiting for you."

Gabe takes my hand and leads me through the unfamiliar home and into the large open kitchen. His mom is at the counter, stirring the stew in the Crock-Pot with a large wooden spoon. The second we step into the room, she lifts her head and hones in on our joined hands.

I try to pull away, but Gabe only tightens his grip.

"Meera, two days in a row," Justin says, standing from his seat at the table. "I'm glad you could join us. I just hope you're up for it. Things get real crazy around here during Saturday dinner," he teases, pulling me in for a hug.

Then and only then does Gabe release my hand.

"What's this?" Evelyn asks as Gabe drops the bread to the counter.

"Meera didn't want to show up empty-handed, so we stopped at the store," Gabe says, his attitude finally dissipating.

"Oh, that's perfect. Do me a favor. Pull the toaster oven out of the cabinet and turn it on," she says, pointing the wooden spoon at Justin.

"Anything for you, my dear," he replies in a singsong voice.

Evelyn pulls the butter out of the refrigerator and sets it on the island. "Grandpa's out back. He brought Dee with him. Did you know those two were hanging out? They played golf today." She shakes her head. "I know he said he would take up golf, but I didn't think he was being serious. Never in all my life have I known him to golf."

"I did not know they were hanging out, but they've been friends for ages, so good for him." Gabe laughs. "Want me to get him?"

"Actually, Meera, can you go grab him? Sophie, go with her and show her where the garden is."

"Sure," I say.

Sophie slides her hand in mine and leads me out the back door. Outside, we're instantly surrounded by lush greenery as far as the eye can see. The porch is covered by a white pergola, and the yard is bigger than I'd imagined. The view from the front of the house is deceiving; from there, the lot looks like a standard size. Though it's not as large as Gabe's, by any means. A gravel trail with potted plants on either side leads to a large brick waterfall near the center. A metal pole runs across two brick beams, and water trickles onto a stack of concrete slabs and beige rocks. Bright purple and blue flowers surround the waterfall on either side, and a reddish-yellow plant climbs a large white wall just beyond that.

As I follow Sophie, my head on a swivel as I take everything in, she whispers, "Grandma likes to garden. I help sometimes. Those hydrangeas"—she points to the side of the yard—"we planted in the spring. And I painted those rocks too." I follow her finger to an assortment of colorful rocks decorated as ladybugs, butterflies, and frogs.

"You did those?" I breathe. "Sophie, you're so talented." I squeeze her hand. She's come a long way in just the few weeks I've known her. She's no longer timid and standing in the shadows. Now she's here, present, and holding my hand.

I let her lead me around the large white wall. On the other side is yet another patio, and that's where we find Dr. Coleman and a woman with short blonde hair sitting beside him.

"Ah, Meera. Evelyn said you'd be joining us today." Both he and the woman stand to greet me. Right away, the yellow tint of his skin is obvious, and I'm left wondering if it's been this way since I met him and I'm only now recognizing it because I'm aware of his diagnosis.

"This is Dee. We've known each other for what, forty years?" He laughs, but it comes out as a hoarse cough.

"Forty-two," she corrects him. "But who's counting? It's nice to meet you, Meera. Edgar has told me so much about you." She hugs me before snagging a tissue from the box on the table and handing it to Edgar.

"Thank you," I say. "Dr. Coleman—"

"Edgar. Call me Edgar. I already told you that. Especially because I'm no longer your boss," he says as a fit of coughing overtakes him.

"Do you need me to get you anything?" I ask with a frown, again wondering how I didn't see how sick he looks until now.

He shakes his head and wipes his face with the tissue. "I'm fine, I'm fine. Just tired. Are we ready to go?" he looks to Dee for confirmation.

"Edgar, we haven't eaten yet. You said you were hungry." She pats his hand and turns her attention to me. "He hasn't eaten much today, so he's a bit confused. We old folks need that protein to keep our brains sharp."

"Old. Ha." He snorts.

"Well, then, it's a good thing we came out here. Dinner is ready."

Evelyn and Justin sit next to one another at their oversized oak kitchen table, while Edgar and Dee sit across from them. Sophie and I fill the side between them, and Gabe sits next to a very hungover Lydia. Conversation jumps from the upcoming school year for Evelyn and Sophie to Lydia's new classes and my apartment renovations.

We laugh over Lydia's drunken escapade last night, and she covers her face in embarrassment. Gabe brushes his foot against my calf from the opposite side of the table on more than one occasion, and while I try to avoid his gaze, it's impossible to ignore the tingles that radiate from that point of contact.

After we help clear the table, Sophie pulls out Monopoly.

Gabe gives her a bewildered look and asks, "You? You want to play Monopoly?"

Her response is an enthusiastic nod that causes Gabe to break out into a grin. He tips his head to me. "If Meera wants to."

I can't say no to her angelic face when she presses her hands together in a plea. So the eight of us play, though we work in teams. Lydia and Gabe are the first to buy property, but Sophie and I are the first to build a house.

When Justin lands on *Chance,* Evelyn picks up a card that reads *Go directly to jail. Do not pass go.*

He throws himself back in his chair and pouts like a toddler, and we all break out into a fit of laughter.

Dee rolls the dice, and just as they fall to the board, Edgar begins coughing again. This time, it's deep and rough and he can't seem to catch his breath. Dee grabs a tissue for him like she did earlier. When he reaches for it, there's a spot of blood on his lower lip.

I look to Gabe, who doesn't seem to notice. No one seems to notice except for Sophie and me.

"Grandpa, you're bleeding," she says.

That observation has every head at the table snapping in his direction.

"I'm fine. I'm fine," he moans, but when he pushes his chair back and stands, he wobbles.

Thankfully, Dee is quick on her feet and steadies him before he can topple over.

"Call 911," I say, jumping to my feet. I reach Edgar first, but Gabe and Justin are right behind.

"Where does it hurt?" I ask.

He doesn't hear me, but he's clutching his side.

Turning to Gabe, I ask, "Can you two get him to the couch?"

When Edgar is sitting and Justin has dashed off to find supplies, I grab his wrist and feel for his pulse. "Edgar." I whisper so the others can't hear the next part. "I know you have stage four prostate cancer. My grandpa had the same thing. Please be honest with me right now. Have you had any treatments?"

He shakes his head.

"Any medications?"

He coughs again, and more blood puddles on his lips.

I snatch a tissue from the end table and dab at his face.

"Dee," he says with a raspy breath. "Dee's been helping me."

Justin is back and strapping a blood pressure cuff around Edgar's arm. When the air releases, he shakes his head. "The ambulance needs to get here fast. His blood pressure is tanking, and his pulse is low."

The rest of the night goes by in a blur. Evelyn and Justin follow the ambulance to the hospital. Gabe, Dee, and I join them there while Lydia stays back with Sophie. After hours of tests, the doctor sits with us and explains that the cancer has spread to his lungs and bones. Dee confesses that he's been sick for a good portion of the year, but he refused treatment. Tears escape more than one set of eyes.

After Edgar is admitted and settled in a room, we say good night to him. Then Gabe is clutching my arm and leading me through the doors. We drop Dee off at home first. When we get to my place, Gabe walks me upstairs, claiming he doesn't want me out alone in the dark. Not with Tom still in town.

And I let him. I unlock my door, and when I turn to face him, I notice for the first time that his eyes are red rimmed and swollen. He ducks his head, avoiding my gaze, and whispers a pained good night.

Without thought, I reach for his arm. I don't know why, other than to let him know that I'm here. To provide comfort. But once my hand lands there, something else entirely takes over.

I pull him into me and slide my arms up his back, holding him closely. He goes rigid at first, surprised by the move. But then he sags and buries his face in the crook of my neck and loops his arms around my waist. I lay my cheek against his chest, over the quick thumping of his heartbeat. Or maybe it's my own, I'm not sure.

Seconds pass before I pull back and slide my hand to his face. I run my fingers across his jaw, feeling the rough stubble beneath my palm.

He closes his eyes and leans into it. When he opens them again, they're heavy and full of sadness. This man. This strong man who plays hero every day is crumbling in front of me.

I know how it feels to lose the people I love. I've lost so many. There's absolutely nothing I can do to help him, and yet I can't let him leave like this either.

"I'll be okay," he whispers, taking my hand and bringing it to his mouth. He flips it over and lays a soft kiss to my forearm.

I inhale sharply at the intimacy of his action, my heart rate picking up speed. Then he pulls his lips away and angles in, pressing his forehead against mine. We stand like that for only a second, and then he's brushing his nose against mine.

"Meer," he rasps against my mouth. The sound of my name falling from his lips spirals through me like an electric shock. It sparks a fire deep inside me, one that's been begging to be lit. And I know in this moment that my "one time" was a lie.

Grasping the front of his shirt, I pull him toward me as I step back into my apartment.

He follows without argument and closes the door behind us.

Gabe has surprised me at every turn, and tonight is no exception. While I'm not sure how the evening would have played out if his grandpa hadn't gone to the hospital, I never expected to be with Gabe right here, right now. Not like this. But there's a pull in my chest that I'm tired of fighting.

"Meer," he groans again. He pulls my face to his, lacing his fingers through my hair, and kisses me with such veracity that I'm a puddle in his hands.

"My room," I gasp once I come up for air.

Without question, he follows me, holding my hand as we make our way through my dark apartment.

It's just the two of us. Alone. And for the second time, in the presence of Gabriel Henry, I feel empowered to go for what I want. I pull my tank top off over my head and drop it to the floor. Then, pushing aside all subtlety, I unbutton my shorts and wiggle them down my hips, making it very clear that I want him.

"Fuck, Meera," he groans, raking both hands through his hair and then down his face. "I can't. I can't do what I did last night and not have you."

I take a step back and lift the lid to a small red antique chest on my nightstand. Tightening my lips, I pull out a box of condoms and hold one out to Gabe.

His eyes go wide, and his mouth drops open, but I cut in before he can speak.

"I've had them for a while. Like a long while," I tell him.

He moves closer, the heat of his body soaking into me. "Dammit, Meera," he growls, clasping my cheeks in his hands. My name on his lips is desperate, pleading, as if he needs me more than he needs oxygen.

I reach for the hem of his shirt and tug.

He slides his hands over mine and helps me pull it over his head. When the shirt lands next to mine, Gabe drops his hands to my hips and pulls me flush against his chest. We're only a breath apart, but he doesn't kiss me. Not on my lips like earlier. Instead, he leans down and presses his mouth to my collarbone. Then he glides his tongue across it, from my shoulder to my breastbone, the slow caress making me burn with desire. I drop my head back and let out a moan.

Gabe trails his fingertips up my ribcage and around my neck. "You're so fucking perfect," he whispers. Guys say stuff like this all the time. They say it to get what they want. It's an easy compliment. But the way he tells me, the rough tone of his voice mixed with the soft touch of his hands, makes me feel like the most beautiful woman alive.

I know I should respond. Say something in return. But all that comes out are more moans. Gabe doesn't complain about that response, though. No, and in the next instant, he's pressing his hard length against me.

I swallow hard, remembering how much of him there is down there. I slide my hands down his abdomen, over his erection, and then back up so I can unbutton his pants, wanting to feel it, to feel him. He helps me tug them past his hips, and then they're falling to his feet. Once he's stepped out of them, he lifts me into the air.

My legs tangle around his waist for only a moment before he's laying me on the bed, climbing over me, and tossing the pillows to the floor.

My breathing is heavy. His breathing is heavy. But everything about this is different from last night. Last night was about pleasure. It was about exploring our bodies, turning one another on, touching spots that hadn't been touched in forever. And I mean that in a literal sense. Gabe found places behind my thighs, along my palms, and even under my arms that sent me past the brink of orgasm.

Tonight is about need. A desire for intimacy.

He parts my legs with one knee, and then he presses his soft lips to my stomach.

"Are you sure?" he whispers, his breath skating across my navel.

I nod vehemently.

He lets out a small groan, the heat of it moving straight to my core, and peeks up at me. "I need to hear it, Meera. I need to hear you consent to this."

Our eyes lock, and that's when I see it. A glimpse of a distant memory. The Gabe I tried to have sex with three years ago. The word *consent* ringing in my ears. "*You'd never consent to this if you were sober,*" he'd said, pulling my dress back up and over my bare breasts. A flash of me pulling it back down, desperate for his touch. His back to me as he strode to his bathroom, only to retrieve a white bath towel. And then I was waking up in his bed.

"You lied," I say to him.

Confusion swirls in his eyes, and he pulls back an inch.

"That night. After the wedding. You said nothing happened."

Instant recognition overcomes him. He edges back another inch, his gaze intent on me. "Nothing did."

I slip my hand around his jaw and pull him to me so we're only a breath apart. "Yes. Yes, I want this. I want to feel you inside me."

Something ignites in me as the words slip into the air. Maybe it's been there all along. Maybe Sadie was right. I may not be the one-night-stand type of person, but I've always been the take-charge type—at least until I'd had it stomped out of me. I just needed someone to pull it out of me. And he's in front of me now. Devouring me with his eyes. His lips. His touch.

I'll reconcile the one-time thing later because I want this man just as much as I know he wants me.

Gabe groans into my mouth. "It's been a long time for me, Meera. I can't promise you a night like yesterday. I can't promise that I'll last long once I feel you."

"That makes two of us." My voice catches as he inches his way down my body, his mouth dragging over the fabric covering my nipple. His teeth catch, and the sensation makes me arch off the bed beneath him. A second later, he's got a hand cupping my panties and he's groaning against my stomach.

"You're wet," he grunts.

"I'm *so* wet," I agree.

He pulls my panties to the side and dips one finger inside me, eliciting matching moans from both of us.

Slowly, he slides his finger out and adds a second, plunging inside again, deeper and with more force, hooking them, finding that perfect spot.

"Gabe," I cry out, bolts of pleasure arcing through me.

"Meera," he pleads. "Help me here." He places the foil wrapper between his teeth and leans forward, his fingers still pumping inside me at a steady rhythm.

I take the condom from him and rip it open. But I lose all sense when his thumb finds me and circles the top of my folds.

"I'm going to need that soon," Gabe groans. He removes his fingers and drags his boxer briefs down his legs.

When they're off, he snatches the condom from me and rolls it down his length. And then he's shimmying my underwear down and pushing inside me. There's an instant relief as he fills me. He takes me one thrust at a time. And I give it to him, taking him with me. Our bodies move as one. It doesn't take long for either of us to shatter with the weight of each plunge.

"Goddamn, Meera," Gabe gasps when we both come undone. His arms shake, but he stays there, above me, inside me, regarding me with those piercing blue eyes as if he needs me again.

CHAPTER TWENTY-SEVEN

Gabe

When I wake the next morning, it's still dark, and it's hailing the size of golf balls. I don't want to get up, but I know I have to. I tossed and turned so damn much, and I want nothing more than to pull the covers over my head and slide into oblivion. I'm typically an easy sleeper. The kind who drops his head to the pillow and is snoring within seconds. But last night? Fuck. I didn't get home till almost one, and shutting my brain off was impossible.

I kept thinking of Meera and her take-me eyes. They weren't the kind that wanted to give me a pity fuck, even if that's what I thought she was doing at first. But Meera isn't the fucking type. She also isn't the type to have sex to cheer a person up. Not even if she was getting something out of it in return.

No. She's a goddamn breath of fresh air. The oxygen my fucking lungs have yearned for, and last night, when our eyes locked and she pulled me in, she wanted me.

That's why I bolted after the second time we made love. Because I was under her spell or some shit. I couldn't just be done after one round. No. I was greedy. She was greedy. The way our bodies molded together. The way she quivered beneath me when I said her name. The way her ass felt in my hands as I pulled her on top of me. And the noises she made that drove me harder and deeper into her core. I wanted her too.

When it ended, she laid her head on my chest, and I soaked her in, trailing my finger across her bare stomach. It wasn't until, in the silence, we heard my phone vibrating, that either of us moved. It was an alert from Lydia. She texted that Sophie was asleep and that I should pick her up in the morning.

That's when it hit me. I should have been at home. I should have tucked Sophie into bed. I don't do overnight bullshit. I don't cuddle. And I certainly don't make love. I'm not romantic. Fuck rainbows and flowers and all that garbage. I'm the asshole who bends a woman over the counter and delivers what she needs and then goes home.

Meera was messing with my brain. I had to get out of there. It wasn't my proudest moment, but I gave Meera a quick peck on the cheek and told her I had to fly. Yes. I used the word fly. Like a goddamn tool.

Now I'm heading back over because I left my wallet in her apartment—of course I did—and I promised to take Sophie out for breakfast.

Meera opens the door, wearing nothing but a long T-shirt. My first instinct is to check out her legs, but she doesn't give me the chance. Without a word, she shoves my wallet into my chest and slams the door in my face.

I deserved that. Hell, I deserved worse. This is why I don't do relationships. Why I don't get involved with women who want more than a night.

I take Sophie to a small restaurant not far from our house and order the works. Eggs, bacon, hash browns, and a side of French toast. Sophie opts for the chocolate chip pancakes with a side of whipped cream. When the waitress walks away with our menus, the door whooshes open, and Sadie, Jack, and Grace rush in, dragging the rain in with them.

"Look, Dad," Sophie says, pointing. "Can they eat with us?"

What I want to say is no. They'll ask about Meera, and I can't get into all that today. I haven't even wrapped my own head around it yet. It was difficult enough when Sophie started in with the rapid-fire questions, but I nod because they're here and Sophie is already waving them over.

"Hey, man," Jack says from the door, closing his umbrella while Sadie peels off Grace's jacket.

"Have a seat." I motion to the empty spot in the booth across from me. "We just ordered."

Sadie and Grace slip in next to Sophie while Jack drops down next to me.

I'm bringing my mug to my lips when Sadie goes in for the kill first. "How'd it go yesterday? Did you get Meera's battery replaced? She never responded to my texts last night, so I figured there was a fifty-fifty shot at it going well or the two of you killing each other." She laughs.

I about choke on my coffee, but I recover quickly. "It's all good."

"She came over last night and ate dinner with us. Then we played Monopoly," Sophie says very matter-of-factly as she hands a purple crayon to Grace.

"She did, did she?" Sadie says, scrutinizing me with one brow cocked.

"Yeah. She was on my team. We were winning until Grandpa got sick and the ambulance came."

"Wait, what?" Sadie's eyes go round.

I set my mug down and prop my elbow on the table, rubbing a hand across my forehead. "He's sicker than he let on. Decided not to inconvenience anyone. They're running more tests today, but it doesn't look good."

"I didn't realize it was that bad. It's cancer, of course, but I guess I assumed he'd start some sort of treatment. Is he going to do chemo or radiation?"

I shake my head. "He waited too long. The doctor won't give us a timeline yet, but he told us to be prepared. We'll know more this week."

Conversation shifts as we dig into our breakfast. Jack and I discuss a few of our clients and which ones we expect to go to trial. Dee comes up in conversation, but I avoid the topic of her being with us yesterday because I don't want to talk about my grandpa again. Instead, I only mention what I already told Dee. That I found Dick's hidden property. And I can't hide the wicked smile that creeps up my face when I tell him that she's finally ready to play some well-deserved hardball.

"That guy was always such a douche. Do you remember that time your dad came back when we were in high school? We were playing that team from Hillside, weren't we? You were up to bat, and Dick and your dad were right behind the fence, talking about Ms. Pruit as if none of us could hear them."

I nod. How could I forget? It was the last time my dad even bothered to attempt to see me. He was passing through town and decided to make a pit stop to see his "only son." As if he had other children out there just as unfortunate as I was to have a deadbeat dad.

Out of the blue, he showed up while we were getting my gear loaded for my baseball tournament. He pitched a fit because I wouldn't ditch my team to hang out with him for a few hours. So, maybe to prove a point to my mom that he wasn't a complete asshole—or maybe because he wanted to look like a complete asshole; I never could figure it out—he insisted on taking me to the tournament.

He complained the entire time. That is, until Dick showed up. The two of them had never met, but when Ms. Pruit, my art teacher, walked by, common ground brought them together. One whistled as the other mumbled something under his breath about her ass, though I wasn't sure who did what. That's all it took. For the rest of the afternoon, the two of them trash talked every female teacher at the high school. Which ones were hot and which ones should retire. Which would be a good screw and which would give the best head. My entire fucking team thought it was the funniest shit they'd ever heard. They never let me live it down.

My dad is the last topic I want to focus on today. So I ask Sadie about the promotion Jack mentioned to me. That does the trick, and the next thing I know, she's explaining her new role as lead sales associate at her firm.

Sadie's phone vibrates on the table, and Meera's name flashes across the screen. "Hey, girl," Sadie says when she lifts it to her ear, then her eyes go wide. "Wait, say that again?"

In the next instant, she's glaring directly at me.

Fuck. Me. I know that look. Meera is telling her everything that happened between us last night.

When Jack catches sight of Sadie's expression, he shifts his gaze to me and mouths "What's that about?"

I shove a forkful of hash browns into my mouth and shake my head. He can wait. I'll no doubt get an earful the moment Sadie gets off the phone.

"Daddy, can I go to the bathroom?" Sophie whispers.

"Yeah. Do you want to wait for Sadie to take you?"

She huffs, and I swear she rolls her eyes like a teenager. "I'm not a little kid. I'll be fine on my own."

"Okay. Make sure to wash your hands when you're finished," I tell her.

When she squeezes past Sadie, my attention falls back to the phone call.

"Yeah, I'll talk to Jack. Sorry about yesterday. Won't happen again." She pulls the phone away from her ear and stabs at the End icon a little too aggressively. Then she carefully places the phone on the table. Her lips are paper thin when she looks at Jack.

My stomach tightens and my throat goes dry. I am so going to get my ass handed to me.

"Can you go through some papers for Meera? Looks like Tom won't leave her alone. He has a flight out tonight and he wants her to sign divorce papers before he leaves, but Gabe here told her that Tom is also demanding she pay two million for abandoning the restaurant and their condo."

Jack chokes on his coffee, the liquid dribbling down his chin as he rushes to grab a napkin. "What?"

"Tom won't leave her alone?" I growl.

But Sadie refuses to acknowledge me. Her stare is fixed on her husband. "You might want to ask your friend here because he already read through the papers. He told Meera that he'd help her with whatever she needed. Then he fucked her, and then, like the douche he is, he dipped out. Now Tom is on her ass and she doesn't know what to do."

"Dammit. That's not what happened," I hiss. "I didn't fuck her. I didn't dip out. Okay. I dipped out, but I didn't fuck her. I—"

"Gabe. What the hell?" It's Jack's turn to question me. He's turned in the booth beside me, his brows pinched.

"Don't *what the hell* me. You're the one who pushed me to help her with her car. You're the one who told me we'd be good together. That I should try—"

"Being good together doesn't mean you fuck someone and then leave."

"For fuck's sake. You know me. I don't do relationships," I say a little too loudly.

In my periphery, Sadie stands and lifts Grace out of the high chair. She stuffs the little girl's chubby arms into a tiny jacket, and then she heads for the door without saying another word.

"Give me a damn break with your *no dating* bullshit." Jack slams his fist into the table. I haven't seen him this angry in years. "This is Meera we're talking about. She isn't some fucking floozy you can sleep with, then drop."

No shit. But I don't tell him that I already feel like shit for what I did. That Meera deserves better. Instead, I get defensive and push the blame right past me. "Meera is a grown-ass woman. If she wanted to sleep with me, then she's allowed to sleep with me. Maybe next time, don't ask me to keep helping your wife's friend with shit."

"My wife's friend? My wife has a fucking name, asshole, and Meera is my goddamn friend too." He shakes his head. "You want to pretend you're this badass single dad, still living this bachelor life, go right on ahead. But don't for a second sit here and think we believe that garbage. Meera stayed the night at your house the other day. She bypassed your golden rule. Something happened between the two of you, and now you're too scared to admit it. So rather than feel something for once in your life"—he pokes me in the chest—"you're going to act like a dick and hurt people in your wake. You're starting to remind me of your dad."

He stands and pushes his plate back. Then he pulls out his wallet and throws some cash onto the table. And without another word, he storms out.

I try to shrug it off. Jack doesn't know shit. My dad was an asshole. He didn't care about anyone but himself. He didn't care who he hurt, so long as he was happy.

When the door to the ladies' room opens, I stand and wave Sophie over. She's subdued. More so than usual, and her eyes are focused on the floor.

"You okay? You were in the bathroom for a while."

She nods.

"Okay, let's get going. Jack and Sadie already left."

As we head back toward the house, wipers at max speed, I can't get Jack's words out of my head. I scrub a hand over my jaw, irritated, but I can't seem to stop the ruminations. Leaving the way I did was an asshole move. It's not lost on me that I gave Meera a hard time after she stayed the night at my place and freaked the fuck out, and now here I am doing the same thing.

But I have a daughter to think about. And Meera deserves better. She's already gone through too much crap with Tom. Fuck. Tom. God dammit.

I take a hard look in my rearview mirror to make sure no one is behind me. And then I look ahead. When the coast is clear, I make a U-turn, bumping over the curb in my fury.

In the mirror, Sophie's watching me, a little crease between her brows.

“I need to stop at Meera’s. I forgot she wanted me to look at some paperwork. It shouldn’t take too long,” I tell her. If Tom won’t leave her alone, I need to do something to help her.

Sophie gives me a melancholy smile and turns to the window.

By the time we pull into the parking lot, the rain has let up and the clouds are clearing.

Above us, Meera’s curtains are drawn closed. The sight gives me an uneasy feeling in the pit of my stomach. She probably won’t even let me inside. Not after my hasty retreat this morning. I’ll be lucky if she even comes to the door. And I wouldn’t blame her. But she can’t do this alone. Jack will give great advice, but he doesn’t fight dirty. And when push comes to shove, he’s a negotiator. I’m not.

CHAPTER TWENTY-EIGHT

Meera

I'm putting away groceries when there's a knock on my door. It's soft at first, but each knock grows louder and more urgent. I grab the can of mace from inside my purse and head for the door, praying it's not Tom. It shouldn't be since we agreed to meet at Betty's Bakery later, but he's lied to me before.

"Meera." A growl erupts from the other side of the door.

Crap. I'd know that tenacious voice anywhere. Gabe is midknock when I fling the door open, ready to yell at him, because while I'm relieved it's not Tom, I'm livid at this man. But outside my door, Sophie stands quietly next to him with slumped shoulders and a sad expression.

"Hi, Soph," I say, ignoring Gabe. "You okay, sweetie?"

"Are *you* okay?" Gabe grumbles. "Is there anybody in there with you?"

His question throws me off, so I shift my attention to him and arch my brows.

He points to my hand. To the mace curled beneath my fingers.

"Oh. No." I turn and set the canister on a small oak end table.

"No, you're not okay? Or no, nobody is in there?" Gabe growls.

"No. I'm fine. And I'm alone."

"Can we come in?"

I want to tell him no. I want to tell him to leave. That I'm still angry about last night. Who does he think he is, giving himself to me the way he did and then running away like I was nothing more than a hookup?

Closing my eyes, I shake my head. I shouldn't have expected anything more from him. This is Gabe. His reputation isn't a secret. And honestly, I didn't expect him to spend the night. But he left so abruptly, so casually, he left me feeling like a piece of meat in the process.

"No?" he asks, a frown marring his face.

"Sorry. Yes. Come in." I pull the door open, and the two of them shuffle over the threshold. "Do you want something to draw with?" I direct my question to Sophie as I grab her hand. "I just picked up a new pack of colored pencils."

If I can avoid Gabe for even five seconds, that's a win in my book.

Sophie nods, but she doesn't crack a smile, which surprises me. Aside from the first day I met her, that's the one thing I've come to count on when she's around. It's small, like she is, but it's genuine and real. Today, though, in its absence are pursed lips and empty eyes.

She releases my hand and climbs the metal barstool at the counter, keeping her attention firmly on the surface in front of her.

I watch her for a beat before turning to the rest of the grocery bags. This isn't like her. Has Gabe noticed? Or is he too busy brooding over whatever the hell brought him here?

I pull out a crate of cherry tomatoes, a green pepper, and a carton of eggs before I finally retrieve the markers and colored pencils. "Ah, here they are," I say, setting them on the counter.

"Can we talk?" Gabe says once I've gotten Sophie set up with a few sheets of white paper.

Here it comes. I don't have any experience with the *it's not you; it's me* shit, but I had a feeling it was coming.

I sweep my arm out, gesturing for him to have a seat in the living room.

He settles on the couch, careful not to sit in the spot where the hole is.

I sit in the chair across from him, making him frown, but I'm taking a play out of Sophie's book right now. I'm not going to pretend to be happy to ease his guilt.

"Meera—"

"It's okay," I urge, cutting to the chase. "I'm not that type of girl. I'm not going to get my feelings hurt just because . . ." I peek over at Sophie and lower my voice. "Because you needed to escape."

He drops his gaze to the floor between us. "That's not why I'm here."

That's—what? That's not why he's here? So he didn't even come to apologize? I shoot a glare at him, but he doesn't bother to look up. Despite my resolve to keep calm, my heart is suddenly threatening to beat out of my chest. "Then why are you here?" I grit out.

"Tom. Sadie said he was bothering you again."

"*Sadie* told you? What the hell? Why is Sadie broadcasting my business?"

"It's not like that." He drops his elbows to his knees and clasps his hands. "We were at breakfast. She and Jack were there when you called."

I huff. Note to self: no more confiding in Sadie.

"She asked Jack to help you. But it'll take time for him to read through the documents. I'm already familiar with them. I read every page. I did the research. And I know the numbers. Plus, Jack doesn't play hardball. It's not in his nature. He negotiates. I don't. I'll fix this for you." He leans forward. "Do you want me to call him? I'll tell him what I think of his demand and tell him to shove it up his—"

"No," I say as I get to my feet, smoothing my shirt. "No, I do not need you to fix this. I wanted Jack to double-check it, but I'm fine now. I did my own research. Jack and I have spoken, and I told him I can take care of it myself. I'll keep him in the loop, but for now, I'm pretty confident things will work out in my favor."

"Please, sit," Gabe says through gritted teeth. "Guys like him don't back down. And I don't want you getting hurt."

"Hurt?" I laugh as quietly as possible. "That's funny coming from you." I turn away and head back to the kitchen, but before I reach Sophie, I pivot on my heel and glare at Gabe. "Don't get me wrong, the last two nights have been great, but I don't know what your deal is, and I'm not interested in finding out."

Once the words leave my mouth, I give myself a mental high five. Old Meera has come a long way. I'm not normally confrontational. And I don't typically blurt things out without thinking them through. But I'm seething, and I'm tired of Gabe waltzing in, hefting his messiah complex along with him, and looking at me with his fuck-me eyes, then not knowing how to put on his big boy pants.

I didn't come to Morganville to fall in love. Maybe one day I will. But Gabe isn't the falling-in-love type, so the sooner he leaves, the sooner I can get back to my life. I've got a job to keep me busy and an apartment to renovate.

When I turn back around, Sophie is standing a few feet in front of me. Her eyes are wide and locked on me, and if I'm not mistaken, she looks like she might cry.

"This is for you." She hands me a piece of paper with a sketch of two people who look very much like the two of us.

"Oh, Sophie, this is beautiful," I say as I tilt forward and wrap an arm around her shoulders. It's instinctive for me to hug, and while she isn't much for showing affection, she's always hugged me back. This time, however, she pulls back, and in the tiniest voice, she asks, "Are you friends with my mom?"

I raise a brow in confusion, but before I can ask her to clarify, Gabe is beside me. "Sweetie, she doesn't know your mom."

Sophie's quiet for a moment, wearing a frown and studying me, looking unconvinced. "I saw her today."

Gabe's eyes widen and his jaw drops. "Wh-What do you mean? You saw her? Where? When?" Gabe squats low so he's at eye level with her.

"At breakfast. She was paying at the counter when I went into the bathroom."

"Sophie," Gabe begins, "that could have been anyone. Maybe the woman at the counter just looked like your mom."

Sophie shakes her head solemnly. "No. It was her."

"Maybe it was your mom. I don't know. But Meera doesn't know her." He looks up at me, and all I can do is shrug.

Sophie turns and points to the kitchen. "Then why is her phone number on her refrigerator?"

My mouth drops and my stomach lurches. But then I connect the dots.

Gabe gets to his feet quickly and stomps into my kitchen. Standing in front of the fridge with his fists clenched at his sides, he glowers at the torn piece of paper with a phone number scrawled on it.

"I didn't know that was her," I whisper. And it's the truth.

"Bre? It's short for Breanna. How could you not put that together? Especially after what I told you about her. How do you even know her?" His questions are rapid-fire and teeming with anger.

"She works at Harbour Animal Hospital," I say, crossing my arms. "I met her the other day when I picked up some medication for your grandpa."

Gabe paces back and forth, scratching his neck.

"I ran into her this morning at the store. We talked for a bit, and then we exchanged numbers. Sadie and Jack are my only friends in town. It was nice to meet someone new." I say all of this as if it matters, but Gabe is already a step ahead.

"Harbour Animal Hospital. That's not even half an hour away." He roughs a hand down his face. "Shit."

"Maybe it's not so bad," I try. "If that is Bre . . . Breanna, she seems to be doing well. She's working, and she just bought herself a car—"

"And you know all this after meeting her once?"

"Actually twice. And yes. She was friendly. Friendlier than most people I know. Forgive me for making pleasant conversation with people who are kind to me."

Gabe huffs and turns to his daughter, who is still standing in the middle of the living room. "Soph, let's go."

Before he can get far, I lay a hand on his arm. "I'm sorry," I say. "I'm just . . ." I try, but I struggle to get the words out.

"I told you not to be sorry. Even with me."

He regards me with those crystalline blue eyes, and for a second, I hate that I don't hate him.

"I know this is none of my business," I whisper so that only he can hear me, "but you should ask Sophie. If she wants to see her mom, that is. Let her make that decision."

The muscles in his jaw tighten, but his mouth stays shut. And then, without another word, he ushers Sophie out the door.

CHAPTER TWENTY-NINE

Gabe

"She saw Breanna? What happened? Did she say anything? Did either of them say anything?" my mom asks. She sets down a wooden ladle and then fills a large pot with water.

I shrug. "I have no idea. She's not saying much."

"Hilary is out of town this week. She said the soonest she can get Sophie in the office is next Tuesday. In the meantime, she said her advice is to focus on what's best for Sophie."

I puff out my chest and exhale. "What does that even mean? What's best for Sophie *isn't* somebody who'll kidnap and neglect her." I rake both hands through my hair and tug on the strands. "Somebody who's not going to get high at every turn and then take off running again whenever the fuck she feels like it."

"Oh, honey," she murmurs, placing the pot on the stove.

Shit. I shouldn't be here right now, complaining to my mom when she has enough on her own plate with my grandpa. But I don't know who else to turn to.

I pace to the window and plant my hands on my hips. Sophie is back there, watering the flowers and plants with the small watering can my mom got for her last summer. She tilts the can until the handle is upside down and the last drops of water fall out. Then she takes it to the hose, refills it, and starts the cycle all over again.

"Have you talked to her?"

My mom's voice pulls me back. I spin to face her again, my heart squeezing at her question.

She tilts her head and presses her lips together, her eyes soft and sad. "Maybe sit down and talk to her. See what she wants."

"That's what Meera said," I say, dropping onto a stool at the island.

"Smart girl. Where is she today?"

"Honestly?"

My mom purses her lips and gives me a sideways glance. "As if I expect anything less."

With a flip of my wrist, I check the time. "She's probably with her ex-husband right about now."

Her brows shoot straight up. "What?"

"Not like that," I deadpan. I straighten and prop an elbow on the counter. And then I tell my mom everything. About Meera's ex-husband's repeated visits and how he's trying to get her to sign away two million dollars. That they aren't actually divorced. How stubborn she is. How she refuses to let me fix this for her.

"That's the guy you punched in the face?"

Pressing my lips together, I nod. "He had it coming. He shouldn't have touched her."

"Do I detect a hint of jealousy?" she teases, and for a second, it's like I'm back in high school. The way we used to talk about girls and life. She knew early on that I had no interest in settling down. I wanted a career. Not a family I could potentially disappoint, so my mom made it clear that there was a right way and a wrong way to be a bachelor. I didn't always heed her advice, but I never led women to believe there was a chance of being more than a hookup. Breaking hearts isn't a hobby I've ever been interested in.

"There's nothing between us. I'm upset she's there alone. I don't want her to get hurt."

My mom lets out a huff. "So I was imagining the way the two of you kept looking at each other the other night?"

"There were no looks," I say, balling my fists on the countertop.

Her expression softens. "You can lie to yourself all you want, Gabriel, but I know you better than you think. I've never seen you look at a girl the way you look at her." She turns back to the stove top and picks up the wooden ladle, turning her back to me while she stirs the red sauce.

I roll my eyes, choosing to ignore her comment in hopes that we can move on to other topics.

"I saw how fast you ran to her at the bar when other men took interest," she continues. "And the way you pulled out the chair for her at dinner . . ." She laughs. "You've invited plenty of people over in the past, but never, not once, have you looked like you were completely captivated by a woman's presence." She shifts on her feet and gives me a knowing smile. "But you need to cool it with trying to solve all of her problems. Give her the space to do it on her own."

"I don't—"

"You're a product of this family. You think I haven't noticed that you're always trying to make things better for all of us? Your profession is built on fixing what's broken. Don't get me wrong. I'm beyond proud of you, Gabriel. But this time, take a step back. Listen to what she needs. She's a smart girl, and from what I can tell, she likes her independence. And truthfully, I don't think you'd be attracted to her if she didn't."

She shoots a look out the window to where Sophie is still tending to the plants. "And if Meera and Breanna are friends, then maybe that's a good thing too."

"Mom . . ."

"Meera seems to have good judgment, Gabe. Maybe give Breanna a chance. Try to see what Meera sees. I'm not telling you to pretend none of this ever happened. God knows I'll never forget it myself. But check in with Sophie and take some baby steps. Breanna is still her mom. Always will be." And with that, she turns back to the stove.

For a long moment, I let my mom's words sink in. I think about Meera's reaction when I showed up to help with the leak under her bathroom sink. When I tried to replace the filter for her air conditioner. The car battery. Every time, I assumed she didn't want to inconvenience me. But I realize now that it was never about that. She wanted to learn how to do things on her own. She didn't need me to *do* those things for her. She just needed the support.

It's obvious from what I've seen of Tom that he was used to controlling her and making her feel small and helpless. Convincing her she needed him to survive. After all that, Meera doesn't want to feel trapped or to be locked under somebody's thumb. That's why she escaped—aside from the obvious.

I look out at Sophie again. Am I making the same mistake with her? Trying to fix and solve and guess every move before it happens? I don't know anything about Breanna right now. Maybe I should have called her back. Given her a chance to voice what it is she wants or expects.

Instead, I avoided it. And now Sophie knows she's here. And that throws a wrench in all of this. Should I give my daughter the choice?

I push out of my chair and head to the back door before I can change my mind.

"Hey, Soph?" I call when I've settled onto the wicker love seat.

She watches me silently for a second, then sets the watering can on the glass table and plops her tiny body next to me.

"I'm sorry," I start. It's as good a place as any. Then I drape an arm over her shoulders and lean back. "I should have told you sooner. About your mom. I only found out a few days ago myself, but I think she's living in Harbour Village. She wants to see you."

Sophie's body tightens, but she doesn't move or say anything.

"I'm not sure how I feel about it, but this isn't about me. This is about you. She's your mom." Once the words leave my mouth, a sense of déjà vu takes over. Only I'm the child in the situation, and my mom is leaning over me, explaining that the divorce had nothing to do with me. That their love for me had nothing to do with their circumstances.

Heart heavy, I realize that I've come full circle. It must have been so hard for my mom. I witnessed some of the hurdles she had to overcome—the bills, keeping up with the house, taking care of me—but I never understood how hard the emotional struggle was until this very moment. Wanting what's best for my child and not knowing if my choices are the right ones.

"Do you think that means she misses me?" Sophie breaks the silence. Her voice is a tiny whisper, shattering my heart into a million pieces.

"She'd be ridiculous not to miss you." I squeeze her to my side. "But yes, I do think she misses you. That's probably why she wants to see you."

She tucks her chin and fidgets with her fingers. And without looking up, she asks, "Can I think about it?"

"Of course." I plant a kiss to her head, the same way my mom kissed mine all those years ago.

Sophie spends the rest of the night reading, coloring, and piecing a puzzle together. As much as I try not to, I spend it thinking about Meera, wondering if she's safe. Hoping she didn't sign away two million dollars this afternoon.

While Sophie takes a shower and gets ready for bed, I pull out my phone and stare at it. I want to text Meera. I need to know she's okay. The unknown of it all is killing me. I must type out a dozen messages and erase each one immediately before giving up. Instead, I keep myself busy by sitting in front of the black TV screen.

"Daddy," Sophie says beside me, pulling me out of my daze.

"Hey, Soph. I didn't hear you turn off the water."

She climbs up next to me on the couch and holds out her brush. She has her pajamas on, and her hair is wrapped in a towel.

Once I unravel it, I bring the brush up to her head and slowly drag it through her wet hair. After several moments of silence, she finally tells me what's on her mind.

"Daddy, if I want to see my mom, you won't be sad, will you?"

Midstroke, I freeze. "Sad?"

"I don't want you to be sad."

"Honey, I won't be sad. I might be worried. But that's because I love you. It's been a long time since you've seen her."

Sophie turns her body so she's facing me. "But you look sad right now."

Ready to argue, I open my mouth. But I immediately snap it shut again, because she's right. Though the situation with Breanna isn't what's bringing me down. I pull my daughter into a tight hug and kiss the top of her forehead, inhaling her clean scent. "I love you. Don't ever forget that. Do you hear me? And if you want to see your mom, we can arrange that. But I want to be honest with you because I expect you to always be honest with me." I take her shoulders and turn her so she can see me. "When you see her, I plan to be there. I don't know where your mom has been or how healthy she is right now, so I won't leave you alone with her. Do you understand that?"

She nods slowly, her eyes locked on mine.

"Do you want me to set up a time to meet for lunch?"

She nods again. "Can Meera come too?"

Her words knock the wind out of me. She's taken a liking to Meera, sure, but I hadn't thought much about it. Okay, that's a lie. It's been hard not to obsess over and examine every facet of the way she reacts to Meera's presence. Because it's something I've never seen from my daughter. But for her to ask if Meera could join us to meet her mom? The significance hits hard.

"I'll see," I say. "Now, how about we get ready for bed?"

Sophie's an easy sleeper. I got lucky with that. So by the time I'm done brushing my teeth, she's already out. Me, on the other hand? I'm a mess. No matter how I fight them, my thoughts keep circling back to Meera.

I climb into bed and throw the sheet over my legs, my gut twisting. Because I don't know whether she's okay after her meeting with Tom. That she managed to leave unscathed. The pain only grows until the twist turns into a full-on squeeze, making it hard to breathe. Knowing I won't be able to sleep until I can put my mind at ease, I pick up my phone again, vowing to text her once, to make sure she's okay. Then I'll leave her alone.

Me: *I'm just checking in to make sure you're okay.*

Meera responds right away: *Yes.*

I should be relieved, but her short response drives me crazy.

Me: *Did Tom leave?*

Meera: *Yes.*

Dammit. She's mad. I get it. I wasn't expecting a full-blown conversation, but something more than one word would have been nice. She's safe. Tom left. That's all I wanted to know. So why is this bothering me so much?

Jack's voice rings through my head. *Something happened between the two of you and now you're scared to admit it.*

He's right. Something did happen, but I'm not scared. I'm fucking terrified.

I crossed the line. Did what I've always sworn I wouldn't. I fucking made love to her. I don't make love to women. I have my way with them. Before Sophie came around, I had one-night stands all the time. I didn't take them home, and I sure as hell didn't spend the night with them. But everything about Meera has been different.

Closing my eyes, I replay the events from yesterday, searching for the moment things shifted, trying to pinpoint exactly when I began to fall for her, because it doesn't matter how much I want to deny it; I know I am.

My heart rate ratchets up as I retrace every interaction. The way she fit in so well with my family at dinner. The drive home from the hospital. My grandpa's retirement party. How she insisted on coming home with me to help with Lydia. Walking barefoot in my backyard. Her fascination with the swans. Falling in the mud and, rather than getting upset about being dirty, shoving me in too. My heart swells when I visualize her mouth dropping to mine.

But that's not the moment things changed. It was before that. Before the party.

When she pulled me on top of her the day I unstuck her windows. That's not it either, but I'm getting closer. My heart is pounding against my ribcage so hard I swear I can hear it.

Meera's only been in town for two weeks. But I've been going to her, finding any excuse to see her, because I've been drawn to her from day one.

Fuck. This is stupid. I suck in a deep breath, hold it, and let it out, willing my heart to calm down. I'm being ridiculous and I'm tired. I need to sleep.

Shoving a pillow under my head, I close my eyes and shut down all the memories. Except it's impossible. They're tattooed in my brain. On my heart.

And there it is. The first memory. When she sauntered through the front door to the Tipsy Brew Garage three years ago. That's the moment I lost the ability to think straight. Ever since that day, I've been a fucking mess. Except it's actually the day I cleaned up my mess. Because three years ago, I fell for a woman I didn't even know. Because breathing the same air she breathed made me want to be a better man. And her presence in my life again after all this time might mean I finally have the chance I missed out on then.

Dammit. I roll over and throw the pillow to the floor.

I fucking blew it. I knew it the minute I laid eyes on her, and yet, even granted a second chance, I still ran off with my tail between my legs.

And Meera deserves so much more than I can give her. She deserves a man who can commit. A man who's there when she needs him, who doesn't run.

CHAPTER THIRTY

Meera

I examine my bruised and swollen wrist and tears escape my eyes before I can hold them back.

My response to Gabe wasn't a lie. I am okay. I'm in my apartment with my door locked, and I'm breathing. And Tom is gone.

Where? I have no idea. But I doubt he made his flight back to California.

I was supposed to meet Tom at Betty's Bakery, in public, where people could see us. Instead, he showed up at my apartment. It was late afternoon, and he was already drunk. That meant only one thing. That what I could expect from him would be somewhere between hostility and rage, and I would be on the receiving end of it all.

He pushed through my door the second I cracked it open. None of this was about the divorce. All he wanted was my two million dollars.

He insisted that he couldn't keep up with the bills. That he'd borrowed from the wrong loan sharks, and now they were after him.

But that isn't my responsibility. So I told him I'd sign over my rights and that he could sell it. Which was apparently the wrong thing to say. And the next thing I knew, he was punching the newly painted wall only inches from my head.

I screamed when his knuckles made contact with the drywall. The noise startled him. Tom wasn't used to me being vocal. I've always taken his threats and his anger and the violence while remaining as quiet as possible, keeping my head inside my turtle shell.

At my small outburst, he grabbed my wrist so tight I thought my bones might snap. "You fucking bitch. You think you can just walk away? That money is just as much mine as it is yours. I waited all this time. I'll keep waiting."

"But will your pregnant fiancée keep waiting?" I snapped back without thinking.

"You think I give a shit about that bitch?" He seethed, squeezing tighter.

I bit down at the pain, nicking the inside of my cheek. Warm blood pooled on my tongue. Then things got fuzzy. The next thing I remember is being pushed against the wall and gasping for air and then my knee making contact with Tom's balls.

Gabe's words had echoed in my mind when Tom had me pinned. *Knee to the balls.*

One second, I could hardly breathe, and then the next, my mouth was filled with a metallic taste, and there was a harsh ringing in my ears.

Tom was curled up on the floor.

"Get the fuck out!" I screamed with as much force as I could muster, but the words came out raspy and hoarse. I held my phone up to him with the numbers 911 on the screen and my thumb hovering over the icon that would connect the call.

He let out a groan, clasping his hands over his crotch. "Goddamn bitch. This isn't over. We're still married, and accidents happen all the time." He got to his feet and glared at me. "All the fucking time."

Then he was gone.

And now, hours later, I'm still sitting with my back to the door, hoping he doesn't come back.

CHAPTER THIRTY-ONE

Gabe

"Hurry up, Soph, Grandma will be here in five minutes."

"Do I have to go?" she complains through a mouthful of toothpaste.

"Yes. I need to get to work. And you need new clothes and school supplies. Plus, Grandma is going to spoil you. You know that."

School starts tomorrow, and my mom has been dying to take her only granddaughter shopping. It's something she loved to do with both Lydia and me, and for the last three years, she's been ecstatic about bringing back the tradition.

Sophie ducks into the bathroom and returns seconds later with a clean face and fresh breath.

"Hello?" my mom calls from down the hall.

"In here," I say, tossing my laptop into my bag. "You two have fun today," I murmur to Sophie, then kiss the top of her head. When my mom steps into the kitchen, I give her a hard look. "And try not to spend too much money, please."

"Can you do me a favor before you go to work?" she asks.

I raise my eyebrows in silent response.

"Can you bring this over to Meera's? She called Lydia late last night. Said she wasn't feeling well and wouldn't be at the clinic today."

Squinting, I study my mom, looking for her angle. "And you couldn't give it to Lydia to take to her?"

"She left early. It's her first official day as owner, and she wants to make sure they won't have to cancel any appointments to accommodate Meera's absence."

I sigh but take the Tupperware bowl from her hand. "Fine. It's not like it's out of my way or anything."

"Good boy," she says and then turns to Sophie. "All right. Make sure you have comfortable shoes on. We have a lot of money to spend today."

After I'm situated in the driver's seat, I fire off a quick text to Meera, giving her the heads-up that I'm on my way. Then I scroll down to *Her* and type in a new message.

Me: *I received the paperwork, and I saw you called. I needed a few days to think about things. We can keep this out of court on a few conditions. We should discuss details first, though. Can you meet for coffee this afternoon?*

Bre's response is almost immediate.

Her: *I understand. And yes, I can meet today.*

Me: *Betty's Bakery? It's on Main Street, not too far from the courthouse. Can you be there at four?*

A few seconds go by, so I start up my engine and buckle my seat belt.

Her: *Yes. I'll see you at four. Thank you, Gabe.*

Fifteen minutes later, I'm in the parking lot outside Meera's apartment. She hasn't responded, so I send another one.

Me: *I'm here.*

Still no response. I grab the container of what I assume is chicken noodle soup from the passenger seat and climb the stairs that lead to her apartment. I knock, but she doesn't answer. So I knock again, louder this time. If she doesn't feel well, she's probably asleep.

"Meera," I call. "Open up. It's me." I bang louder, worry creeping through me. She may be a heavy sleeper, but even if that's the case, her apartment is small, so she should be able to hear me knocking. I should leave her alone if she isn't feeling good, especially after how we left things yesterday, but my gut is telling me something's off.

I balance the container of soup in one hand and dig my phone out of my pocket with the other. With my thumb, I scroll to her contact, then put the phone to my ear. The ringing in my ear is echoed by a corresponding sound on the other side of the door.

Fuck. I bang again, this time with as much force as I can muster.

"Meera," I call again, panicking. Why isn't she responding?

I hit End, and without a second thought, I dial 911.

"911. What's your emergency?"

What is my emergency? I don't even know.

"My name is Gabriel Henry," I choke out. "I think my girlfriend is in trouble. She's diabetic and lives alone. I'm at her door right now. When I call, I can hear her phone ringing, but she isn't answering. I need a wellness check and an ambulance. Immediately."

CHAPTER THIRTY-TWO

Meera

"I don't understand. Why didn't you call anyone?" Sadie scolds as she rushes toward me. When she's standing beside my bed, she wraps her arms around my shoulders and squeezes.

She pulls back and catches sight of the cast on my right wrist, and her face crumples in concern. "He broke your arm?"

"It's fractured," I correct her, as if that makes it any less terrible. What I don't tell her is that Tom crushed my wrist so badly, I won't be able to operate for at least six months. And that's if it heals right and I regain full mobility.

The idea of Tom taking yet another thing from me sends tears slipping down my face and a sob breaking free of my chest.

Sadie sits on my bed and places a hand on my good wrist. "Meera Beara, you're not alone in this. You have Jack and me. I mean it. You're family. We'll find that asshole. It's not like we don't know where he lives." She cracks a smile, but it's a sad one.

She rubs my arm. "You have a lot of people worried about you. Gabe's out there. Did you know that?"

I swallow and nod, draping my hair over my shoulder. I heard Gabe's voice when the paramedics wheeled me into my room. The nurse asked him to leave, told him he could sit in the waiting room and she'd update him later. But he refused, and security had to escort him out. I only knew he was still there because I overheard the nurses gossiping outside my room. In all the chaos, he'd earned himself a nickname: Sexy Caveman.

"I don't want to think about what would have happened if he hadn't stopped by." Sadie blows out a breath. "Do you know how much longer you have to stay?"

I shrug. "They mentioned running another bag of fluids when this one is finished, so that might take a while. But you don't have to wait. I know you need to get back to work. I can text you when they discharge me."

Sadie hauls herself to her feet and plants her fists on her hips. "You're crazy if you think I'm leaving you alone. Lucky for you"—she raises an eyebrow—"Gabe said he's taking you home and he won't take no for an answer."

I open my mouth to protest, but Sadie continues. "As mad as I am about how he acted the other night, I'm thankful he's here. Do you want me to tell him it's safe to come in now?"

Do I? I give an awkward grimace in response. It's not that I don't want to see him. But I don't want him riding in on his high horse.

"I don't know what's going on with him, but maybe give him a chance. He's bullheaded and stubborn, I'm not denying that, but that's part of his exterior, a wall he uses to protect himself. He's made himself unavailable his whole life, but the one time he gave it a go, he was actually pretty nice. Caring and thoughtful and all that, believe it or not. He'd never purposely hurt someone. Honestly, I think you scare him."

"Me?" I scoff. "Scare him?"

"Girl, you're so easy to fall for. Do you not see it? Jack thinks Gabe's terrified because he's never been in love before, and his first reaction is to push away those feelings."

That tidbit of information has my heart plummeting. I turn toward the window, frowning, wondering how that's supposed to be helpful.

"Gabe has never had to face those types of feelings. Ugh. I'm making this worse." She palms her face. "Ignore everything I'm saying. Just let the man come in here already. He did pretty much save your life."

I regard Sadie for a long second. She's ridiculous, but she's right. I owe him a thank-you.

"Okay," I finally agree.

When Sadie leaves, I slump back against my pillow and close my eyes. Images of last night flash before me. I should have called the police. The logical side of my brain knows this. If I did, I would have gotten up. I would have known my blood sugar was tanking, and I would have eaten something. Then I wouldn't be here, sitting in this godforsaken hospital bed.

When I open my eyes, my heart stills. Gabe is standing in the doorway. He looks like shit, but in the best possible way. I can see why the nurses dubbed him the Sexy Caveman with that tousled hair and the disheveled clothes that somehow make him look more attractive.

He's silent, his expression carefully neutral, like he's waiting for me to say something. Like he needs my permission to come in. But shame washes over me suddenly and hot tears stream down my face.

He's at my side in an instant, sitting in the spot Sadie just vacated. Then he pulls me against him and wraps his arms around me. I instinctively do the same and bury my face in his chest. I'm a puddle of emotions, and I can't seem to get my eyes under control.

"Meera," he whispers, threading his fingers into my hair, "you scared the shit out of me. When the paramedics pulled out that glucagon pen and you still didn't wake up . . ." he chokes out, his words laced with fear. "The doctor said you were lucky. Your blood sugar was so low you could have easily slipped into a diabetic coma."

My tears turn into sobs then. Not because of what the doctor told him. But because of Gabe. His hands on me. The closeness of our bodies. I hate that he makes me feel protected. I hate that he was right about Tom. I hate feeling ashamed and foolish while also wanting Gabe to never let go.

"I'm sorry," I say, crying into his shirt.

Gabe pulls back, gripping my biceps gently. "Sorry? Stop that shit. Every time you say those words, you're taking responsibility for something, and you didn't do anything wrong."

I exhale, but before I can get another word in, Gabe pulls my hair away from my neck, lifting it ever so gently. His touch on my bare skin soothes me, and I almost forget why my hair was there in the first place.

But then he goes rigid. "What the hell is this?" he growls, his eyes narrowing to slits.

My body stiffens, and I shut my eyes. Dammit. If I could go back in time, I wouldn't have opened that door. I would have ignored Tom's banging. I would have called the police right away.

"Meera. What the fuck happened? Is this from Tom?"

I press my lips together and nod, dropping my head, overwhelmed by another wave of shame. This one big enough to sweep me away. I can't lie to Gabe. He'll see right through me.

"Look at me." He tilts my chin up. His voice is brash, but his touch is tender.

When I don't open my eyes, he scoots closer. "Meera," he whispers, "for the love of God, please look at me." The warmth from his breath skates across my cheeks.

My eyes well with tears again, but I do as he says. "I didn't lie." I shake my head, wanting Gabe to understand. I *am* fine. My response to his text wasn't a lie. "I did what you told me. When he grabbed me, I kneed him in the balls."

Gabe drops his forehead to mine. "And your arm? Was that him too?"

I nod.

His chest rises sharply, but he releases a few deep breaths before he continues. "Did he do anything else? Did he—"

I shake my head, knowing what he's thinking. Tom is violent, but he's never tried to force himself on me.

"I'm going to fucking kill him," Gabe growls. "Do the police know?"

"Yes. I mean, they will." I find my voice. "I told the nurse. She said the police would be notified, and then they'll take my statement."

"And you're pressing charges?"

My stomach clenches. "Yes," I croak.

"Good," he says, and then he does something I don't expect. He places his hands on either side of my face and dips his head, brushing his nose against mine. "I'm going to kiss you right now. Please don't pull away."

He searches my face, his blue eyes filled with vulnerability and need, waiting for some sort of acknowledgment. So I nod, ever so slowly, my focus locked on him.

And with that, he sets his lips to mine, taking me somewhere I don't think I can ever come back from.

CHAPTER THIRTY-THREE

Gabe

I sit with Meera until the police show up. When they ask me to leave, I stand and straighten my shirt, then shuffle for the door. But Meera demands that I stay and tugs me back down to her side.

"He stays or I can't do this," she tells the officers.

The younger of the two pulls out a notepad and takes down her information. Name, birthdate, address, that sort of stuff. Then he asks about the details that led up to Meera's attack. She downplays it. She says it wasn't so much an attack as it was Tom being drunk and violent.

"If he hurt you in any way, it's considered an attack," the older officer chimes in. "Did you invite him into your home?"

"No."

"Did you ask him to leave?"

"Yes, multiple times."

"Did he hit you?"

This is when Meera grows quiet. I know this kind of silence. I've seen it before with my mom.

"Ask her that in a different way," I say.

Meera and both officers turn to me in unison.

"She doesn't want to lie to you. She won't say he hit her if he didn't actually hit her. But ask her if he hurt her. Look at her wrist. Look at her throat."

"Can you walk us through what actually happened? If we have questions, we'll address them as they arise," the one with the notepad says.

With a solemn nod, Meera begins. She tells them everything she told me, all the way until she kicked Tom in the balls and threatened to call the police. I can't help but feel a bit of pride when she repeats that last part. Because she took my advice, and that might have been what saved her life.

They jot down Tom's information, including the tidbit about his scheduled return flight to California last night.

"We'll check with the airlines first. We'll find him. But in the meantime, is there anything else you want to tell us that we may not have covered?"

Meera's shoulders slump, and she picks at an invisible piece of lint on the sheet covering her lap.

My stomach drops. Dammit. There's more, and she's clearly more hesitant to tell us this than she was about the assault.

"He told me accidents happen all the time."

"You're not going back to your apartment alone," I growl once I get Meera into my truck. "Not with Tom still out there."

"But you can't miss your date with Bre," she says, her bottom lip pulled between her teeth.

"It's not a date," I grumble. "And yes, I can reschedule." There's no way I'm leaving her alone. Not with the threat of an "accident" looming over her. She needs to rest, and she can't do that if she's worrying about Tom.

"No." She sighs. "This is about Sophie. You and Bre need to talk. I'll be fine."

I work my hand over my jaw and check my phone, then look back up at her with my brows raised and a smile on my face.

"What?"

"You'll see."

CHAPTER THIRTY-FOUR

Meera

An hour later, we're sitting in the corner lot behind Betty's Bakery. Gabe took me home so I could change, but instead of letting me rest, he demanded I pack clothes for the next two nights. "You're staying with me until the cops have Tom behind bars."

When I huffed at his ridiculous suggestion, he grabbed a bag from the top shelf of my closet and pulled out a drawer, ready to pack the damn thing himself. With a frustrated huff, I pushed him out of my way and tossed clothing and my toiletry bag into the duffel he refused to set down. Then we hopped back into his truck, and Gabe drove the two blocks to the bakery so I wouldn't have to exert any "unnecessary energy."

"No," I say. "I can't get in the middle of this."

"You won't be getting in the middle. If anything"—he clears his throat and drops his gaze, looking sheepish—"you'll be helping me."

"Helping you?" I laugh, holding up my casted arm. I'm not in any sort of shape to help anyone.

His shoulders deflate. "You're impartial. I'm too angry to make a decision one way or the other. I want to keep Sophie safe, but Sophie wants to see her mom. Just sit with us and listen. If I get obnoxious, I give you permission to put me in my place." He laughs. "I want this to work out. I really do. But I can't be naïve about it."

I sigh, still unconvinced.

Then he adds, "Having a friendly face might help Breanna too."

There's sincerity in his voice, and while I'm still worried about how I can help, I unbuckle. "I'll go in there on one condition."

He arches an eyebrow.

"You take me home and let me sleep in my own bed afterward."

He snorts. "Not a chance."

Betty's is small, so when we step inside, I see Bre right away. She's at a table in the corner wearing a solid black shirt beneath a brown cardigan.

When she sees us, she tilts her head and bites her lip, then tugs at her sleeves.

I give a small wave and mirror her expression. This is such a bad idea.

She stands and looks at Gabe. "I ordered you a coffee, but I didn't know anyone else was coming." She clears her throat and frowns. "I didn't know you two knew each other."

Gabe motions us to sit, so I take the chair across from Bre, and he sits next to me, immediately scooting his chair close.

"I wasn't aware that the two of *you* knew each other either," he growls.

Under the table, I lay my hand on Gabe's thigh, hoping that'll remind him to take it easy.

"What happened to your arm?" Bre asks, shifting in her seat and eyeing the hot pink cast on my right wrist.

"Just a little accident."

"*Not* a little accident," Gabe grumbles. Sexy Caveman has turned into Asshole Caveman.

Bre looks from me to Gabe and then back to me.

"I'm sorry, Bre. Bottom line, none of us knew about our mutual connections," I say, getting things back on track. "I work with Gabe's grandfather. When I met you the other day, I had no idea you were Sophie's mom."

Bre tugs at her sleeve again, a wary look crossing her face. "You've met Sophie?"

I nod. "She's a sweet girl."

Her expression softens, and a smile forms at her lips. Then her eyes dart back and forth between Gabe and me. "Are you two dating?"

I almost choke at her words and rush out a *no* as Gabe nods and grits out a *yes* through his teeth.

Eyes wide, I turn to him and shake my head. "No. We are not." I remove my hand from his leg and cross my arms.

Gabe lets out a small chuckle, but then he turns his focus back to Bre. "Meera said you're working at Harbour Village Animal Hospital?"

Bre tightens her lips and nods. "I've been there for almost a year. I have an apartment a few blocks from there. I wanted to get my life in order before I contacted you. So you'd know I was serious."

"You've been back for a year, and you haven't said anything? Do your parents know?"

"Yeah. I reached out to my mom about six months ago. I needed her to know I was serious too. That this wasn't just another failed attempt at getting sober."

"You're sober?"

"Eighteen months tomorrow." She gives a wry smile. "That rehab you sent me to in Savannah . . . it helped. Until it didn't."

"What does that mean?" Gabe growls.

"That was my first real attempt at getting sober." She swallows thickly. "At that point, I couldn't even remember how it felt to not shoot up. I thought I had everything under control. I figured I could check myself out and be fine. But I didn't have a backup plan. So I relapsed.

"But I'm okay with that. Relapse is part of recovery. If I'd never gone there, I wouldn't have started attending NA meetings, and then I would never have met my sponsor. She eventually helped get me admitted to a rehab facility in Florida. They helped get me into sober living and then, when I was finally ready, I moved back here."

"NA?" Gabe asks, his voice still laced with anger.

"Narcotics Anonymous. I attended meetings every day for the first few months. Then it was a few times a week. Now I go a minimum of once a week."

"That's wonderful," I say, hoping for a little break in the tension, but instead, it does the opposite.

"Wonderful? Yes, I'm so happy to hear you've gotten your shit together while Sophie hasn't had her mom in her life."

"Gabe," I snap.

"No. It's okay. I deserve it. And you're right. I'll live the rest of my life trying to make up for what I've done to her. But I can't change my past. I can't even promise I won't relapse. But I'm here right now. I'm not asking for anything more than visiting rights. You can be there every step of the way. I just want to see her. I want to tell her I'm sorry."

Gabe reaches for the coffee that Bre ordered him and takes a sip while silence fills the space between us.

Finally, he sits back and looks at Bre again. "It's been three years."

"I know," she rasps, her eyes filling with tears she doesn't let fall.

Behind us, the front door to the bakery jingles, and while I don't look up, it's hard not to notice Bre's expression change. Her mouth drops, and she pulls her shoulders inward, like if she can make herself small enough, she'll be invisible.

Gabe and I turn and follow her line of sight at the same time. Declan is standing just inside the door, wearing a similar shocked expression. When his eyes drop to us, he's quick to close his mouth.

"Hey," he says to us. Then he turns to Bre. "I didn't know you were back in town."

She bites her lower lip and nods. "I'm in Harbour Village."

"Are you working in town today?" Gabe asks Declan. He's still turned in his seat with his arm resting on the back of my chair.

"Yeah, we're working on houses in the new development a few blocks south of the school. I'll be there for the next few months," he says, not shifting his attention away from Bre. "Does your mom know you're back? My mom hasn't said anything."

She nods and keeps her eyes trained on the table in front of her, where she's got her hands clasped around her coffee cup. "I asked her not to tell anyone."

"Does that mean you're staying?" His voice cracks at the end.

"I hope so." She looks at Gabe.

After an awkward pause, Declan finally turns and looks at us. "I'm sorry. I didn't mean to interrupt." His eyes snag on my cast, and he tips his chin toward it. "You'll have to tell me what happened there some other time."

I nod.

"Maybe I'll see you around sometime, then? Maybe at your mom's?" Declan says to Bre.

"Yeah, maybe."

Their eyes linger on one another, and I can't help but wonder what I'm missing. If there's some kind of history between them.

After Gabe helps me into his truck, he takes the seat belt and wraps it over my shoulder before snapping it into place.

I bite back a smile. I can buckle myself, but I don't say anything, because it wouldn't make any difference. He's hell-bent on taking care of me. And while I can take care of myself, it's starting to feel nice having someone to lean on. Long term, I'm not sure I want it to be Gabe, but in this moment, there's no one else I'd rather have holding me steady.

"That wasn't so bad," I say once he's fastened his own seat belt. "You two worked out a great compromise."

"I don't know," he grumbles. "Having her see Sophie on her first day of school sounds like a bad idea to me. It might backfire. What happens if she acts out and doesn't want to go to school for the rest of the week?"

"You can't control how she reacts. She has a right to have her own feelings. And on the flip side, what happens if seeing her mom after school tomorrow makes going to school the rest of the week even better?"

Gabe snorts. "Not everything is sunshine and roses."

I don't know what he means by that, but I let it slide. I'm too tired to argue. Yawning, I rub at my eyes. The lack of sleep is finally catching up to me.

"So what's the deal between Bre and Declan?" I ask, leaning my head against the window.

"They were best friends. They grew up next door to each other. We'll be home in five minutes," he adds, as if reading my mind.

But I'm out before we reach the driveway.

CHAPTER THIRTY-FIVE

Gabe

"Shh," I say, reminding my mom and Sophie to keep their voices down when they push open the front door. "Meera just fell asleep."

They toss a dozen shopping bags onto the table, and both grimace as the sound of crinkling plastic practically ricochets off the walls.

Like I knew she would be, my mom was concerned about Meera when I called her from the hospital to fill her in. But I hadn't expected her to recommend bringing Meera back to my house.

Sophie, on the other hand, does not know what happened, so when she asks why Meera is sleeping in the guest bedroom, I hold my breath and rack my brain for what to tell her.

My girl is far more mature and observant than she should have to be, so I decide to go for a version of the truth. If I don't, she'll probably figure it out on her own anyway.

"Meera is sick, kind of. She has a condition called diabetes. It's where her pancreas," I say, pointing to my stomach and hoping I'm somewhere in the right vicinity, because I studied law, not biology, "can't produce enough insulin to help regulate her blood sugar."

She scrunches up her nose as she climbs into a chair. "What does that mean?"

"Well," I say, ruffling her hair, "it means she has to check her blood sugar all the time to make sure it's not too low or too high, or she can get really sick." I think about my grandma, but I don't bring her up because Sophie never met her, and I don't want to scare her with things she doesn't need to know. She already carries the weight of way too much for a kid her age.

"Does that mean she can't eat sugar?" she asks.

"She doesn't have to cut out all sugar. She just has to watch how much she has. The doctors didn't think it was a good idea for her to be alone until she can get a monitor that will help track it better and alert her if it's too low like it was this morning."

"Oh," she says, as if it all makes sense.

"Do you want to show me what you and Grandma bought?" I change the subject, snagging a bag from the table.

Sophie tugs it out of my hand before I can open it. "Not until Meera wakes up. I want to show her the outfit I picked out for my first day of school."

Her excitement is something I've rarely witnessed. I turn to my mom to see if she's as shocked as I am and find her grinning from ear to ear. "Meera is going to love it. Now why don't you take these bags to your room so your dad doesn't have to?"

When Sophie hops off to her bedroom, my mom finally sits. Her shoulders slump, and she lets out a long breath. "The doctor called about Grandpa today."

"And?"

"He was diagnosed over a year ago."

"*A year ago*?" I echo back.

She pinches the bridge of her nose and nods. "He refused treatment. It had metastasized to his bones before they caught it. They called his oncologist, and his office sent over their last scans. It spread to his liver and his lungs. They want to keep him for a few days while they decide what to do next."

She blows out a breath, and a single tear trickles down her face, but she's quick to wipe it away. "The doctor said he's still confused, and he was agitated when Dee went to check on him this afternoon. He wasn't making a lot of sense, so they suggested I wait until tomorrow to visit. I just don't understand why he never told us."

I round the table and pull my mom up from her seat so I can wrap my arms around her. When my grandma passed away, she didn't have the chance to grieve the way she should have. Instead, she became the thread that bound our family together, taking the role my grandma held for so long. She took care of my grandpa, checking in on him day and night. She cooked his dinners, cleaned his house, and even bought his groceries. And while I don't think my grandpa needed nearly as much attention as my mom thought he did, it's what kept her going.

"We'll get through this. Just tell me what you need," I say.

She pulls back and studies me. "I don't need anything." She pats my chest and sits again. "Tell me about today. How did it go with Breanna?"

I glance over my shoulder to make sure Sophie isn't within earshot and then drop to the seat beside her and fill her in.

"When do you plan on telling her?" my mom asks.

I puff out my cheeks and release a ragged breath. "I don't know. I guess tonight. This way she can prepare for it."

She puts her hand over mine and gives me a sympathetic smile. "It's going to be a rough week for all of us."

After my mom leaves and Sophie starts her nighttime routine with a shower, I head down the hallway and check on Meera. She's only been asleep for a few hours, and while she needs to get some rest, she really should eat.

I tap my knuckles lightly on the door in case Meera is awake, but when she doesn't respond, I turn the knob and walk in. The shades are drawn, and the only light that streams in is from the kitchen down the hall.

When my eyes adjust to the dark, I find her curled up beneath a blanket with her bare legs poking out. Her long brown hair cascades across her neck and spills onto the pillow. She's adorable and sexy as hell at the same time. If she didn't need to eat, I'd let her sleep until morning.

"Gabe?" Meera says, her voice small. She lifts her head and rubs her eyes. "Is everything okay?"

Everything is not okay. Meera is sleeping in my house. Under my roof. Again. But I don't want her here. I want her in my bed. I can't deny my feelings anymore. For so long, I've tried to push every thought of her out of my mind, but it's impossible because she's everywhere.

"You need to eat," I growl.

"Ugh," she sighs and rolls over. "I know, but I'm tired."

"C'mon. You can go back to sleep after you put something in that mouth." The second the words are out of my mouth, they register.

And Meera hears the way they sound too, judging by the way her body stills.

Ignoring the elephant in the room, I yank the blanket off her and then head back down the hall.

A few seconds later, she's following behind.

CHAPTER THIRTY-SIX

Meera

Unsure of how I got here, I survey the man standing in front of me as he wraps my cast in a plastic bag. Gabe didn't give me much of a choice in terms of my physical presence. But emotionally, I don't know how I let myself fall so hard, so fast.

Once we got back to his place, I stumbled into his guest room and passed out. I was exhausted from the lack of sleep, and his spare bed is a hell of a lot more comfortable than the worn-out mattress in my apartment. I would have slept there all night if he hadn't woken me up to eat. Though I begged him to leave me alone, he forced my hand when he tossed the blanket to the floor and said Sophie was waiting.

When I made my way into the kitchen, Sophie stood in the doorway that led to the back deck. "We're having dinner outside tonight," she'd said, wearing a hint of a smile.

I raised an eyebrow and pinned her with a look, but she didn't flinch. Like eating under the stars was part of her normal routine, something I don't think I'd ever done in all the years I lived in California.

Three tall candles sat in the center of the table, surrounded by three plates full of food. Gabe grilled chicken and made mashed potatoes, and not the box kind. He actually peeled and chopped the potatoes himself, the sight of which I wished I'd seen.

When Sophie finished eating, she scampered off, excited to show me her new clothes. She put on a fashion show of sorts, parading around in her new jeans, T-shirts, dresses, and sweaters. At the end, she came out in the cutest T-shirt that read *I like animals better than people.*

"Is that the shirt you want to wear on your first day?" Gabe laughed.

She nodded, wearing maybe the brightest smile I'd ever seen from her.

"I love it." I laughed. "I wish I had one just like it."

Sophie bounced over and hugged me, and in my periphery, I caught Gabe's expression shift. I knew that look. The way he pressed his lips together and his cheeks lifted. He was happy, and it made me happy.

When we finished, I volunteered to clean up, but Gabe took the plate from my hand and suggested I take a bath instead. How was I supposed to argue with that?

Now, here I am, standing in front of Gabe as he wraps my cast in plastic next to the oversized tub filling with hot water. After he triple-checks the bag to make sure there's no opening, he sets a towel at the edge of the tub and excuses himself, closing the door behind him.

With a little effort, I wiggle out of my clothes and let everything fall to a heap on the floor. I haven't taken a bath in years, maybe even decades, so I let myself enjoy the hot water as it hugs my body. I soak until my fingers are wrinkled and a knock interrupts my thoughts.

"Are you still okay in there?" Gabe calls from the other side of the door.

I lean over the tub and check the time on my phone. It's later than I realized, and I'm sure Gabe wants to get to bed. "Yes, I'm getting out now," I call out.

When I step out of the tub, I wrap the towel around my body. Dread takes over when I contemplate the pile of clothes on the floor. How the hell am I going to get them back on? I let out an exasperated huff.

Determined, I slip my feet into my underwear first, but pulling them up with one hand proves a challenge. Even as I alternate tugs on either side, they don't want to go any farther than midthigh. I groan out of frustration. I can do this. I know I can. But after my underwear, I'll still have my bra to deal with.

I don't want to give Gabe the satisfaction of helping me, not after the way he kissed me at the hospital today. He's confusing, and I don't know if my heart can handle his hands on me tonight, but I don't have much of a choice.

A soft knock rattles the door again, but before Gabe gets a chance to say anything, I bite the bullet and open it.

"I need help," I tell him.

Gabe towers over me. His bare chest is on full display. I take a step back and have to bite back a groan. Of course he took his shirt off. It's well past bedtime. He should be sleeping right now, but he's waiting for me to get out of his bathroom.

His chiseled abs flex as he inches his way closer, denying me the space I was trying to give myself.

When I step back again, desperate for breathing room, I stumble over the clothes on the floor, but Gabe grabs me just in time.

My heart flutters at his touch. I try to tell the traitorous organ that there is nothing between us. That my attraction to him is purely physical. But the connection is there, a desire begging to be unleashed. And I worry that before long, I'll crack and give in.

"I can't get dressed by myself," I say, pulling from his grasp and shutting out the emotions his proximity stirs. "Here." I toss my panties at him. "I can't pull them up."

Gabe doesn't smile like I thought he would. I figured he would have a field day when I gave him permission to touch my underwear. Instead, he nods and lowers to one knee. He holds them out so I can step into them. Then he pulls them up. When he reaches the towel, he drags his hands up under the terry cloth until the band of my underwear sits along my waist.

"Breathe, Meera," he says when he stands back up.

Breathe. Yes, that's a good idea, breathe. I let out a quick breath. That wasn't so hard.

He does the same for my shorts, which are easier because they're loose.

My bra, however, is a completely different story. I don't even look at it as I hand it to him, my face going hot.

"I don't think I've ever put a bra on anyone before. I'm usually the one taking it off."

I roll my eyes, making no effort to hide my defeat as he helps me slide each arm through the straps. I don't like feeling helpless or relying on other people. But this feels different. He wants to help me. And while I didn't want to give him the satisfaction of it at first, I wouldn't want it to be anyone else.

"I'm sorry," he murmurs, interrupting my thoughts, "but you have to drop the towel."

I clench my jaw. He's already seen me naked. This shouldn't be a big deal. It's not like my breasts will be on full display or anything.

I hold my bra in place, awkwardly grasping the bottom of the cup with the hand in a cast as I release the towel. Gabe's fingers glide across my skin as he ensures it's fastened correctly, the sensation causing my body to shiver in response.

"Is this good?" he asks, dragging his hands over my shoulders to untwist the straps.

I arch in response, then moan or make some other equally embarrassing noise. I curse myself, knowing Gabe heard me by the way he shifts his body closer to mine.

"You're so fucking beautiful, Meera." His voice is velvety smooth and laced with desire.

I crave that voice. I want those lips on my skin. But Gabe doesn't want me. I have to remember that. He may want to be inside me. But he doesn't want me.

Closing my eyes, I take in a slow breath, ready to tell him that I can't do this. I can't sleep with him again. Because no matter how much I want to, it's a terrible idea. There's no way I won't get more attached, that I won't fall even harder for him.

But before I can force the words out, Gabe's warm breath skates across my skin.

"I'm sorry, Meera," he rasps, pain evident in the way he says my name. "I'm so fucking sorry I ran out the other morning. I shouldn't have left. I never should have left." He presses his chest to my back and wraps his arms around my waist.

I snake my hands over his and tilt my head, allowing him to nestle into the crook of my neck. I shouldn't let him, but I like it too much to stop him.

"Why did you leave?" I whisper. It's a dangerous question, but I can't accept his apology until I know what happened. I may not like the answer, but I need to know the truth, regardless.

He sighs, his hot breath on my neck. "You scare me. Everything about you scares me."

Frowning, confused by his truth, I spin in his arms. His brilliant blue eyes are full of sadness.

"What do you mean? How do I scare you?" I drag my hand across his jaw, feeling the stubble graze my fingers.

"That," he says as he nuzzles my hand. "When you touch me. When you're near me. Your voice. Everything about you. How you light up a room. The way you care so deeply." He drops his forehead to mine. "The way you make me feel. I feel so damn much when I'm around you."

Speechless, all I can do is close my eyes and soak in his words.

"You didn't deserve to be run out on like that. You don't deserve anything less than a man who can give you his whole heart. Who will treat you like you're the most important person in the world. And I kept telling myself that person wasn't me. But this morning, when you wouldn't wake up, when those paramedics stabbed you with that glucose pen and you wouldn't respond . . . the fear I'd been running from? It was nothing compared to what I felt then."

"Gabe . . ." My voice is all air when I say his name.

He shakes his head. "No. I'm not done." He slides his hands to my jaw and cups my face. "I'll never deserve you. No one will. But I'll live every goddamn day trying to be worthy."

"Gabe," I say again, because no other words will come.

He tilts his head back and sighs, his eyes locked on mine. "Tell me I'm crazy."

I swallow. I can't. Because if he's crazy, then so am I. Instead, I press up on my toes and nip at his mouth. But he doesn't press forward. He doesn't kiss me back. He's waiting. Watching. He needs to hear me say it.

"You're not crazy."

That's all he needs. And in the next instant, he's lifting me off my feet. His fingers dig into the backs of my thighs as he wraps my legs around his waist. Instead of laying me on his bed like I expect, he turns around and sits at the edge of his mattress so I'm straddling him.

"I'm serious, Meera." He runs a hand up my neck and snakes it into my hair. "I want to make dinner for you every day. Run you a bath before bed each night. Take long walks and curl up on the sofa next to you and watch movies. You like movies, right?"

I nod with a soft laugh.

"I'll watch whatever you want, even cheesy romantic comedies or those Hallmark movies. God help me, please say you like more than just romance." He brushes a strand of my damp hair away from my face.

"Gabe." My voice cracks.

"Nope. Still not done." His hands move to the small of my back. "I tried everything I could to ignore it, but I started falling the second I set eyes on you. But after what happened this morning and seeing you out there with Sophie once again, I don't want to ignore it anymore. I want you. Every part. And I'll do whatever it takes to prove that I'll never walk away again."

He's ruining me, but in the best possible way. I can't take it any longer. If he tells me he's not done one more time, I'm going to lose it. "Will you shut up now and kiss me?"

His eyes go wide, and his mouth drops open, and all he does is stare.

"Well?" I ask.

And then he's crushing his lips to mine and flipping me over so my back is on the bed, his arm still circling me. His mouth is soft, but he's forceful, taking me like he can't get enough. Like he's scared he'll lose me. I kiss back the same way. Like he's giving me life. When he slips a hand out from beneath me, he holds my jaw with his thumb and forefinger, the movement causing my hair to fall away from my neck.

Gabe lets out a low growl at the bruise, then peppers it with the gentlest kisses. He's somewhere near my ear when a phone chimes nearby.

"I think that's your phone," Gabe says in a hushed voice. He sits up and leans over to the nightstand next to us.

And then his expression changes. "It's him," he growls, placing the phone in my hand.

My heart comes to a crashing halt when I see the familiar number. "I can't answer it."

"Send it to voice mail."

I do, and when the phone rings again, Gabe takes it from me and sends him to voice mail himself.

Tears form at the edges of my eyes. I can't help it. I don't want to cry, but I know why he's calling. It's the same thing every time this happens. He'll say he's sorry. That he got carried away. That he won't do it again. And then he'll somehow turn it back to being my fault. He'll remind me that I'm the one who set him off. If only I'd signed the papers. If only I'd done what he wanted, then none of this would have happened.

Gabe wipes at my damp cheeks. "Call the cops. Tell them he's calling you. They should have found him by now, anyway."

CHAPTER THIRTY-SEVEN

Gabe

The scent of cinnamon and oranges and the sound of classical music fill the space around me as I wake. I roll over and check my phone. It's already seven o'clock. How the hell did I sleep so late?

I push myself out of bed and shuffle to the kitchen, where Sophie is giggling, and Meera is spinning her in circles on the tile floor. Sophie is still in her pajamas, which surprises me. She's usually dressed before I am. And she knows she has school today. Meera is wearing the same pair of black cotton shorts and the gray tank top she wore to bed. She's beaming as she laughs along with my daughter.

I don't know anything about classical music, but the song they're dancing to sounds familiar. They sway and shake, but not in sync and definitely not to the beat of the melody. Charlie circles them, trying to work his way into the fun. When the music comes to an end, Sophie reaches for the hem of her nightgown and bows. Meera mirrors Sophie but presses her cast close to her chest when she bends forward.

Finally, when the tempo shifts into another piece, I clap.

Meera snaps her shoulders back, and her eyes go wide. Sophie, on the other hand, runs to me and throws her arms around my waist.

"Daddy," she says, resting her chin on my sternum, "Meera was teaching me about Beethoven. Did you know he played the piano, but he couldn't hear anything?"

I pull her close and squeeze her tight, not wanting to let her go. This isn't the Sophie I know. The girl I've spent every morning for the last three years with dresses as soon as she wakes up and quietly pours herself a bowl of cereal.

This Sophie, though, is loud and giggly and full of energy.

"He couldn't hear?" I croak, feeling like I'm inhaling deeply for the first time in years.

"No." She shakes her head. "He was deaf."

"I didn't know that." I did, but I don't want this moment with her to end. "How could he play the piano if he was deaf?"

"That's what I said, but Meera told me he didn't let that stop him from doing what he loved. He taught himself to hear with his body."

"You went to college. You didn't take any introduction to music classes?" Meera asks, blushing. She turns away and slides an oven mitt over her good hand.

"What are you doing?" I ask, rushing to her side and snagging her arm. "That's a good way to burn yourself." I snap the mitt off her hand.

When my bare chest presses against her back, her whole body tenses.

"And to answer your question, no. I did not take introduction to music. I took art appreciation."

Meera turns around, but I have her caged between the stove and the island. Her eyes don't stray from mine, the deep pools giving away her thoughts of last night.

"The cinnamon rolls are going to burn if you don't pull them out," she says, her words coming out one by one, as if she has to think carefully about what she wants to say next.

I shift my position a fraction so she can squeeze by. "Can I help you frost them?" Sophie calls out.

I have the oven halfway open when Meera replies. "Of course, sweetie."

My heart almost goes into fibrillation at the term of endearment she chose for my daughter. Does Meera not know what she's doing to me? I'm having a hard enough time controlling myself around her because she's so fucking gorgeous. But then she has to go and do shit like that with my daughter. Making breakfast for her. Dancing with her in the kitchen. Teaching her about classical music.

"Daddy, do you need help?" Sophie asks when I take too long.

Fuck, get it together.

"No. I'm fine." I pull out the tray of oversized cinnamon rolls and place it on the wire rack next to a pitcher of orange juice.

"Where'd this come from?" I ask, knowing Sophie polished off the last of the juice in the fridge a few days ago.

"Meera showed me how to make orange juice." Sophie lifts a small glass. "Do you want to try it?"

Fresh-squeezed orange juice? We had oranges?

"Sure," I say.

I take the glass Sophie offers me and bring it to my lips. "Wow. This is great. Did you help Meera since she only has one hand?" I shift my attention to the woman in question and raise a brow. I told Meera to take it easy, but I already know she doesn't listen.

"You did all the heavy lifting, right, Soph?" she says, averting her gaze. Then she moves around to the other side of the island, still trying to avoid physical contact with me.

But I make it hard this time.

She edges around me, reaching for where she left the frosting, but I scoot closer. When she realizes I'm not budging from my position, she finally looks up. Her eyes are heavy with desire, and she's got her lip caught between her teeth, yet she still avoids my touch.

"Looking for this?" I say, producing the bowl of frosting. I hold it close to my chest, taunting her, daring her to come closer.

Meera tightens her lips and sighs, refusing to budge. She's so damn sexy when she pouts.

I bark out a laugh, which causes her to glare at me. "Okay, okay. You win." I extend my arm and let her take the bowl.

She brings it to Sophie and directs her to stir it again. Then she glances back at me. "Can you bring the cinnamon rolls over here? It'll be easier for Sophie to frost them on this side."

I place them exactly where Meera points, and then I pour myself a cup of coffee, watching and listening as she shows my daughter what to do. And Sophie listens too, as if she's captivated by the plastic spatula and all the wonders it can produce with a simple flick of the wrist. Meera struggles a little with her cast. She keeps forgetting about it, wanting to grab things that won't fit between her fingers and thumb like she wants.

When Sophie plops her first mound of frosting on top of a cinnamon roll, I make my way back over to them, detouring to pick up Meera's sling from where it's sitting on the table.

"Put this on," I whisper, bringing it to her.

She tries to ignore me, but I'm persistent. With one hand, I grasp her waist and turn her so she's facing me. Then, without saying a word,

I drape the strap over her shoulders and work her arm into the sleeve. She doesn't fight me this time. After I adjust her arm and move her hair out from under the strap, I catch her eye and smile, because she's no longer pouting.

"Aren't you going to be late for work?" Her words are breathy when she speaks.

"I'm not going to work today. It's Sophie's first day of school, which means"—I turn to my daughter, who's in the middle of licking the spatula—"you need to get dressed if you want to ride the bus this morning." Plus, there's no way in hell I'm leaving Meera alone.

"Will she be here when I get home?" Sophie asks. Last night, while Meera was in the tub, I told Sophie that Meera and I met her mom earlier in the day and that we agreed she could come over after school. Sophie didn't say much, but when I asked if that was all right with her, she nodded.

"As far as I know, she will be."

She sets the spatula on the table and then jumps down from the chair. "You'll still be here too, right?" she turns to Meera.

Meera looks from Sophie to me before looking back at her. "If you want me here, I'll be here. If you don't—"

"Yes, I want you here," she says. And then she turns on her heel and slips away to her bedroom with Charlie at her heels like always.

Meera shifts her attention to me. There's a small smile pressed to her lips, but once her eyes land on mine, her smile quickly disappears. She places her good hand on her hip and scowls at me, which is sexy as hell and might be my new favorite look on her.

I inch closer, but when I do, she takes a step back.

She places a hand between us and says, "Not out here."

Frustrated, I growl out my protest, but she's right. Sophie is just down the hall, and she wouldn't understand if she witnessed me kissing Meera.

I shift my gaze to Meera's mouth. "After Sophie leaves, I'm taking those clothes off. And then I'm taking my time with you."

CHAPTER THIRTY-EIGHT

MEERA

Gabe doesn't waste any time. Sophie is barely on the bus when he's gripping at my hips.

He gives me a devilish grin, and his eyes burn bright with desire. I don't think I've ever experienced this. The way he looks at me like I'm the only person in the world. Like he can't get enough of me. Like he needs me the same way I need him. So when he lifts me off the floor and slings me over his shoulder, I bask in the attention. I'm falling hard. I don't want to stop it from happening. And I couldn't if I tried.

I can't trust that tomorrow will be the same as today. Or that Gabe won't change his mind about me next week. But maybe it'll be me who changes my mind about him. Maybe how I'm feeling right now will be short-lived.

But I'm okay with that. We both deserve to see where this leads us.

"Hold on," Gabe whispers in my ear, patting me on my ass and striding to his room.

He eases me onto his bed, and then, like he said earlier, he takes his time undressing me. Or did he say he was going to take his time with me? I can't remember. Either way, he makes good on his promise.

Sliding his fingers across my body, he explores me like a treasure map. He starts at my lips, then traces small circles down my neck. With his nose, he brushes the shell of my ear. His lips are on my skin next, tasting me. He continues downward, and his warm breath catches on the fabric over my nipples.

I moan and tug at his hair, trying to guide his mouth where I want it, desperate for more, but Gabe is stubbornly slow.

"This has to go," he says, slipping the material of my shirt between his fingers. He lifts it unhurriedly, inch by tiny inch, over my head. Then he works his way to my bra. To the thin material that separates my breasts from his mouth.

With one finger, he slides a strap down my arm, kissing the flesh above my breast as he does. He repeats this on the other side, and then, when my chest is heaving and my heart is pounding, Gabe pushes my bra to the side.

"Meer," he growls against one pink peak. His breath is warm and feathery and light.

An inarticulate sound forms in my throat, and I've lost all ability to focus on anything other than the way he makes me feel.

With his nose, he brushes against the most sensitive area of my breasts. His lips follow behind, skating across each nipple.

He inches farther south, trailing kisses down my stomach. When he reaches the waistband of my shorts, he tugs at them until they slip from my hips. And like my shirt, he's slow and methodical as he pulls them down each leg. He repeats this with my panties.

When I'm naked below him, Gabe glides one hand under my leg and lifts it so my knee is bent and his face is close to my center. He groans as he lays a kiss to the inside of my thigh.

I moan with him, all the air releasing from inside me. "I need you," I say, my words barely a whisper.

"Not yet," he responds, his voice a rumble.

He licks his lips, but he doesn't dip closer. Instead, he lifts my other leg slowly. He drags me close, and when he presses his lips to the inside of that thigh, the stubble from his jaw rubbing against me, I shut my eyes and inhale sharply.

"Look at me," he groans.

It takes me a moment to have the wherewithal to obey, but when I do, he drops his head, and holy hell, the sensations that course through my body are too much to handle. "Gabe," I whimper, my eyes fluttering shut again. My back bows, but Gabe presses me down with the palm of one hand while he grips my thigh with the other. He nips with his teeth and explores with his tongue. And then—

"Gabe," I exhale. "I'm—" My words get lost in the sudden wave that takes hold.

"Tell me," he grits out. I can barely hear him over my pounding heart and the blood rushing in my ears, but I know exactly what he needs to hear.

"Don't stop," I pant. "Please, don't stop."

A deep, guttural groan erupts from inside him. I never had a chance. His fingers slide into me, and with his tongue, he's ruined me.

"Meera." Gabe whispers my name, brushing the side of my face with gentle fingers.

"Mmm," I say, not wanting to open my eyes. I must have fallen asleep. Between the sun and the humidity, I didn't stand a chance of staying awake after what Gabe and I did in his bedroom a short while earlier.

"The police are here."

That wakes me up. "The police?"

He grins. "They found him."

CHAPTER THIRTY-NINE

Gabe

When we enter the police station, Meera slips her hand in mine. "I know you don't agree, but I think this is the best option for me," she insists.

She's right. I don't agree. I think Tom should rot in jail, but Meera's heart is too damn big.

A deputy leads us down a long hallway and opens a door. Inside, Tom is sitting at a brown table with his hands bound by cuffs. He's wearing black slacks and a cream-colored button-down shirt. There are two buttons missing and a stain over his left breast pocket. His blond hair is matted, and there's a bruise forming under his left eye. I look at Meera, wondering if this is the result of her, but from her wide eyes, it's clear she's just as surprised as I am.

When Tom sees us, he stands, but the deputy puts a hand on his shoulder, urging him to sit back down.

"Meera, I'm sorry," he stammers.

"What the hell happened to you?" Meera waves a hand at his face.

His eyes drop. "I don't know."

The room is silent as Meera and I sit across from him. When Tom looks back up, I meet his gaze and stare hard into his eyes. With Meera's hand still locked in mine, I rest my forearm on the table and squeeze gently, reminding her that I'm here. But I also do it for Tom's sake. I want him to know that I have her back. That if he ever touches her again, he won't just have the police to worry about.

Turning his attention to Meera, he speaks first. "They said you were pressing charges. That I could go to jail for assault. But this was all a mistake. I didn't mean to hurt you. I was drunk. I don't remember much of anything from yesterday."

"Tom, what you did to me *was* assault. Do you see this?" Meera tosses her hair over her shoulder, displaying the black and blue bruise along her neck. "You did this. You choked me. You broke my wrist. You could have killed me." She takes a breath. "You should be charged with attempted murder."

"Attempted murder?" he croaks, looking at the deputy and then back to Meera. "I didn't—"

She holds her hand out to stop him. "I don't want to hear it. I don't even need to be here since you left proof."

"Proof?"

"My landlord, bless his heart, installed cameras around the perimeter of my apartment when he lived there. He doesn't trust easily. There's footage of you barging through my door and then additional footage of you with your hands on my throat. But do you want to hear the best part?" she says proudly, sitting straighter. "The camera also caught me kicking your ass."

I try to suppress a laugh, but it escapes me anyway.

Tom shifts his eyes to me, but quickly, he locks on Meera again.

"I'm not here to gloat. But I am here to cut you a deal. I'll drop the charges if you agree to a few things."

"Like what?" he asks, his jaw hard.

I don't blame him. I almost didn't believe it myself when Meera told me her plan.

"One, you agree to attend AA for the next year. Ninety meetings in ninety days and then weekly meetings thereafter."

Tom's mouth drops, but Meera ignores it.

"Two, when you get back to California, you volunteer at an animal shelter. Once a week, minimum. Three, you sign our divorce papers right here, right now. My lawyer drafted a new set, eliminating the part where I have to buy you out of my share. You can keep the restaurant and condo, free and clear, but you won't receive a penny from me. And last, you agree not to step foot in the state of Georgia so long as I live here."

Tom narrows his eyes. "I'm not going to AA. I don't have a drinking problem. And I'm definitely not volunteering at an animal shelter."

"Okay. Enjoy your time in jail, then." Meera scoots her chair out and plants her feet, ready to stand.

"Fuck," Tom growls, making Meera pause. "Okay, I'll go to AA. But you know I don't like animals. Why would you make me volunteer at an animal shelter?"

"Because animals will help ground you. You'll learn patience. You'll learn how to put their needs before your own. You'll get to play with them, which will, I hope, teach you better coping mechanisms for your stress."

I shift my hand under the table and squeeze Meera's leg. I'm so fucking proud of her. She believes in rehabilitation and all that garbage. Personally, I still want to kick his ass. But this isn't about me.

"Do you have a pen?" Tom mutters.

When we get back to the truck, Meera collapses in the seat beside me. "Pinch me."

I raise an eyebrow and put my hand on her forearm, but I don't actually pinch her.

"No. For real. You have to pinch me. I have to know if that was real." Her words come out excited and fast.

I laugh. "That really happened. I witnessed it. You were a badass in there."

Meera throws her hands over her mouth. "Oh my God. Does this mean I'm finally divorced?"

I hate having to burst her bubble, especially when she's so happy, but someone has to do it. "Not yet. That just means he agreed to the terms."

Her shoulders slump, and she sticks her bottom lip out.

"We'll file this in California. The process will be quicker that way. Georgia requires you to be a resident for at least six months prior to filing, and then it can take another six months before a hearing is scheduled."

"All right." She blows out a breath. "I waited this long. I guess I can wait a little longer."

I turn the key in my ignition just as my phone vibrates in my pocket. I dig it out and check the display. "It's Sophie's school," I say, confused. "Hello?"

"Mr. Henry? This is Lisa, the secretary at Morganville Elementary School. We noticed Sophie wasn't in class today, and you didn't call in an absence. Will she be out all day?"

My heart plummets. "She's not at school?"

For a long moment, there's nothing but silence on the other end of the line. Meera looks at me, her eyes dipping with concern.

"Um, no. Her teacher marked her absent."

I swallow past the boulder lodged in my throat. "Sophie got on the school bus. I watched her. Are you sure she isn't there?"

There's another pause, but there's chatter in the background.

"No. She isn't in class. We'll do an all-call for her and check the bathrooms. Is there somewhere she may have gone instead?"

I throw my truck into reverse and peel out of the police station.

Ten minutes later, Meera and I are pulling up to my house.

"She's got to be here somewhere," I say. "She did this when she was in kindergarten. It was a week after we got her back. She didn't want to go to school, so she ran all the way back here."

Meera unbuckles and jumps down from the truck.

"You check inside. I'll go around and check out back."

I nod and then run up the three stairs that lead to the front door. "Soph?" I yell out when I'm inside. "Sophie?"

Charlie doesn't come bounding down the hallway to greet me the way he usually does, so he's probably keeping her company, wherever she may be hiding.

I scan the kitchen and the living room and then make my way down the hall. It's quiet. Too quiet.

"Shh." A tiny whisper comes from behind the door to Sophie's bedroom.

Letting out a sigh, I drop my shoulders and slowly push her door open. Charlie is sitting on Sophie's bed, his tail thumping excitedly against the lump beside him.

Carefully, I lower myself to the mattress and pet the underside of Charlie's chin. "Good boy," I say. Then I pull back the covers.

"Soph. What happened?"

Her hair is a tangled mess, dangling over her face, but she doesn't make any effort to move it.

"Soph. Talk to me." I pat her shoulder.

At my touch, she pulls away and turns toward the wall.

I take in a deep breath through my nose and let it out slowly. I don't understand what happened. She was fine this morning. Excited even. She wanted to meet her new teacher and see her mom.

"Soph," I plead, "I can't fix this if you don't talk to me."

From the doorway, Meera clears her throat. When our eyes meet, she motions me to her.

"Can I try?"

I nod and inch out into the hall. And then she shoos me away.

CHAPTER FORTY

Meera

"Hey, sweetie. You had us worried," I say as I kneel at Sophie's bedside.

Charlie sticks his nose under my hand, begging me to pet him.

When Sophie doesn't budge, I move to the floor and fold my legs beneath me. Then I pull out my phone and flip through my song list until I find the perfect piece. I click play, and the sweet and familiar high notes of Beethoven's *Fur Elise* come alive. It plays for two minutes before I feel the bed shift behind me. I don't turn. I don't open my mouth.

When the song ends and the room goes quiet, Sophie finally speaks. "Was that Beethoven?" Her voice is tiny, and there's a hint of a sniffle in there.

"It was," I muse. "It's beautiful, isn't it?"

Sophie slides down next to me, and Charlie plops down next to her. "It sounded sad."

Her words send shivers down my arms. "You have a good ear, you know that? Before I started listening to classical music, like really listening, I thought there was a playfulness to this piece. My mom loved it. I'm not sure if it was her favorite, but she played it a lot when I was your age. Then, after she died, the song took a different direction for me. It became nostalgic."

"What does nostalgic mean?" Sophie asks, showing genuine interest.

"Well," I begin, "it means you remember something that happened in the past and it makes you feel a certain way. Anytime I hear those keys being played, I remember my mom, which makes me happy. But she died when I was a teenager, so it also makes me miss her, which makes me sad."

Without another word, Sophie looks down at her hands.

"Sweetie, you don't have to tell me what happened today. But you need to know it's okay to have feelings. Something must have upset you. When things upset me, I like to listen to music. It's safer than running away."

"But I didn't run away. I came back home."

Pressing my lips together, I put my hand out in front of her, palm side up.

She inspects it for a long moment before placing her hand on top.

Slowly, I lift her up so she's standing in front of me and direct her to my lap. She follows, which surprises me, but I don't draw attention to it. "You know what I mean."

"If I tell you, do you promise not to get mad?" Her big blue eyes are locked on mine and brimming with tears.

"Sweetie, nothing you say is going to make me mad."

She sighs, and her shoulders sag. “When I was on the bus, Jamie and Chloe were talking about their moms. Jamie said her mom took her to get her hair cut, and Chloe said her mom took her to get her nails painted.”

I close my eyes. I know exactly where this is going. My heart hurts for her so much. Not having her mom around to do those things can be tough on any girl, but it’s got to be so much harder for someone like Sophie, who’s gone through so much in her short life.

When I reopen my eyes, Sophie has her chin tucked and is fidgeting with her fingers.

“Then,” she murmurs, “Jamie asked where my mom took me.”

“Sophie,” I say, brushing her hair away from her face.

“I was going to tell them my grandma took me shopping, but then Joey yelled at them to not talk about my mom because my mom was a crackhead.”

My mouth drops. I look up to see if Gabe is standing in the doorway listening, but he’s not.

“So I kicked him in his balls. Daddy said if a boy hurts me, I should kick him hard. So I did. But then the bus driver yelled at me.”

I cover my mouth to stifle a laugh. This has Gabe written all over it. “You what?”

“You promised not to get mad.”

“Sophie. I’m not . . . I don’t know . . .” I don’t finish my sentence. Instead, I loop my arms around her and hold her tight. “I’m not mad, but we need to talk to your dad.”

She pulls away from me and wipes her eyes. “Meera, what’s a crack-head?”

CHAPTER FORTY-ONE

Gabe

"I can't believe my little girl kicked a boy in his junk," I say once Sophie is out of earshot.

"Right? I'm not going to lie. I'm kind of impressed," Meera says. "It's the one thing my dad and grandpa forgot to teach me. But somehow, you managed to get two of us to do it in the course of twenty-four hours."

We're sitting on the couch, looking out the large windows where we can watch Sophie and Breanna. They're sitting side by side on the wooden swing with a foot or so of space between them. Breanna pushes with her feet while Sophie's legs dangle in the air.

"We have to call the school, right? She has to apologize to that boy."

"Definitely call the school. But that boy should also apologize for what he said to her."

I nod, then rest my hand on Meera's knee. "Thank you. What you did in there with Sophie—"

"It was nothing," she says before I can finish.

"It wasn't nothing. You got her to open up. She's not normally a talker."

We sit in silence for a while, both focused on Sophie.

When Meera inches closer and nestles into my side, I wrap my arm around her shoulders, reveling in how right she feels there.

Meera clears her throat. "Gabe?"

"Mmm?" I like the way my name sounds coming from her mouth.

"I should probably get back to my apartment. They found Tom, so he's not a threat anymore."

"No." I squeeze her closer to me and thread the fingers of my free hand through hers. "His flight doesn't leave until tomorrow, so no, you are not leaving. Not yet." If it were up to me, she'd never leave.

She doesn't respond. And neither of us mentions it again.

An hour later, Breanna says her goodbyes, and Sophie runs upstairs to take a shower. Charlie chases after her, per his usual.

"Thank you. Both of you. You don't know what this means to me," Breanna says, wiping tears from her eyes.

Meera leans in and gives Breanna a hug. "Do you want to get coffee with me tomorrow? I'm not going back to work till next week, so I'll have extra time on my hands in the morning."

Breanna shifts her weight and then turns her focus to me. "Would you be okay with that?"

"Honestly? I don't know. This all makes me nervous." I'm more than nervous. I'm still angry, but I'm trying to do what's best for Sophie.

Breanna's shoulders sink. "I understand."

"But," I continue, "I want this to work, so yeah. You two should get coffee."

Breanna sucks in a deep breath and smiles. "Thank you, Gabe," she says softly. Then she turns to Meera and adds, "Do you want to meet at Betty's at ten?"

"Make it eleven," I say, "so we know Tom is gone."

"Tom?" Breanna asks.

Meera shakes her head and pulls Breanna in for another hug. "I'll tell you tomorrow."

After Breanna leaves, I take Meera by the hand and lead her back to the couch. "Just sit with me," I say, wanting to savor this moment a little longer. And she does. She drops to the cushion next to me and snuggles into my arm. And together, we stare out the windows, watching as the night sky falls.

After her shower, Sophie finds us in the living room and asks Meera to put her to bed. Meera grins and chases her down the hall, making my little girl squeal in delight.

My stomach flips at the sight of them disappearing behind Sophie's bedroom door. A calm settles over me in a way I don't think I've ever felt. I never imagined what it would be like for Sophie to have a woman around, other than my mom and sister.

Maybe it was easier not to think of it because I didn't do relationships. But Meera? She's doing something here. To Sophie. To me.

A few years ago, when my sister was a senior in high school, she asked if I believed in soulmates. She'd just had her heart broken by a dumb jock she thought she was madly in love with, so I knew better than to laugh. Instead, I sat next to her on her bed and explained that the idea of one true love in a sea of billions seemed far-fetched. That if someone threw a needle into the infamous haystack, I would never go searching for it. I argued that, logically, we could find many people worthy of love, but it was up to us to find the best in them and to make that love last.

"So you don't believe there's one person out there for you? Waiting for you to find them?"

I scrunched my nose and shook my head.

"That's so sad, Gabe. And you think it would be as easy to create love with a random stranger as it would with someone like Mack from down the street?"

Side-eyeing her, I said, "Not Mack. But yes. You'll meet tons of people in your life. You'll connect with a lot of them. But at the end of the day, I think you fall in love with who you choose. Not one person the universe says you're destined to be with."

Lydia huffed and dragged a blanket over her lap. "Do you think maybe you don't believe in soulmates because you haven't found yours yet?" Her voice had shifted, almost hopeful. "Maybe she's out there, right now, waiting for you." She paused, and then, as if suddenly becoming very aware of something, her eyes grew wide. "I just got it. A needle in a haystack. You'll never find it, but it'll find you. When you least expect it, you'll be busy living your life, and then, bam"—she threw her arms out—"you'll get stuck with one end of the needle."

I threw a pillow at her head, laughing. "Remind me to stay away from haystacks."

But now, as I sit here, I can't help but relive that conversation, reevaluating every word we exchanged that night. Was Lydia right all along? I'd never been invested enough to fall in love, but maybe that's because I hadn't met the right person.

A soft melody floats down the hall, snapping me out of my thoughts. I get up from the couch and turn off all the lights and make sure the front door is locked. Then I make my way down the hallway and stop outside Sophie's door.

Inside, my girls are lying next to one another, whispering about things I can't quite make out. When the music comes to an end, I tap my knuckles gently on the doorframe.

They look up in unison.

"Good night, Soph. Time for bed. You have school tomorrow," I say to her.

Meera rolls out of the bed and pulls the blankets up to Sophie's chin.

"Good night, Daddy. I'm sorry about today. I love you."

I kiss her forehead and tell her that I love her too. Then, just as I turn to leave, Sophie adds, "Good night, Meera. I love you."

The room is silent for only a split second before Meera responds. "I love you too, sweetie. I love you too."

And with that, my heart stops beating in my chest. Instead, it's lodged in my throat somewhere, and it's cutting off my airway. Those three little words shouldn't be a big deal. Kids hand over their hearts easily. They love with abandon. The ability to love others comes so much easier for them than it does for us adults. But Sophie isn't a normal kid.

Ever since Meera showed up, she's smiling bigger, talking more, hugging, and dancing. Come to think about it, Sophie hasn't dragged Charlie to the hospital in a week. There haven't been any more concerns over missing Lego pieces.

I take a step back and gasp for air as Meera goes in for another hug.

I turn, and before I know it, I'm outside, standing on the deck with my arms at my sides. It's brisk out tonight, as it will be for many more nights as summer draws to an end.

I'm somewhere midpanic when the screen door slams against the metal frame behind me. But I can't turn. I can't do anything but breathe in and out, trying to calm my nerves.

The wood creaks below Meera's feet as she makes her way to me. She snakes her hands around my waist and presses her cheek to my back, her chest brushing against me with each breath she takes. I wonder if she can hear how fast my heart is beating.

"Gabe," she says.

But as usual, I don't let her finish her sentence. At the sound of her voice, I spin around and take her into my arms, and then I crush my lips to hers. It's more forceful than I intend, so I pull away and wipe her mouth before going back for more, this time softer. When my lips brush hers, I finally find my voice.

"I need to say something, but I don't want you to panic." I'm already panicking enough for the both of us.

Meera pulls back and tilts her head in confusion. Already, there's fear swimming in her eyes.

With both hands pressed to her cheeks, I pull her so close that our noses touch. "Close your eyes."

She bites her lip, but she listens. When they're closed, I drag her good hand to my heart and press it firmly against my chest. I can't believe I'm doing this, but Jack was right. I was scared. I'd fallen for Meera, and I didn't know what to do with that. But I won't hide anymore. I'll face these feelings head-on, and if Meera doesn't feel the same way, then I'll deal with that later.

"I don't know if you believe in soulmates or not," I rasp out breathlessly, studying her face for her reaction. "I never did. I always laughed at the notion that there was one person out there, crafted and designed for each of us. I'm more of the *you make your own magic happen* type of guy. But Lydia was right. You're my needle."

Meera blinks open her eyes, confused.

"I didn't have to find you. You didn't have to find me. We quite literally collided. And from that moment on, I've known. You're my needle."

Meera sucks in a sharp breath, her chest heaving.

That's when I say it. Those terrifying words that I've kept inside me my whole life because I've had no one to share them with. "I'm in love with you, Meera."

Her lips part, but I keep talking. I have to get it all out before she responds.

"Shh, don't say anything. It's not fair for me to say it so soon. You probably think I'm crazy. Hell, I probably am. But it's true. I've been falling for you from day one. And after watching Sophie in there, so free with how she can give away her love, I couldn't wait another minute."

"Gabe," Meera says, pulling away.

All the air in my lungs escapes me, and while there is a part of me that thinks maybe I should have waited, an enormous sense of relief drowns out that thought. It's like a weight has been lifted from my shoulders. I suddenly feel light and free.

She bites her lip. "I came out here to tell you . . . maybe a bit more subtly . . ." She ducks her head and gives it a shake. "That I'm falling for you. But of course, you had to do it first. You have to beat me at everything, don't you?" There's a sheepish grin plastered to her face.

I want to smile, but I'm too stunned. "Wait, did you say . . .?"

"Yes, Gabe, I'm falling in love with you too."

The last word isn't even out of her mouth when my lips crush against hers again.

Meera is the first to pull away this time, but only far enough for her to whisper into my ear. "Take me to your room."

Fuck. She doesn't have to tell me twice. I lift her up, and before I know it, we're both falling onto my bed. We tear at each other's clothes wildly. Okay, it's mostly me, because Meera still struggles with her cast.

She's vocal. She's not afraid to tell me what she wants, and that makes me fall in love just a little more.

I grip at her hips as she tries to tear open a condom package. It takes too long, so I snatch it out of her hands and rip it open. She helps slide it over my erection, and then, just as I'm about to press into her, I pause and survey her.

"Yes. Yes, I want you inside me." She laughs up at me.

I dip down and nip at her lips as I enter her.

And then, feeling her body shift, I change tempo. We go from feverishly fast to slow and unhurried. I take in the way her body moves, where her hands go, and when her legs tighten. When she pulls me into her, I take her hard with every thrust. When she holds me back, I pull out so slowly she can barely contain herself. I listen to her body as it begs for more. We change course more times than I can count. I never want it to end.

"I love you. I fucking love you," I growl into her chest. At my words, she tightens around me and her body bucks beneath me as she tightens her grip in my hair.

"I love you, Gabriel Henry," she moans in response.

CHAPTER FORTY-TWO

Six Months Later

Meera

I crack one eye open, only to find Gabe's handsome face staring back at me.

"Good morning," he whispers, brushing a few stray strands of hair over my shoulder.

"Good morning," I say back, a warm tingling sensation rushing through my body.

"How does it feel to wake up as a divorced woman?"

I grin. Gabe flew to California with me so I didn't have to be alone during the final hearing. We stayed just long enough to hear the judge bang his gavel, and then we flew home on the red-eye. "How does it feel to wake up next to a divorced woman?" I throw back at him.

He growls in my ear and presses his length against me so I can feel for myself. But before we can take things further, there's a loud banging at my front door.

Gabe jumps up first and throws a T-shirt over his head.

I follow behind, tugging on a pair of sleep shorts.

"Meera. Are you in there?"

I let out a sigh of relief and lay a hand on Gabe's shoulder. It's Mallory, the girl who runs the boutique downstairs. I open the door, and there she is, tall, tanned, and gorgeous, her blonde hair swaying in the wind.

"We got an eviction notice," she says, holding two red papers up in front of her face.

I narrow my eyes. "What do you mean? Tanner can't evict me. I pay my rent a month in advance."

"It's not from Tanner. It's the bank. Looks like they want to tear it down and rebuild. My friend, Joshua, works with a developer who's interested in putting in a bid and said that Tanner hasn't been paying on any of his properties. They're giving us thirty days."

"They can't do that, can they? Where's Tanner?" I reach for my phone, but Mallory stops me.

"He's in jail. Distribution of meth. We all have to relocate. Dawn and Craig are scoping out other buildings in the area, but we're never going to find something in this price range."

Dawn and Craig rent out the shops next to hers. Dawn runs a secondhand store that sells beautifully refurbished furniture. Craig is a fitness coach and yoga instructor. His place is small, but it draws in a big crowd on Thursdays when he hosts hot yoga.

"I figured I'd catch you while you were here since you're not around much." She gives Gabe a wry smile. "And honestly, even though this throws a wrench in my plans, I'm glad he's off the streets. I just hope the charges stick this time around."

After she leaves and I shut the door behind her, Gabe throws his head back and guffaws. "Well, I *have* been asking you to move in with me for the last six months."

I shoot him a mock-glare. He's right. He's gone to all kinds of lengths, even pleading on his knees, to get me to move in with him and Sophie. I'm there enough, but the idea of giving up my apartment so soon after I moved to Morganville makes me nervous. It's been nice having a place I can call my own.

Then an idea hits me. I bite my lip and grin. "You know I love you, right?"

He nods at me slowly, squinting. "Yes. Why? What are you thinking?"

"Let's go meet Dee for breakfast. I'll tell you on the way."

CHAPTER FORTY-THREE

Gabe

It's been three months since my grandpa passed away, but Meera and I still meet Dee and her son for breakfast once a week. Sometimes my mom and Lydia join. Other times it's Helen and her boyfriend. Even Jack and Sadie tag along when they have the chance.

We started doing this when my grandpa was sent home on hospice. He'd long passed up any opportunity for treatment, and he was okay with that. My mom and Lydia struggled with it. But with a little time, they came to terms with it and did everything in their power to make him more comfortable.

We had him moved into my house since it was the largest and afforded us the opportunity to have Dee and her son come by daily. Dee, the caretaker that she is, sat at his bedside when he was too tired to sit and made him get up and move when he spent too much time lying down. It was her idea to do breakfast at Betty's once a week. She said he needed something to look forward to. And so we did, sometimes taking up the entirety of the small bakery.

Dee stands from the table and greets us when we step through the door at Betty's, then pulls each of us into her tight embrace. "I hear congratulations are in order." She smiles. "Happy divorce."

"Thank you," Meera says.

We all sit, and before we can order our coffee, Meera is sharing the details she just discussed with me.

"I want to purchase the building I live in," she says after explaining the situation with Tanner. "I have the money just sitting in an account. By doing this, I could save a few jobs. And the corner unit is vacant. I could turn it into a place where women can go for self-defense classes, therapy, stuff like that. Nonprofit. I just don't know how to get something like that started."

Dee's eyes light up. "Meera." She places a hand on top of hers. "That's an incredible idea."

The two of them chat, working out details and who to call. By the end of breakfast, it's decided. She'll partner with Meera since she too has an abundance of money she's been sitting on since we took her ex to the cleaners, and she'll start making calls to people in the community she thinks can help them get the process started.

EPILOGUE

Another Six Months Later

Meera

"Yes. Right there. That's perfect," I say. "Don't stop there. Keep going."

Gabe has a few more frames to hang, and if he doesn't finish tonight, there's no telling when it'll get done. Next week is the grand opening, and I want every inch of this space radiating comfort and relaxation with a touch of *I can kick ass* appeal.

Dee and I won the bid once my building went up for auction, and only a few months later, we've reconstructed the empty office space into an open gym designed for self-defense classes with a few private rooms for counseling services. We'll offer routine appointments as well as supply resources to help women and children who live in abusive households. And every Tuesday evening, it'll welcome recovering addicts as Morganville's new NA meeting sight.

"Say those words to me again," Gabe growls from the ladder.

My face heats at the innuendo.

I don't know how I got so lucky. He really is the perfect man. He's an amazing dad, the sweetest boyfriend, and the most forgiving person I've ever known. He takes care of us. All of us. He's learned to back off when I want to do things on my own, but he also encourages me to accept help when I need it, especially when it comes to my diabetes. I've tried three monitors in the past year, and each time, Gabe was right there, at my side, taking care of me. He's shown me a type of love I didn't know existed before him. That, and he's a good kisser and great with his hands.

"Gabriel. Sophie is right outside." I turn toward the door, but Sophie isn't there. She's nine now, which is like thirty in suburb years, but that doesn't stop me from panicking. "Oh my God, where did she go?" I'm about five feet from the door when a hand lands at my waist.

"She's upstairs. I figured tonight would be as good as any for her to spend the night with Bre."

Gabe loops his arms around my waist and pulls me to him. Since Bre moved into my old apartment last month, we've discussed the idea of letting Sophie have an overnight with her mom.

Things have been good. Really good. Bre and I have grown close. She has a soft spot I gravitate toward. She's lived a hard life, and she's humbled by it. I'm sure it also helps that Bre and Gabe never had any real chemistry and that their relationship was brought on more by Bre's desire to make somebody else jealous. She gravitated to me quickly too, because when we met, I didn't know about her past. During those first encounters, she said it was such a relief. And even after I learned about her past, she felt comfortable with me, knowing that I didn't judge her.

Bre is a strong woman. While I don't know her full story, I admire her for the effort she puts toward being sober as well as being a mom. She loves Sophie. The story the private investigator told Gabe about how she offered to sell her daughter to get high doesn't mesh with the woman I know. But that's all moot since it's in the past.

This woman loves her daughter with her whole heart. And she's always careful to blend affection and thoughtful conversation tactics with time and space. She eats dinner with us twice a week, always on Tuesdays and Thursdays, so Sophie is prepared.

I created Me First not just for myself, but for people like her. It wasn't until months after we met that I discovered her history with her father. I did it for Sophie too, so she can have her mom close by. And I did it for so many other women who've yet to learn the true nature of how aggressive and controlling some relationships can be. I know I can't help everyone. But maybe, just maybe, I'll find that one girl who only needs that extra push to believe in herself. To understand her true worth. And maybe I can show her that she doesn't have to live out of a car to find it.

"Sophie will have a great time. She's ready," I breathe as I inhale Gabe's evergreen scent. And I mean it. That little girl has come a long way too. Gone are the days of supervised visitation. Those disappeared once Sophie and Bre recognized their shared love for the library.

Gabe nods into my neck, his warm breath skating across my skin. Sliding his nose up and under my earlobe, he leaves small, tantalizing kisses that turn me into mush along the way.

Then he nips at my ear and whispers, "Marry me."

For a second, I'm not sure I hear him correctly. I'm wrapped in an array of sensations, each one consuming me in its own right, as Gabe continues to press soft kisses along my neck. But then the fog lifts, and I take a step back.

He's still holding me, but now he's watching me, his blue eyes intent and swirling with affection. Then, as if he's just remembered, he drops to one knee and takes a small black velvet box from his pocket. Inside is a stunning round-cut diamond ring I can't help but gawk at as he removes it and slides it over my finger. It shines and sparkles, catching the light from the sun hanging low in the sky outside the window.

My heart pulses. I knew this was coming. He's hinted at it for months. But it still takes me by surprise.

He waits, holding me hostage with a look of pure adoration.

We've only been together for a year. After he told me that he loved me, things moved quickly. And now, he's rotating the ring around my finger, making sure it fits. That it's not too loose and not too tight. And I know there is absolutely no way that I'm going to say no.

I nod. Slowly at first. Then quickly. "Oh my God, yes." The emotions take me by surprise, and before I know it, my eyes are brimming with tears. "Yes," I say again, a little louder.

Gabe's grinning one second and then laughing the next. He scoops me into his arms and swings me around before he places a kiss to my lips. "Do you like the ring?" he asks.

"It's beautiful. Does Sophie know?" I smile so wide my cheeks hurt.

"Who do you think picked it out?"

My eyes lift to meet his. "Did she know you were asking me tonight?"

He shakes his head. "No. I was torn between doing a grand gesture or winging it when the moment felt right. I hadn't made up my mind until ten minutes ago."

I scrunch my nose at him. "What happened ten minutes ago?"

Without hesitation, Gabe responds, "I looked at you."

I run my hand over his firm jaw and say, "I love you, Gabriel Henry." I lean in, suddenly desperate to press my lips to his, but come to a screeching halt inches away and pull back. "Can we go tell Sophie?"

"Absolutely not. You're mine for the rest of the night," Gabe groans, tugging me so I fall into him and sliding his hands down my waist. "I want you naked and under that pergola. And then I'll show you exactly what's perfect."

Half an hour later, the sun dips behind the treetops, casting shadows from below the slotted wood of the newly built pergola. An assortment of red, pink, and yellow rose petals surrounds us as Gabe makes good on his word by peeling my clothes off in a hurried frenzy. Then he drops me onto an oversized lounge chair.

Before he joins me, he pulls the curtains closed, offering up a bit more privacy, though we're already tucked away at the far end of his property, near the tall oak trees with Spanish moss his grandma used to hang lanterns on.

There are lanterns again, but this time, they're strung together, rather than hanging haphazardly, with electricity running through them instead of candles.

Gabe has made a lot of progress on the long list of things he wanted to do here. From updating his grandparents' home to reflect a more modern bed-and-breakfast to transforming the backyard into a peaceful retreat. It's a scene right out of a romance movie.

There's still a lot of work to be done, but bushes have been trimmed, flowers are blooming, and the dirt path that snakes around the property line is now dotted with paved stone so we can walk around it in the rain without slipping into any more mud *if* we wanted.

We're hopeful that by this time next year, we'll welcome our first wave of guests. People excited to get away from the hustle and bustle of city living. We want this to be a place they can rest their feet and enjoy a night of peace and relaxation.

But for now, I plan to enjoy this night with the man I love. To soak in the sight of Gabe tearing his shirt off and climbing over me.

"Are you sure you want to spend the rest of your life with me?" Gabe whispers. His eyes penetrate mine, as if he's cataloging this moment so he can recall every detail later.

I imagine us out here in ten years. He's holding my hand as we meander our way around the pond. The two of us lost in each other as we discuss our day. And then in twenty years, when Sophie gets married. Gabe has salt-and-pepper hair in this vision. And he's smiling at me in the same serious way he is right now, with intense eyes and a small curve to his lips. And then in fifty years. Gabe is more salt and less pepper. He'll hand me a cup of tea, and we'll share a blanket as we watch the setting sun beneath the oak tree out beyond the pergola.

And then Gabe's mouth is on mine. He's soft yet forceful as he consumes me. And I give to him as much as I take in return.

When we come up for air, he runs the pad of his thumb across my swollen lip. "You have the most perfect mouth," he says quietly. Then he trails his thumb down my neck and into the hollow of my throat, following behind it with his lips, planting tiny kisses along the way. "And the most perfect neck." His voice grows deeper.

My breathing picks up as I lose myself in sensation. Gabe is attentive and knows exactly what makes me tick.

He glances up when he notices, giving me a devilish smile as he slides his fingers across my shoulders and drags the straps of my bra down to my elbows. Then he shifts his attention lower, brushing his nose against my skin and nipping at my collarbone. "This right here. This is perfect."

"Gabe." A breathless moan escapes me. I thread my fingers into his thick dark hair, then drag them down the length of his back.

His only response is more kissing. More touching. He slips his fingers into the cup of my bra and finds the peak of my breast, hard and firm beneath him.

I gasp in pleasure, closing my eyes and biting my lip, wanting more. The sensation is all-consuming. Gabe knows this is my undoing, so he takes his time. It's simultaneously a curse and a blessing.

In an instant, he takes one nipple into his mouth and uses his thumb and forefinger to work the other, pulling and kneading and rubbing.

When his teeth skate across my flesh, I buckle and press firmly into his length.

"More," I whisper.

A deep growl erupts from his throat. "This"—he uses his tongue to circle one nipple—"is perfect."

The heat from his breath sends ripples across my body. A pulsing ache burns deep inside my core. I want him. I want him inside me. So I reach for him. Hurriedly, I unzip his jeans and reach inside to feel his thickness. I stroke him while he cups my breasts, one by one.

"Take off your pants," I manage to say between breaths.

Once he's shucked them off, our hands are everywhere. I'm on top of him, and then he's back on top of me. There's only so much room on this lounge chair, but it's suddenly my favorite piece of furniture.

"Right there," I moan into Gabe's ear as he drags a hand south. "Right . . . there."

"Meer," he moans back, gripping at my thigh with one hand while finding my center with the other. He trails his warm lips down my abdomen. "I need you right now."

"Quick," I say, not wanting him to stop touching me but desperately wanting him to be inside me too.

Gabe reaches for his pants and pulls out a condom.

When my eyes land on it, I bite my lip and press a hand to his chest.

He looks up at me, searching my face, and I shake my head.

"Tell me I'm crazy," I begin, my heart thrumming in my ears. "I can't believe I'm about to say this, but . . ."

He tilts his head, confused.

I swallow, ready to try again. And this time, Gabe runs his finger along my jaw and down my neck, calming me. He's so good at that. When my anxiety gets the best of me, he's right here, working through it with me.

I breathe in and out a few times and finally say it. "I want a baby. I want to give Sophie a sibling. And . . ." But I stop there. If I say too much, I'll cry, and this should be a happy moment.

Gabe's face morphs in front of me. The desire that was exploding from him a moment ago changes to love and adoration. The blue flames in his eyes go soft. "Then let's make a baby."

ACKNOWLEDGMENTS

I am a different writer today, than I was when I began this journey two years ago and I owe a great deal of this to the writing and reading community on social media. It is because of them, mere strangers, that I've grown as a storyteller. I'll forever be grateful for their insight, direction, and support.

To my editor, Beth at VB Edits. You are incredible. After that first round of edits, I was blown away. You took what I thought was some of my best writing, and finetuned it, elevating it into the story we see today. You are a dream to work with and I feel like the luckiest author on the planet to have you in my corner.

To my cover designer, Amanda Walker, PA and Design Services. Can I just say 'Wow' and let it sit there for a minute? Because I'm still speechless at your ability to create something so breathtaking with what little I give you. You are brilliant beyond words.

Huge appreciation goes out to my proofer, Sarah Burr at Reed Editorial Service. You complete me. None of this would be possible without your final touches.

And lastly, to my husband and children, my family and friends, thank you for your love, support, and patience. Maybe one of these days, I'll write one of you into a story.

OTHER TITLES BY MANDA MAZANEC

And There You Were, A Beach Brew Novel

Under The Maple Tree, A Beach Brew Novel

ABOUT THE AUTHOR

Manda Mazanec is a United States Marine Corps veteran and educator, committed to shaping a better and brighter future. While being an avid reader, writer, and runner, Manda is also an advocate for breaking the stigma associated with mental health illness, bringing to light how trauma can affect our everyday lives. Manda lives in Illinois with her husband, three daughters, and her two dogs and two cats.

 instagram.com/mandamazanec

 goodreads.com/mandamazanec

www.ingramcontent.com/pod-product-compliance
Lightning Source LLC
LaVergne TN
LVHW010602100826
845148LV00014B/2807